Books by Suzanne Woods Fisher

Amish Peace: Simple Wisdom for a Complicated Life

❧ LANCASTER COUNTY SECRETS ❧

The Choice

The CHOICE

ℒ LANCASTER COUNTY SECRETS ℓ
Book 1

The CHOICE

A NOVEL

Suzanne Woods Fisher

Doubleday Large Print
Home Library Edition

Revell

a division of Baker Publishing Group
Grand Rapids, Michigan

Published by Revell
a division of Baker Publishing Group
P.O. Box 6287, Grand Rapids, MI 49516-6287

Printed in the United States of America

ISBN-13: 978-1-61523-875-0

Scripture used in this book, whether quoted or para-phrased by the characters, is taken from the King James Version of the Bible; or *The Message* by Eu-

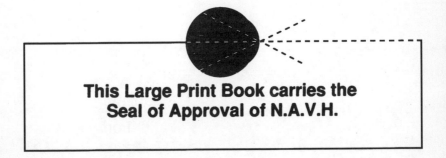

**This Large Print Book carries the
Seal of Approval of N.A.V.H.**

To my family, whom I love.

1

Carrie Weaver tucked a loose curl into her cap as she glanced up at the bell tower in Lancaster's Central Market. The clock had struck 2:00 p.m. more than ten minutes ago, and an English couple was haggling with her stepsister Emma over the price of a crate of strawberries. After all, the man was saying, the market was closing for the weekend. "Certainly, you Plain folks wouldn't want this fruit to go to waste now, would you? Tomorrow being Sunday and all?" He rested his hands on his round belly and fixed his gaze on Emma, a satisfied look on his red face—as red and ripe as a late summer tomato—as he waited for her to buckle.

But this red-faced English man didn't know Emma.

Carrie saw Emma purse her lips and hook her hands on her hips in that determined way and knew where this standoff was headed. Emma wouldn't drop the price of her strawberries to anyone, much less an Englisher whom, she was convinced, had a lost and corrupted soul. Her sister would plant her big feet and squabble over the price of strawberries until the sun set.

Carrie picked up the crate and handed it to the man. "Abgschlagge!" *Sold!*

The man and his wife, surprised and delighted, hurried off with the strawberries as Emma spun to face Carrie. She lifted her hands, palms out. "Have you lost your mind? My strawberries are worth twice that price! What were you thinking?"

"I'm thinking that it's past two and the market has closed and the van is waiting." Carrie pushed the leftover crates of red ripe strawberries into the back of the van of the hired driver and slammed the door shut, pinching her thumbnail. Wincing from the pain, she knew she didn't dare stop to get ice. There wasn't a moment to waste.

"Dummel dich net!" Emma muttered as Carrie opened the passenger seat door for her. *Don't be in such a hurry!* "You've been as jumpy as a jackrabbit all morning."

Carrie reached out an arm to clasp her younger brother on the shoulder, pulling him back as he started to climb in the van behind Emma. "I need to run an errand and take the bus home later today. Andy's coming with me."

Andy's eyes went round as shoe buttons, but he followed Carrie's lead and hopped back out of the van.

Emma twisted around on the seat. "What errand?" she asked, eyes narrowed with suspicion. "You know your dad wants you home to visit with Daniel Miller."

Carrie blew out a big sigh. Silent, solemn Daniel Miller. He and his father, Eli, were staying with the Jacob Weavers this summer. Eli Miller and Jacob Weaver made no secret of the fact that they had a hope for her and Daniel. Well, they could hope all they liked but Carrie's heart was already spoken for. Spoken for and claimed, and the thought warmed her.

"Daniel's mighty fine looking, Carrie," Emma said. "Your dad is hoping you'll think so too."

"If you think Daniel is such a looker, why don't you visit with him?" Carrie stepped back from the van to close the door. That had been mean, what she said to Emma, and she reached out to give her sister's arm a gentle squeeze in apology before she swung the door closed and the driver pulled away. Dear Emma, nearly twenty-seven and terrified that she would end up an old maid. Carrie felt a smile pull at her mouth and fought it back, as an unbidden image of a large celery patch popped into her mind—Emma and her mother, Esther, grew celery in the family garden in hopes that this would be Emma's year.

Carrie shook off her musing and grabbed Andy's hand and hurried to the bus stop. She wanted to reach the Lancaster Barnstormers' stadium before Solomon Riehl would start pitching. Last night, Sol told her he might be a closing pitcher in today's scrimmage, so she should be in the stands by the last few innings.

"What kind of errand?" Andy asked Carrie.

She shaded her eyes from the sun to watch for the bus. "It's a surprise for your birthday."

"I won't turn nine 'til October."

Carrie looked at him and tousled his hair. "Consider it an early birthday present." She knew she wouldn't be here on his birthday.

As Carrie and Andy climbed on the bus and sat among the English, she felt the happiness of her secret spill over her. She didn't even mind the pain radiating from her throbbing thumb. She was entirely preoccupied with the conversations she had been having with Sol lately. Last week, he called her at midnight, as planned, from the phone shanty across the road from his father's farm. During that call, he had talked to her about leaving the community and trying to make a living as a baseball player. And he told her he wanted her by his side, as his wife.

※

Sol had been crazy about baseball ever since he first held a ball in his hand. Although competition was discouraged on the schoolyard, Sol stood out. He could throw a ball faster, farther, and with more accuracy than anyone.

Just a few months ago, a baseball scout happened to be driving past their youth gathering and had pulled his car over to watch Sol pitch, mesmerized. The scout had quietly slipped a business card into Sol's hand and whispered something to him.

On the buggy ride home from the youth gathering, Sol had pulled out the card and showed it to Carrie. "They're having open tryouts next week. He wants to clock my pitch. He said he hasn't seen a fastball like mine in years."

Stunned, Carrie turned the card over. "You aren't serious. Sol, you can't try out for professional baseball. You shouldn't even go to a game! You know that. The elders will be at your folks' door by day's end."

"Not if they don't find out," Sol said, grinning mischievously. Then his face tightened and the smile disappeared. "I'm tired of all the 'shouldn'ts' and 'can'ts' in my life. *Can't* go to the movies. *Shouldn't* listen to the radio. *Can't* ride a bicycle. *Can't* own a car."

Carrie gave him a sideways glance. All Sol talked about lately was how smothered he felt, being born and raised Amish. At first she felt alarmed by such talk. But she'd grown used to it and didn't take his complaints too seriously. She was sure he couldn't really leave his family and church behind. Or her. He would never leave her behind. Of that she was confident. "Not being allowed to own a car sure hasn't stopped you. I still don't know how you've kept that heap-of-rust you call a car hidden from your folks for so long."

Sol's face relaxed into a grin. "Six months now." He turned the buggy off to the shoulder and faced Carrie, taking her hand in his. "It's *just* a tryout. There will be plenty of other guys pitching, guys who have been training their whole life for a tryout. Most likely, I won't even make callbacks." He lifted her chin so she would look at him. "But I've decided. I'm going to go to the tryouts next week. Now's the time in my life to have a taste of what the world has to offer. That's what the running-around years are for, aren't they?" He leaned over to kiss her, featherlight, on the lips, then gently rubbed his nose against hers before slapping the reins to urge the horse forward.

As the horse lunged ahead, Carrie mulled over Sol's reasoning. Was Rum-springa a time for trying worldly things? To be tried and found lacking? Or, just by try-ing, did it make a person long for another kind of life than the Plain one? Her father had a saying, "Was mer net hawwe soll, hett mer's liebscht." *What we are not meant to have, we covet most.*

Sol laughed when she quoted her fa-ther's saying to him and told her that even Jacob Weaver was young once. Sol made it sound so easy. He made everything sound so easy. Besides, she thought, dis-missing concern about Sol's restless na-ture, he probably wouldn't be picked by that team. He's just feeling his oats.

One week later, Sol had tried out for the Lancaster Barnstormers and was offered a one-season contract with promises of more. The pitching coach had been impressed with this Amish kid who could throw bullets. And when Sol stood on that pitcher's mound in the Clipper Magazine Stadium, he was hooked, ready to sign. There was no turn-ing back.

Carrie was the only one who knew about Sol's baseball contract. He had hidden the fact from his father, telling him he was working a construction job for an English company. It wasn't entirely a lie; he did work on a construction site in the morning, but come noon, he clocked out, with the foreman's permission, and rushed to the stadium for spring training. Sol and Carrie knew this ruse wouldn't last. Next week, the Barnstormers would start a three-game series on Long Island. It was time to come clean with his folks. Sol would be leaving and he told Carrie he wanted her with him.

"But what about your folks, Sol? And my dad and Andy?" Carrie had asked him, still unsure if she could live with herself after leaving home. Like Sol, she had mixed feelings about joining the community. They both struggled to believe the way their par-ents believed, and oh, the world with its infinite choices, it was calling to them.

"We haven't bent at the knee, Carrie," Sol reminded her. "It's all the difference.

We won't be shunned. We can still visit and write letters and eat with them. Be glad we haven't been baptized yet. Trust me, they'll understand. They were young once."

After a few more late-night conversations with Sol, Carrie came to see things his way. But the next morning, she watched her father and Andy talking and laughing together, and she felt all churned up again. How could she do this to them? How could she leave them?

As soon as she had a chance to see Sol face-to-face, she told him that she had changed her mind.

He patiently listened to her and answered her concerns, even those she had about God turning his back on them. "If it doesn't work out, we can always go back to the church," he assured her.

And then he kissed her, first on each cheek, then her forehead, before grazing her lips with his finger. By the time his lips found hers, Carrie's objections had evaporated.

Still, Carrie wasn't so sure their parents would understand. She was even less sure that God would understand. But one thing

Carrie didn't doubt was that she wanted to be wherever Sol would be. She loved Sol *that* much.

❧❧

Warming up his arm in the bull pen, Sol Riehl felt a deep satisfaction he hadn't dreamed possible. He certainly never felt it when he was mucking out stalls or plowing a field. Here he was, an Amish kid plucked right off the farm, pitching for a professional baseball team. Who had ever heard of such a thing? It felt like a dream that he didn't dare to wake from.

The catcher gave Sol a signal to throw some pitches. "You sure do pack some heat, Sunday Sol," he told Sol, slapping him on the back as the pitching coach called for the two to come up to the field. Sol tossed the ball to the catcher and followed him out of the bull pen. He scanned the seats above the dugout for any sign of Carrie. He had told her exactly where to sit, right behind the catcher, so she would have the best view of the pitcher's mound. He frowned, disappointed that she wasn't there yet.

Then Sol heard his name announced over the loudspeaker as the closer. He hoped Carrie was somewhere in the stadium so she would hear that announcement. He tried, without success, to keep the grin off his face as he took his first jog out to the mound.

⁑

As Carrie and Andy plopped down in the stadium's hard plastic seats, she breathed a sigh of relief, hearing Sol's name announced over the loudspeaker. Sol had told her where to sit so he could see her from the pitcher's mound. It was one of the things she loved about him; he had everything planned out.

She saw him jog out to the mound and look up, right to where she was seated. He gave her a quick wave, did a double take when he noticed Andy, then turned his attention to the catcher to practice a few more warm-up pitches.

When Andy realized it was Solomon Riehl on that pitcher's mound, he blurted out, "Ein Balleschpieler?" *A baseball player?*

"Best not to tell Dad and Esther about this birthday surprise, Andy," Carrie said, flashing him a warning. "Nor Emma."

Andy nodded, sealing the pact, eyes glued on the field. "Dad wouldn't mind." A slow grin spread over his face. "Esther would, though."

Carrie laughed. "Yes, Esther would mind something fierce."

As she watched Sol pitch, her heart felt so full she didn't even notice that tears were running down her cheeks. She knew that feeling so proud was wicked, but she couldn't help herself. Down on the field was Sol Riehl, in a sparkling white-with-red-pinstripe uniform, pitching in front of thousands of people in a baseball stadium. Her Sol.

※※

At dinner that evening in the Weaver house, all that was spoken of was Eli Miller's purchase of an apple orchard. Carrie was grateful that no one asked her where she and Andy had been all afternoon.

Carrie's father, Jacob Weaver, knew of an orchard owned by an English neighbor who wanted to retire to Florida. It wasn't even for sale yet, but Jacob and Eli spent the day talking with that neighbor. When they returned, hours later, Eli was the new owner of a twenty-acre apple orchard. Jacob was so pleased to help his friend that he couldn't keep the smile off of his kind face.

"I'm mighty fortunate to have a friend like you, Jacob," Eli told him, matching Jacob grin for grin.

"Fortunate for you, Eli, that you had money to buy land," said Esther, Jacob's wife, in a thin, tight voice.

Carrie braced herself, keeping her eyes fixed on her plate. She knew that Esther couldn't tolerate letting Jacob be the center of attention.

"This farm belonged to my first husband. Jacob was penniless when I met him. Penniless with two small children." Carefully, Esther buttered a roll and began to delicately eat it as an awkward silence covered the dinner table like a blanket.

"And a blessed day it was when I met you, Esther," Jacob answered back softly, dark brown eyes twinkling, causing everyone to laugh. Even Esther softened. He was long accustomed to Esther's sharp tongue and had a way of defusing her.

Carrie looked fondly at her father. Once she had asked him why he married Esther in the first place. "Carrie girl," her father said, "folks marry for all kinds of reasons." He hadn't really answered her question, but she thought she knew what he meant.

Eli rose to his feet and clapped his hands together. "Daniel, it's time we set off to the bus depot." Like his son, Eli was a man of few words and only gave a nod of thanks to Esther.

Daniel crammed one last roll into his mouth and hurried to join his father outside, helping him hitch the horse to the buggy. Before the sun set today, Eli planned to be back on the bus to Ohio. He wanted to finalize the sale of his farm, auction off his equipment, and fetch his widowed mother, Yonnie. Daniel was to remain at the Weavers' to finish up details of the sale of the orchards.

Why Eli was in such a hurry was a mystery to Carrie, but she didn't really concern herself with the Millers. Her mind was on Sol. Leaving with Sol.

"And," Emma told Carrie as they cleaned up the kitchen after dinner that evening, "I heard Eli tell Daniel to try and woo you while he was gone."

"Woo me?" Carrie asked, drying a bowl before tucking it in the cupboard. "Maybe he should woo you."

"I'm too old for him. Besides, I think Daniel likes you. He kept stealing looks at you during dinner tonight."

"Emma, please." Carrie rolled her eyes. "He's such a brooder. Haven't you noticed he never smiles or laughs?"

Emma handed Carrie another wet bowl and gave her a suspicious look. "You'd better not be holding out for that Solomon Riehl. You know how your dad feels about Sol. He thinks he's a fence jumper."

Carrie stiffened, irritated. "*One time*, Emma. *One time*, Dad saw Sol working in the fields with his shirt off. That doesn't make him a fence jumper."

"Well, my mother says it does." Emma put her hands on her hips. "I heard her tell your father that Sol Riehl was a fellow walking with one foot in the world and one foot in the church. She said that he was always spoiled, being the only boy after all those girls. She said that his parents never expected enough from—"

"Emma!" Carrie held up a hand in warning. "Wer lauert an der Wand sei eegni Schand." *If you listen through the wall, you'll hear others reciting your faults.*

The kitchen door burst open, interrupting them. "Carrie, it's set up!" Andy shouted.

Carrie threw the dish towel at Emma

and hurried outside to join Andy in a game of horseshoes before the sun set.

※

Watering the vegetable garden, Mattie Zook heard Andy and Carrie's voices in their yard. She dropped the watering can and ran down the hill to see her friend. Now that Carrie was working at the Central Market, Mattie hardly saw her anymore. What little free time Carrie did have lately was taken up by Sol Riehl.

All of the boys were crazy about Carrie, but she acted as if she didn't notice or didn't care. Sol was the only one who had ever caught her interest. Mattie could see why Carrie was so sought after. Sometimes Mattie thought she looked like an angel. Big blue eyes fringed with thick black lashes, skin the color of cream in summer, a dimple in each cheek that framed a bow-shaped mouth. And her hair! Good thing the boys couldn't see her hair too, Mattie thought. Thick, honey blond curls that cascaded down her back. But Carrie was more than just pretty, she was smart and kind, and had a little bit of mystery to her, as if she always had something else on her mind. The boys had to work hard to get her attention. Whenever Mattie told her that, Carrie would laugh and say she was just imagining things. Mattie loved Carrie's laugh. It reminded Mattie of the church bells she heard ringing whenever she was in town.

As Mattie reached Esther's rosebushes that bordered the property, she slowed to avoid thorns. She and Carrie had beaten a path through those bushes the very first summer Carrie's dad had married Esther and moved to her farm. The path had made Esther furious, which secretly delighted the girls.

Carrie waved to Mattie to join them. "I bet I know why you're here, Mattie!" she called out, laughing. "But Daniel isn't here. He and Dad took Eli to the bus stop."

As Mattie broke into a run to join Carrie and Andy, she wondered why Carrie would assume she was interested in the Weavers' houseguest. Like most of the girls, she had noticed Daniel Miller at the Sunday Singing. And he was handsome, she couldn't deny.

But Mattie's heart belonged to one man: Solomon Riehl. She had loved Sol for as

long as she remembered. Long before
Carrie had even met him.

Mattie would never reveal those feelings, though. She loved Carrie too much.
She wasn't sure what the future held, but
she trusted that God had given her this
love for Sol. And she knew God was trust-
worthy.

❧❧

Near midnight, Carrie quietly tiptoed
downstairs, jumping carefully over the
squeaky third step because Esther had
ears like a hawk. She slipped out the kitchen
door and glided into a run as soon as she
turned onto the road. When she reached
the phone shanty, she jerked the door open
and stared at the phone impatiently, willing
it to ring.

While she waited, drumming her fingers,
her thoughts drifted to the talk she'd had
with Mattie tonight. She nearly confided to
Mattie about the plans to leave with Sol, but
she held her tongue. It wouldn't have been
right to have Mattie keep such a secret. The
truth, she realized, was that she didn't think
Mattie would understand. There was something about Mattie that seemed . . . pure.
Holy, almost. Like those orchids sold at

Central Market. Once the Orchid Lady had told Carrie that she kept the orchids in the greenhouse because they were so delicate. That's what Mattie seemed like. Too delicate for Carrie to share her tangled thoughts.

The phone rang, startling her out of her muse. She lunged for the receiver and smiled as she heard Sol's deep voice.

"Did anyone ask where you were this afternoon?" Sol asked.

"No," Carrie said, still smiling. "Dad and Eli were so excited about purchasing the orchards that it was all anyone was talking about."

"Surprised me to see Andy with you. Think that was wise?"

"Aw, it was a birthday present for him. He won't tell." Carrie was quiet for a moment. "I won't be here for his actual birthday." Her heart caught for a moment.

Sol didn't seem to notice the quiver in her voice. "So we'll tell our folks Sunday afternoon, just like we talked about. On Monday, I'll be on the team bus to Long Island, but you can follow on a Greyhound as soon as you can. I thought we could get married in New York, the day you arrive. How does that sound?"

Carrie didn't answer right away. She glanced back at the big white farmhouse. The moonlight shone behind it, casting a bluish hue over it. The night was so quiet and peaceful; the house and the barn filled with sleeping people and animals. An owl hooted once, then twice.

Her eyes caught on a shadowy figure and she gasped. Daniel Miller was sitting on the fence across from the phone shanty, watching her.

"Carrie?" Sol asked, his voice tight.

She pulled her attention back to the phone. "Daniel's here."

"That fellow who's staying at your house? What does he want?"

"I have no idea."

Sol snorted. "I have a pretty good idea. He stuck to you like flypaper at last Sunday's singing."

Carrie rolled her eyes. "Sol, he didn't know anybody else."

"He knew Emma and he didn't get anywhere near her."

Carrie smiled. Sol had a jealous streak. She shouldn't be pleased, but she couldn't help it. "Maybe I should find out what he wants."

"Carrie, you haven't answered my question. Have you changed your mind?"

She turned away from Daniel's gaze. "I haven't changed my mind."

"Ich liebe dich," he said. *I love you.*

A blush warmed her face. She'd never said the words before, because it was not the Plain way. But Sol said the words often. He admired how the English expressed themselves openly. "Ich auch," she whispered. *Me too.*

"So tell Daniel Miller to find another girl."

Carrie waited until she heard the click of Sol hanging up before she put the receiver back in the cradle. She turned slowly and opened the door to the phone shanty.

"Evening." Daniel's low voice came as a shock in the whispering stillness of the night.

"I guess I didn't see you on the way here." She pulled the collar of her nightgown close around her neck. "Why are you up so late?"

He shrugged. "Too hot to sleep." He crossed his arms. "You?"

She glanced back at the phone shanty. "Business call. For Central Market. They get up early."

moment, he lifted his head. "It was too late by the time Esther found him—"

"Esther found him?" Carrie's hands flew to cup her face. "She didn't call the ambu-ance, did she?" She started trembling. Esther didn't think he ever needed infu-ions. She said they cost too much and idn't believe they were necessary." She tarted to gulp for air. "She has the money, ou see. This farm, it belongs to her. She ever lets him forget that."

Daniel took a step closer to her.

"And then the last time Dad was hurt," arrie continued without stopping to breathe, he talked him out of having an infusion. took him months to recover. The blood oled in his joints and caused him terri- pain. But if his head was ever injured, would be in serious trouble because the ood would pool in the brain. The doctor d so. I heard him say so. Esther knew t." She was visibly shaking now. "She ew that."

Carrie looked to Daniel, hoping he would mit that it was a prank, a bad joke. That ob was waiting for her and for Andy in kitchen. But Daniel wore such pain in eyes that she knew it was real.

"My, my. That is early," Daniel said, sounding amused.

She stared at him and he stared back. Then her cheeks started to burn as if she'd been standing too close to a stove. She dropped her eyes and spun around to leave. "Well, goodnight."

"Wonder what Esther might say about you having a midnight phone call."

Carrie froze. She did not want Esther to know she was out in the night, on the phone. Once Esther locked on to some-thing, she wouldn't let go until it thundered. For the first time, she thought that Daniel Miller might just have a thought or two in his quiet head. She pivoted around to face him. "Do you plan to tell her?"

He gave a short laugh. "She reminds me of a bear that treed me once. Not sure I want to be on the wrong side of that woman." Daniel took a few strides and passed by Carrie. "You got more business calls to make?"

In the moonlight, Daniel looked less stern and tense, a little gentler. She decided that Emma was right, he was a looker. He used more words tonight than he had all week.

"Wait up. I'm coming," she said, matching his stride.

�֍

When the van dropped Carrie and Emma off from work the next day, Daniel and Andy were waiting for them at the gate. Andy's face was red and puffy from crying.

"Nau, was is letz, Andy?" Carrie asked. *What's wrong?* Something terrible must have happened; Andy never cried.

"Dad," he sobbed, gulping for air. "It's Dad." He threw himself into Carrie's arms and buried his face against her.

"Was fehlt ihm?" Carrie's heart started to pound. *What's wrong with him?*

Daniel explained that Jacob had been shoeing a horse when it kicked him.

"Someone's taken him to the hospital, yes?" Carrie asked. Her pulse quickened as her breath came up short.

Daniel shook his head. "He's on the couch in the kitchen." He took a step closer to Carrie.

"We must get him to the hospital. He has hemophilia. He's a bleeder. He needs an infusion of Factor IX." She stroked Andy's hair. "Alles ist ganz gut, Andy." *All will*

be well. She looked up at Daniel. "Did call for an ambulance?"

Daniel glanced up at the house. " rie . . ."

Emma gasped as she seemed t derstand what Daniel couldn't say. nee! Ach, nee! Er is dot, zwahr? Ach Mamm!" *Oh, no! Oh, no! He's dead he? Oh, dear Mom!* She ran towa house.

Carrie heard Emma's cries, but the dipped and swirled like barn swall her mind. She watched Emma dis into the house, heard her shout for Andy had tightened his grip arou waist, his small body wracked wit wrenching sobs. She took in the co look on Daniel's face and then the f of what Emma said struck her, gripped her chest so tightly that sh her heart had stopped beating. *M must be a mistake.*

"He was kicked in the head. late—"

"Du bischt letz," she told D voice that was too calm. *You ar*

Daniel rubbed his forehea

My father is dead. He's dead! A small startled cry escaped from her throat.

Daniel stepped closer and wrapped his arms around both of them—a grief-stricken woman and a sobbing little boy—and held them tight.

2

Jacob Weaver's body was embalmed by the English undertaker and returned, the next day, to the farmhouse for the viewing. All afternoon, Carrie, Esther, Emma, and Andy received friends and neighbors offering condolences, doing errands of kindness. It was a soaker of a day, gray skies that poured down rain, matching Carrie's dark, troubled mood.

Carrie was worried about her brother. Andy was silent, never far from her side. She wasn't sure how to help him. It was one thing to grieve the loss of a parent, but after Esther's outrageous accusation last night, she wasn't sure he would ever be himself again. There was no balm for this wound.

It started when Andy had arrived late to supper, having lost track of time. Andy's absentmindedness was a constant source of irritation to Esther, and last night she told him that Jacob's death was his fault.

"Your father had told you to come to the barn straight from gathering eggs in the henhouse," Esther said, pointing a long finger in his direction. "If you had just obeyed your father, instead of getting distracted like you always do, he could be alive today. You *knew* he was a bleeder. Every minute counted."

Carrie exploded at Esther's accusation. "Sie ist schunn ab im Kopp! Er ist ein Kind! Mei vadder hett's net erlaabt! Du settscht dich scheme!" *You are crazy! He is only a child! My father would not permit such talk! You should be ashamed!* Her fists shook as she screamed, her chin quivered with rage. "You don't care, Esther! You never did!"

Esther stared into Carrie's eyes, a stand-off, before abruptly turning and leaving the kitchen.

Carrie rushed to put her arms around Andy, crumbled with grief, weeping silently. "Andy, Andy, don't listen to her. It was Dad's time. The Lord God decided that, not you. And not Esther, either." Carrie scooped Andy up on her lap and held him tight against her.

It surprised Carrie to hear those words about God burst out of her mouth, as naturally as if they came from her heart. Triggering a fresh wave of grief, it sounded like something her father would have said.

❋

When Sol arrived with his family to pay respects, he slipped a note to Carrie to meet him in the barn. As soon as he viewed Jacob's body and shook Esther's hand, he hurried to the barn to wait for Carrie. He knew she had to wait until an opportune moment; no one was supposed to have any idea they were courting. Funny, he thought, leaning against the horse's stall, they both tiptoed so carefully around the brittle requirements of the church. In two short days, they would no longer need to worry.

The heavy barn door slid open with a rumble. Carrie waited until her eyes adjusted to the dim light, then ran to him.

"I'm so sorry," he mumbled, folding her into his arms. For a long time, neither of them spoke.

Keeping her head tucked under Sol's chin, Carrie broke the silence. "I should have been here. We came back late from the market. Maybe if I'd been here, I could have gotten him to the hospital. She didn't even call for an ambulance."

"It was just an accident, Carrie," Sol said, tipping her chin up to face him. "Esther is a lot of things, but she isn't cruel." He knew how Carrie adored her father. That was one reason he wanted them to leave before they were baptized. He didn't want Jacob to have to shun Carrie.

"Neglecting a head injury when someone has hemophilia is cruel."

"A kick in the head is pretty hard to recover from, bleeder or not."

"But she didn't even give him a chance."

"Aw, Carrie, be fair. From what I heard, it was too late by the time anyone found him."

She sighed deeply as if her argument had run out of steam. "Maybe you're right. Dad was unconscious by the time Esther got to him."

Sol pulled her close to his chest. "Things have a way of working out, Carrie."

She pulled back from him, a confused look on her face. "What?"

"I've been thinking this over. I know how hard it was going to be to say goodbye to your father—"

She tilted her head. "What are you saying?"

"Just that, maybe it's a sign. That it's right for us to leave."

"God gave us a sign to leave by letting my father die?"

Sol put his hands on her shoulders, but she flinched, shrugging them off. This wasn't going the way he had hoped. He decided to change subjects. "I struck four batters out yesterday and threw a runner out at second base. You know what they're starting to call me? 'The Riehl Deal.'"

Her eyes widened as if his words had hit her, a solid slap. "Sol, I can't leave Andy. I won't leave him with her."

"You can't be responsible for Andy for the rest of your life."

"Maybe not. But I'm responsible for him until he's grown. I'm his only sibling. We have no one else, Sol."

Sol felt his stomach tie itself into a square knot. "Carrie," he said, choosing his words with great sympathy, "we have to face facts. We need to be practical. I can't take care of a wife *and* a little boy. Especially one with hemophilia. Andy needs to stay on the farm, with his people. They can help him with his medical bills. I can't do that."

"I realize that," Carrie said. "But there's another choice."

He lifted his hands, exasperated. "Such as?"

She looked at him as if it was the most obvious thing in the world. "You could stay."

❊❊

After Sol left with his family, Carrie went back to the house, so exhausted and emotionally spent that she felt numb. She was certain that Sol would think everything over and agree with her. It shocked her to hear him still talk about leaving. Why couldn't he see it? Remaining in the church was the best choice. The only choice.

When the entire Riehl family came to her father's funeral on Monday and Sol was absent, she tried not to panic. Then she thought of how he had kissed her in the barn before he slipped back out to join his family, and she knew. It was a goodbye kiss. She hadn't wanted to admit it to herself, but she knew. Er hat sei verlosse. *He had left, without her.*

Carrie didn't think it was possible that a heart could break twice, in just one week.

❧❦

One month after her father's funeral, Carrie thought she might just commit murder. Esther had discovered that Andy had left the gate unlocked, and the sheep had wandered down the road into other neighbors' fields. It had taken Esther all afternoon to gather them. Afterward, she took a switch from the willow tree and beat Andy's backside.

When Carrie returned home from the farmer's market and saw Andy's bruises, it was like someone lit a match to kerosene, her temper flared so hot and fast. She marched to the barn to prepare the horse and buggy to take Andy to the hospital. She grabbed the bridle and hurried to the stall, clumsily thrusting the bit into the horse's mouth, her hands were shaking so badly. "Es dutt mir leed," she whispered, apologizing to the horse, trying to gain control over her emotions.

Later, at the hospital, Carrie sat by Andy's bedside in the emergency room as a long tube snaked from an IV bag into his vein, filling him with Factor IX to help his blood clot. Mesmerized by the television hanging on the wall, Andy watched it, slack-jawed. The sight made Carrie smile. It felt rusty, that smile, but it felt good.

With Andy occupied, Carrie grew restless and noticed a newspaper left on a chair. She picked it up and automatically turned to the sports section, just as she did every time she worked at the Central Market, scanning for news of Sol. Just last week, she had read that he was the closing pitcher for every game.

As she turned a page, her heart skidded to a stop. There was a picture of Sol, celebrating a win, with his arm wrapped around a girl. An English girl. A pang of longing pierced her heart. Carrie stared at the picture so long that she didn't even notice Daniel, standing at the door, until he cleared his throat. Startled, Carrie dropped the newspaper.

"Heard about Andy," he said, pulling up a chair to sit down next to the bed.

Carrie gathered the newspaper and

tossed it in the wastebasket. It occurred to her that Daniel had a curious way of appearing out of nowhere. But she found she didn't mind. Daniel was good at just being there.

A few hours later, after Andy was released, Daniel and Carrie took Andy home. Carrie settled her brother into bed and read until he was asleep. Esther had gone to bed, a relief to Carrie. She still felt a mutinous anger toward Esther for harming her brother. She went out to the front porch to look at the stars and search out the tail of the Milky Way. It was something her father had liked to do. He said it gave him great comfort to see God's handiwork in the heavens. Sorely missing him, Carrie wished she could borrow some of her father's faith. Especially now.

The kitchen door creaked open. "Another midnight call?" Daniel asked, holding the door open as if waiting for an invitation.

"No," Carrie said. "I'm not expecting any calls." Not now, not ever again, she realized.

He closed the door and stood beside her, arms crossed, gazing at the sky, not saying a word.

"When is your father expected?" Carrie asked, breaking the silence.

"When? Or what?"

Carrie glanced at him, not understanding.

"He's due on Friday." Daniel cleared his throat. "But he's expecting that by now I've asked you to marry me." He kept his eyes fixed on the stars.

Carrie's eyes went wide with surprise. She opened her mouth but no words came to the surface. Suddenly, an image of Sol with his arm around that girl bounced, unbidden, into her head. She wanted to hurt Sol as much as he had hurt her. What could hurt Sol more than knowing she had married? Without thinking, she blurted out, "Andy comes with me."

Daniel gave a nod.

Carrie's mind started to spin. "I've started baptism instructions this summer."

Mattie had persuaded Carrie to take the classes together. Carrie finally agreed, hoping Sol would hear that she was going to be baptized. She knew his mother wrote to him each week. Sol had been right about that one thing; it wasn't like he was under the ban. His folks were deeply disappointed in him, but they held out hope that he'd get over sowing his wild oats and return home.

Well, Carrie wasn't waiting for him. As far as she was concerned, he chose baseball over her and nothing would ever change that. "I'll be baptized in a few weeks. Then I'd like a wedding soon after." She glanced up at the direction of Esther's bedroom window. "As soon as possible."

Daniel gave another nod.

Carrie took a deep breath. "I have to be honest about something. I don't love you."

Daniel smiled, a slow unraveling. "Makes things simpler," was all he said, leaning over the porch railing, gazing at the moonless sky.

Carrie looked at his profile for a long time, trying to understand him. She had a feeling that she never would. "I don't know how they do things in Ohio, but here, you need to speak to the deacon who will speak to me. About marrying, I mean. He acts like a go-between."

Daniel straightened up and turned to her, looking her straight in the eyes. He held out his hand. "Deal?"

Carrie's eyes dropped down to his large

open hand and she shook it, sealing the bargain.

❦

Not long after the deacon's visit, Carrie and Daniel set the day for their wedding. As Carrie pinned the top of her blue wedding dress, she felt as if she might faint dead away, caught in that horrible place between regret and resolution. She wondered how Daniel was feeling right then, if he felt as sick as she did.

She fit the organza prayer cap over her hair bun, tying the strings under her chin, feeling as if her world had just become very narrow and she couldn't get enough air. For one fleeting moment, as she heard the churned-up gravel made by the arriving buggies, she thought about running away. Finding Sol.

But then she thought about her father. And Andy.

A fierce grief welled up within her, nearly to the point of bursting. One thought spilled into another and soon Sol filled her mind again. Cold fury displaced grief, renewing her determination. She finished tying the cap and smoothed the creases on her apron.

Carrie was just about to go downstairs when she heard a gentle knock on the door. She took a deep breath and opened the door to find Yonnie, Daniel's grandmother.

Soft wrinkles creased Yonnie's face as she studied Carrie. Then, a satisfied smile covered Yonnie's face, warm as a summer day. "So. Today is your wedding day," she said, in a voice tender and shaky with age.

In her arms was a bundle wrapped in tissue. It looked as though it weighed more than she did. Carrie took the bundle from her and helped her sit down on a chair.

"You can open it," Yonnie said.

Carefully, Carrie unwrapped the tissue and found a quilt inside.

"It's called a Crazy Quilt." Yonnie's words were slow and faltering, her voice as thin as a trail of smoke. "It seems more fitting to have brought you a Double Wedding Ring, but for some reason, I felt as if this one was the right one."

Carrie gave her a sideways glance. She fought a wave of guilt as she realized Yonnie assumed she loved Daniel.

Yonnie pointed to some blue triangles.

"I used the scraps from Daniel's clothes. They're from his growing-up years."

Carrie's chin snapped up. "You made this quilt all by yourself?"

"I did." The strings on her organza kapp bobbed as she nodded. She wasn't being proud, just stating a fact.

"You're a fine quilter, Yonnie. It's wonderful." Carrie laid the quilt out on the bed, the place where she and Daniel would spend their first night as man and wife. Her last few nights in Esther's home, she realized, relieved. Last night she had learned that Esther's eldest daughter and her husband were moving in to take over the farm, dispelling any doubts that she had made the right decision. At least, for Andy's sake.

Yonnie's Crazy Quilt was stunning. Deep-colored jewels of purple and green set among bright turquoise. The pattern practically popped in the room against the stark white walls and simple furniture. It snatched Carrie's breath away, the same feeling she got after the first snowfall each year.

"Truth be told, some people don't like the Crazy Quilt so much," Yonnie said, gently smoothing her weathered hand across the tiny stitches. "It's usually made of scrap cloth. But for some reason it's one of my favorites. Daniel's too." She paused to take a breath.

"Thank you, Yonnie. I will always treasure it." Carrie's life felt like a Crazy Quilt right now, long before the pieces were brought together into a pattern. Would they ever?

Carrie looked in the mirror one last time, took a deep breath, and followed Yonnie down the stairs to go marry Daniel Miller.

❦❦

All of the furniture in the front room had been moved out for the wedding to allow room for seating. The traditional celery-filled vases had been placed around the house, and a mountain of food had been prepared by the ladies in the church. As Carrie stood beside Daniel in front of the bishop, her name was forever changed from Carrie Weaver to Carrie Miller.

The wedding lasted the entire afternoon and evening. Two meals were served for over three hundred people. Emma was happiest at weddings, Carrie thought, watching her move from table to table like a bumblebee over a field of flowers.

Carrie and Daniel were seated for meals

at the Eck, the corner table reserved for the bride and groom. She noticed that her school friends seemed childish and silly compared to Daniel. Many of them hadn't been baptized yet and were still in the throes of their Rumspringa, sampling temptations that the world had to offer before re- nouncing worldly pleasures for good. All but Mattie, Carrie realized, watching her as she talked to Andy. Mattie never seemed to need a Rumspringa to know who she was. She was born knowing. She was like the hymn sung at the wedding ceremony, al- ways sung in the same, sure way.

Later that night, after the last buggy pulled out of the gravel driveway and the last dish had been washed and put away, Carrie went upstairs to get ready for bed. She felt all trembly and shaky too, as if she'd been sipping on Esther's sweet rhubarb wine. Her stomach felt like a knotted fist. This was the moment that she had been dread- ing, ever since she had agreed to marry Daniel. She reviewed in her mind all of the reasons she had married Daniel—that she needed a home for her and Andy, that her father had approved of Daniel and hoped for this union. In a far corner of her heart, she knew this was the right thing to do. But she had dreamed about her wedding for years now, and the man in her dreams who would be knocking on her door should have been Solomon Riehl.

She gazed out the window at the sliver of a new moon. Not a moment later, Daniel knocked at the door. Carrie cleared her throat. "C-come in," she said.

Daniel came inside and closed the door behind him, hand on the doorknob. He stood there for a moment, looking at her, his expression unfathomable. She wondered if he could tell that she was shaking, though he was across the room. It seemed to her as if he was in the middle of deciding something. Then the moment passed. He walked over to the bed and grabbed a pillow and Yonnie's quilt. As he spread out the quilt on the floor, he said, "Seems best to wait. I'll sleep here."

Carrie didn't know how to respond. "Daniel, I mean to be a good wife to you," she finally said, lifting her chin bravely.

He nodded. "We can wait. Till you're ready." He took his vest and shirt off and hung them on a peg on the wall. Then, as comfortable as if he had been doing this every night of his life and she wasn't even in the room, he took off his shoes and pants, stripped down to his longjohns, and stretched out on the floor, pulling the quilt over him. "Night," he said.

Arms crossed, Carrie remained at the window, hugely relieved. She listened as Daniel's breathing settled into the even rhythm of sleep. She realized how little she knew about Daniel Miller, this man she had married. She didn't even know how old he was, or what his birthday was, or his favorite meal, or how or when his mother had passed. She didn't even know he would be so kind.

3

A few days after Carrie and Daniel's wedding, a group of men arrived at the Millers' newly purchased property early in the morning to get to work on the house. There was a lot of work to do, undoing modern conveniences to make it suitable. They disconnected the electricity, unhooked telephone jacks from the wall, lugged out a washing machine and an electric dryer, pulled screens off the windows.

About midmorning Carrie went outside to get some fresh air. She spread old quilts over the pieces of plywood resting on sawhorses that would serve as makeshift tables. Then she set out jars of coleslaw, bean salad, and applesauce that she and Emma had canned last summer. She spotted a big boulder on the lawn, soaking up the sun, so she went over to it and sat down, resting a minute.

Carrie leaned back on her elbows, grateful for the sun's warmth on her face. She looked up at the big house, at the white clapboard siding and the green shutters with little cut-out pine trees, at the stone foundation the house rested on. It was fancier than the simple Amish farmhouses she was used to. A pretty house, to be sure, but would it ever be a home to her? Would she ever learn to be content in this life she chose? She felt so strange inside. Sad and lonely and missing the life she thought she would have.

A small red car without a top on it suddenly swerved onto the circular gravel driveway and parked by the front door. Out hopped a young woman, talking to herself. She had an odd black clothespin attached to her ear. She didn't notice Carrie as she hurried to the door. She pressed the doorbell, glanced at her wristwatch, then pressed the doorbell again.

Carrie watched the stranger for a while, amused by the woman's growing irritation. She had red hair, long and sleek, held back by a dark band around her head. Her white shirt hugged her body, with the shortest skirt and the longest legs Carrie had ever seen. The heels on her shoes were so tall that Carrie wondered how she could walk on them without tipping over.

Finally, the stranger turned around impatiently, scanning the yard, and noticed Carrie. "Miss? Oh miss?" She waved. "Your doorbell doesn't work."

"No. I guess it doesn't." Carrie got to her feet, dusted off her apron, and went over to finish setting the table for lunch.

"Are you the homeowner?" she asked, hurrying over to Carrie.

Carrie looked up at the big house. "Yes, I suppose I am."

Relief smoothed out her face. "Good! My name is Veronica McCall. Here's my business card."

The woman was very pretty, Carrie thought. She had creamy white skin, even features, but her green eyes . . . they had a sharpness to them, like the glint of a frozen pond reflecting a winter sky.

Carrie took the business card, read it, then slipped it into her apron pocket. "Hello, Veronica McCall." She gave her a nod and started to put cups at each place setting.

She trotted behind Carrie. "And you are . . . ?"

"I'm Carrie Miller." It sounded strange to her tongue to stick Miller after her name.

"Well, Carrie, if you don't mind giving me a few minutes of your time, I'd like to discuss purchasing your property."

Carrie laid out forks and plates at each spot. "Thank you, Veronica McCall, but this property is not for sale."

Veronica McCall was not easily dissuaded. "I can guarantee a profit for you."

Carrie smiled and shook her head. She had forgotten napkins, so she turned to head back into the kitchen just as Davy Zook, Mattie's brother, burst outside, holding a big metal box.

Veronica McCall stared at him as he hoisted the box in the wagon. "Is that a microwave?"

"Would you like it?" Carrie asked her. "We have no use for it."

She looked mystified.

"You're welcome to anything in that wagon, Veronica McCall."

Her eyes were locked on the wagon's contents: an electric stove, two window air conditioners, a room heater, electric wall lamps. "Are you moving out? Or in?"

"Moving in. Fixing the house up. Soon, they'll be pulling down the walls inside to make it so we can fit a large gathering for Sunday meetings." The confused expression on her face amused Carrie. "Are you new to our county, Veronica McCall?"

She shook her head as if trying to remember why she was here. "Yes. I just moved here from San Francisco."

"Earthquake country."

"Well, yes, but I'd take an earthquake any day over these lightning and thunderstorms." She scanned the skies for any threatening clouds, frowning.

"It would take a leap of faith for me to live in earthquake country," Carrie answered. Suddenly, she smiled. She was trying to decide on a name for her new home but hadn't settled on any. Maybe she should call it Leap of Faith Farm. Or better still: Blind Leap of Faith Farm. That's exactly what it felt like. Like she was taking a gigantic leap of faith. With her eyes closed shut.

Veronica McCall laughed. "I hope we can become friends, Carrie."

Carrie thought she saw a glimmer of sincerity behind those cold, glittering green eyes. But maybe not.

"Anyway, as you can see on the business card—"

Carrie patted her apron pocket.

"—I'm in business development for my corporation. We're very interested in acquiring property we can convert into a golf course. Finding land around here is nearly impossible. Yours has ideal topography." She paused for a moment, looking out across to the even rows of trees in the orchards.

"The slopes help to minimize frost damage to the apples," Carrie said. She had heard her father tell Eli that very thing.

Veronica ignored her. "It's possible that the house could be converted to a clubhouse, and that area there"—she made a sweeping gesture with her hand—"could be torn down and used for parking. Really, it's perfect. We're hoping we won't even need double fairways." She turned to Carrie.

"Safety can be a factor with double fairways, you know."

Carrie didn't understand her words, or the meaning behind them, so she answered with silence.

"Of course, we have to get rid of that old carriage house and that barn. So many rickety old barns in this area." She made a clucking sound.

"There's a saying in the Plain life: 'A farm is not a farm without its barn,'" Carrie said.

Veronica opened her mouth to say something, then snapped it shut and tilted her head at Carrie, puzzled.

"The Amish build their barns first. When the farm is successful, a good house follows. To the Amish, a barn is more important than a house."

Veronica shook that thought off, then resumed her sales pitch. "And this property holds excellent proximity to Honor Mansion, which is really why I'm here." She spun around to face Carrie. "The hotel was recently bought by my corporation, Bonnatt's Development Company. First, we have plans for a major renovation on the mansion. You know, day spa, tennis courts, and then, a golf course." She flashed a brilliant smile, revealing white, even teeth. "So, Carrie, how much would you like for it?"

Carrie admired this woman's tenacity, but she had work to do. "Thank you, but as I said, it's not for sale."

Veronica sighed. "Is there anyone else whom I could speak to?"

"You could talk to Eli Miller. He's just coming up from the barn now." Eli, Daniel, and a few other men were walking toward them from the barn. They had been examining where to put the blacksmithing shop that they planned as a sideline business. Apples alone weren't enough to pay the bills.

"Which one is he?" Veronica asked. "They all look alike! Blue shirts, black trousers with suspenders, straw hats—"

"He's the only one with whiskers. Only married men wear whiskers. The bachelors are clean shaven." Daniel's jawline just showed the shadow of a new beard.

She squinted her eyes. "The one who looks like he's got a shoehorn wrapped around his chin?"

"That's Eli."

"So a beard takes the place of a wedding ring?"

She nearly surprised a smile out of Carrie, the way this woman talked. Carrie nodded.

"Thank you, Carrie!" Veronica called out, as she hurried toward Eli.

Carrie couldn't resist a grin when she saw how quickly Eli shooed Veronica McCall off. They all stood and watched as she zoomed away in her little car. Her red hair flew behind her like a flag waving in the wind.

"Englisch," Eli muttered, shaking his head as he passed by Carrie to head into the house.

❧❦

With help from neighbors, Carrie and Daniel moved into the farmhouse at the apple orchard by week's end. Since Carrie and Daniel married in September, with their apple crop ready to harvest and sell, they skipped the honeymoon visits to relatives.

Carrie knew that Andy was never fond of school, but she couldn't understand why, after the first few weeks, he seemed reluctant to leave the house each morning.

"You're sure you're not sick?" she asked him, putting a cool hand to his forehead.

"Nah," he said, pulling away from her. "But maybe you should pack me another brownie. I get awful hungry."

"But I packed you two yesterday. How could you still be hungry?" Carrie asked, frowning. "And put your shoes on. You are not to go barefoot. Ever, ever, ever. You know that. Too much risk of cutting yourself."

Andy sighed wearily and bent down to put his socks and shoes on. Daniel was sipping his coffee, his eyes on Andy, narrowed slightly in the way of a man studying a mildly perturbing question.

Carrie packed up a third brownie and handed Andy his lunch pail, then opened the door for him. "Go, Andy! You'll be late!" Andy poked his head out the door, looked both ways before stepping out on the porch, then lit into a sprint and flew down the lane.

Carrie leaned against the doorjamb watching Andy for a minute, puzzled. As she closed the door, Daniel blotted his mouth with his napkin and got to his feet. He scooped his straw hat off of the peg and stepped around her.

"Where are you off to, Daniel?" she asked. "To the orchards? Should I tell Eli you'll meet him there?"

He was halfway out the door when he tossed a "no" over his shoulder. Then he hopped onto a blue scooter, resting against the house, to catch up with Andy.

Carrie turned to Yonnie and shrugged, exasperated. "Why use two words when one will do?"

Yonnie smiled and continued to drizzle white icing over cinnamon rolls, hot from the oven. "Daniel doesn't say much because he's busy listening. He hears what others miss because he listens more than he talks."

Carrie looked at her, puzzled.

"He feels the sounds deep inside him."

❧❧

Solomon Riehl didn't receive his mother's letter until he returned to Lancaster after traveling with the Barnstormers to Maryland, New York, and New Jersey. All of the team mail for the players had been held at Clipper Magazine Stadium. Sol had started to receive so much fan mail that he didn't even notice his mother's familiar handwriting until he had read halfway through the

passed by them one morning in her buggy
as she came to help Carrie cut up apples
to dry on racks for snitz.

"Morning, Carrie."

Somehow, Emma could make a simple
greeting sound worried, Carrie thought, as
she hung Emma's bonnet upside down on
the peg, hanging next to hers and Yonnie's like three black coal scuttles. Emma
lived most of her life in a near panic.

"You know why Daniel's doing that, don't
you?" Emma asked.

Carrie bristled, irritated by Emma's nosi-
ness. "Of course I know why." Though the
truth of it was that she didn't really know
why, but she was grateful that Daniel took
an interest in Andy. Andy needed a man in
his life. At least, that was Carrie's reasoning when she told Esther she was taking
Andy with her to live. Carrie thought Esther would have been relieved, but instead,
she reacted with a cold fury. She barely
spoke to Carrie during the wedding and
hadn't come to visit Carrie at all since. Esther always had something to be angry
about, Carrie knew. She had learned long
ago that the only way to handle her was to
stand up to her, but Esther nursed her

pile of letters. He read the letter, then re
it. A clear stream of fear pooled from
throat to his stomach, the quick panic
comes when you realize something
gone terribly wrong, something that it is s
ply too late to fix.

"Who's that one from, Amish boy?" as
Pete, an outfielder on the team. "From
look on your face, you just got dumped."
guffawed loudly.

Sol looked over at Pete, not really see
him. He took his mother's letter and hurri
outside of the locker room, then ran to l
car. The keys shook in his hand as he stu
bled to unlock the door. Some paint flak
off in his hands as he yanked the do
open to climb in. Carrie had called his c
Rusty because it had so much rust und
its chassis.

Carrie, he thought, *how could you d
this? How could you have married some
one else?*

He locked the door, sank down low i
the seat, and cried like a baby.

⁂

For the next few days, Daniel rode Andy
to school on the scooter and met him
each afternoon, as school let out. Emma

grudges with the same loving care she gave to her roses.

Emma pulled up a chair to sit down, eager to divulge her news. "Well, I heard that your new English neighbor boys take Andy's lunch on the way to school. They wait for him at the end of the lane."

Carrie looked out the kitchen window. "Who told you that?"

"I heard it at a comfort knotting at Ada Stoltzfus's farm. You should have gone to the frolic, Carrie. Yonnie too. You learn all kinds of things."

Carrie frowned. She wasn't ready for a frolic yet, for all the questions about married life. "So, what's he like then, this Daniel? What sort of man is he?" her well-meaning friends would ask. Carrie wondered those questions herself. She wasn't sure she knew Daniel any better today than she did a few weeks ago.

"Why would those boys be taking Andy's lunch?"

"Well," Emma started out breathlessly, cheeks turning pink with pleasure, "they found out he's a bleeder, and they told him they want to see him bleed. They're picking a fight with him so he'll bleed."

Carrie threw the dish towel down and ran down the lane. By the time she reached the end of the lane, Daniel was on the way back.

"Emma told me!" she said, out of breath, when she reached him. "About the boys teasing Andy."

Daniel glanced over at the neighbor boys, who were throwing rocks at a tree-top, trying to knock down a bird's nest. The mother bird flew close by, making distress calls.

Carrie saw them too. She frowned at them, but said to Daniel, "You can't take him to and from school for the rest of his life. Maybe I could speak to their parents so they'd understand how serious hemophilia is." Andy was small, built like Jacob, and looked younger than his years. She worried about him. She always worried about him.

Daniel's eyebrows lifted in warning. "And shame him with a fuss?"

"I'm not making a fuss," she said indignantly.

Daniel's gaze turned toward the boys. "As soon as the weather gets cold, they'll lose interest in meeting him so early." Daniel put one foot on the scooter. "Coming?"

She sighed and hopped on behind him for a lift.

※

"Mother, you ought not to be eating dessert for breakfast," Eli said quietly when he came inside from the barn one morning.

Yonnie was seated at the kitchen table having a slice of pie. "The way I see it, just in case the day doesn't turn out well, at least I've had my dessert."

"I like that way of thinking!" Andy said, bouncing down the stairs.

Eli looked at Yonnie and shook his head. Carrie handed him a cup of coffee as he sat down. "You see, Mother? You're a bad influence on the boy. Carrie, I'm counting on you not to let her get away with this nonsense."

Carrie smiled at the teasing, but she knew Eli was counting on her for much more than minding Yonnie. She knew he had hopes that Carrie would be able to turn Daniel around from his burden. Daniel seemed to have an invisible cloud of sadness hovering over him. She hadn't figured out what Daniel's burden was, but she had a hunch it had something to do with Abel, his cousin, raised as a brother to Daniel, who had left the family during his Rumspringa. Every so often, a letter from Abel would arrive and she would see Daniel quietly tuck it into his pocket. The letter's contents were never discussed. But for the rest of the day, Daniel and Eli would go quiet, even by their standards.

Carrie was filled with wonderings about this Abel fellow, whether he was younger or older than Daniel and where he was now. But it was Daniel's place to tell her these things and he was not one to volunteer information. Abel's name was hardly spoken between Eli or Daniel, or even Yonnie. It was like he had stopped living, like he was shunned, even though that couldn't be right. Carrie knew Abel hadn't been baptized, so he wouldn't be shunned. Yonnie had let that slip once. Carrie tried asking Yonnie more, about where Abel was now, but she could see Yonnie's mind drift off to another place and another time. Yonnie never did answer. Yonnie was a Miller, to be sure.

Carrie had wanted a home of her own and a future for her brother. In exchange, she received the hidden secrets and heart-aches of the Millers.

※※

In the middle of the night, Carrie woke and went downstairs, out to the porch to look at the stars. A few minutes later, Daniel joined her, wrapping a quilt around her shoulders.

Daniel was a deep sleeper. He could fall asleep instantly, she could tell so by the sound of his breathing. But he always seemed to know when she left the room. Maybe it was part of his listening, she realized. Even in his sleep, he seemed to listen.

"I had a nightmare," she said, hoping he would stay for a moment. "Andy had fallen and needed my help, but I couldn't get to him. It was like I was in quicksand. He kept calling for me and I couldn't get any closer."

"Just a dream," he said.

Carrie pulled the quilt tightly around her. "If anything ever happened to Andy . . ." Her voice drizzled off.

"It won't." Daniel leaned on the porch railing and looked up at the night sky.

A barn owl flew over them so closely they could hear the whir of its wings.

"The winged tiger," Daniel said, watching the owl disappear into the treetops.

Carrie tilted her head toward Daniel. "That's what my father used to call owls! They fly silently as moths and seldom miss their prey." She gave a short laugh. "Esther would correct him and say they're just flying rat traps."

"You miss him." He said the words simply, his voice low and flat.

"I do miss him. So much that at times I . . ." She shrugged, pressing her lips together.

Daniel nodded, as if he understood.

"Mattie said that all of creation is meant to remind us that God is nearby. She said that God is closer than our own breath." She turned slightly to face Daniel. "Do you think she's right?"

She saw a flash of something in his eyes, the echoes of a longing, a sadness. "I'm not the one to ask." He went to the door and held it open. "Don't stay up too late. Morning comes early."

Sometimes, she thought, turning back to gaze at the night sky, trying to talk to Daniel felt like trying to pump a dry well.

❦

One afternoon, Carrie went to town to run some errands. When she returned to the farm late in the day, Daniel came out of the barn to help her down from the buggy.

"I'm sorry I'm late. I'll get dinner started right off," she told him as he unhitched Old-Timer from the tracings.

Carrie hurried to the kitchen and saw Yonnie at the stovetop, stirring a sauce. Glancing at the table, she noticed it was already set for dinner. "Oh, bless you, Yonnie!" She hung her bonnet up on the peg and untied her cape when she remembered that she had left a few packages in the back of the buggy and rushed down to the barn to get them.

As she reached the partly open barn door, she saw Andy drag a sack of oats over to Daniel, talking as he pulled.

"He used to be Amish but now he plays baseball," she heard him say.

Daniel stopped in mid-turn. "The baseball player? The one everyone talks about?"

"Yeah. He's the one." Andy held up an English newspaper, pointing to the headline about the Lancaster Barnstormers, about Sol's pitching.

Carrie had found the newspaper abandoned on a bench near the hitching post in town where she tied Old-Timer's reins. She had picked it up. When she was nearing home, she had turned down a quiet lane and pulled the buggy over to the side to read the article about Sol. She read it and reread it, then realized how late it was. That foolish action had made her late getting home, late starting dinner. She clapped her hands to her cheeks. How could she have been so careless to have left the newspaper in the buggy?

Andy held the sack of oats open so Daniel could scoop them into Old-Timer's bucket. "Solomon Riehl was courting Carrie, but then he disappeared, right when my dad passed. So she married you."

Carrie slid open the barn door and walked in. "Andy!" she said sharply.

Startled, Andy nearly knocked over the sack of oats.

"Geh zu Yonnie im Haus." *Go to Yonnie in the house.*

Andy looked at Carrie in mute astonishment, surprised by the sharp tone in her voice, but he hustled past her to go to the kitchen without a questioning word or glance.

Daniel turned back to filling the bucket with oats as if nothing had happened. Carrie picked up the newspaper and folded it. She wasn't sure what to say. Maybe she didn't need to say anything at all. She turned to leave and stopped when she heard Daniel ask, "So Solomon Riehl was the midnight caller?"

Carrie spun toward Daniel, who still had his back to her. "Yes."

Daniel put the bucket down and turned to face Carrie. "It was like Andy said?"

Carrie looked down at her hands nervously, avoiding Daniel's steady gaze. "Yes," she answered quietly.

Daniel didn't say a word, he just stood there, waiting for her to continue.

"Sol wanted to play for the Barnstormers and wanted me with him. We had made plans to leave. We were going to be married that very week when my father died. But . . . then everything changed. I couldn't leave Andy." She looked down at the hay-strewn floor. "Sol left anyway. The night that Andy was in the emergency room, after Esther had taken the switch to him, I knew I had to get Andy out of Esther's home. When you asked me to marry you, it seemed like . . . an opportunity." She lifted her eyes to gauge his response, but his face was expressionless. "I told you that I wasn't in love with you. I've never tried to deceive you."

He glanced out the barn window. "But you didn't mention you loved someone else."

The silence between them felt as real as a brick wall. Finally, she asked softly, "Daniel, why did you marry me?"

He didn't move for a moment, didn't say anything. She couldn't read him well enough to know what he was thinking. Finally, he took a few steps toward her and gently lifted her chin so that she would look at him. They were inches apart, close enough to feel each other's breath.

"Same as you, Carrie. Trying to forget."

Daniel strode past her, out of the barn and into the orchards, not returning home until long after dark.

4

The pitching coach slapped Sol on the back as he jogged in from the mound after practice on Monday. "We clocked you at over 95 miles per hour! Fastest ever!" He was nearly bursting with pride. "Not sure what you had for breakfast, but keep it up, Sol."

Sol nodded, before heading into the locker room for a shower. The other guys on the team congratulated him as he peeled off his uniform. "You must be as pumped up as a hot air balloon after that practice," said Rody, the catcher.

Sol shrugged. "Just a good day, I guess."

But he knew why. Every time he wound up for a pitch, the image of Carrie in another man's arms popped into his head. He pictured the catcher's mitt as the man's face—he could barely remember what Daniel Miller looked like—and he threw that ball as hard as he possibly could.

"Some of the guys are going out for a cold beer." Seeing his hesitation, Rody threw a wet towel at him. "Come on. I'll treat."

Sol slammed his locker shut. "Okay. Give me ten minutes to shower."

※

Veronica McCall dropped by on a weekly basis to ask Carrie if she was ready to sell the property. Each time, Carrie said no. Today, Emma was visiting to help Carrie can applesauce. Veronica smelled the freshly brewed coffee and helped herself to a cup.

As she poured the coffee into the mug, she glanced out the kitchen window. "Do all Amish men look like him?"

"Who?" Carrie asked, cutting the apples and tossing them into a big pot.

"Him. He's a hottie." She pointed out the window. "He could be on the cover of *GQ*."

She turned to Emma to explain. *"Gentleman's Quarterly.* It's a magazine that has a gorgeous hunk on its cover every month."

Carrie put her knife down, wiped her hands on her apron, and looked out the window to see who Veronica meant. "Why, that's Daniel!"

"Who's he?" Veronica asked.

"Carrie's *husband*," Emma said, raising an eyebrow.

"He's my grandson," Yonnie added, in a voice of quiet pride. Seated at the kitchen table, Yonnie had been peeling apples for a pie. She had a trick of peeling the entire apple skin in one long ribbon—a talent that impressed Andy.

Veronica shrugged. "Your husband is a babe, Carrie. He could be a male model." They watched Daniel lift a bale of hay from the wagon and toss it onto a wheelbarrow. "He's got muscles in his arms that look like ropes."

Carrie looked at her as if she was speaking a foreign language.

Emma pointed her paring knife in Veronica's direction. "Lusting after another woman's husband is a sin."

Veronica turned to Emma with catlike

eyes. "There's nothing wrong with admiring nature's handiwork." She glanced at her wristwatch. "Gotta go." She picked an apple slice out of Emma's bowl of cut apples and sailed out the door.

"Carrie, we need to keep an eye on *that* woman," Emma said, scowling, turning her attention back to her apples. "The English aren't like the Amish."

"And the Amish aren't like the English, Emma," Yonnie said. "My Daniel does not have a roving eye."

Carrie stood by the kitchen window, watching Veronica as she walked over to Daniel. She wondered what Veronica said to make him laugh. Before turning from the window, she did happen to notice that Veronica was right. His arms did look like thick pieces of rope.

❧❦

Mattie had asked Carrie to help her sew a new dress. After purchasing the fabric in town, they returned to Carrie's house to use one of her patterns. While Carrie hunted for the patterns upstairs, Mattie started some coffee in the kitchen. She inhaled the aroma from the coffee grounds as she scooped the coffee out of the can and into the filter.

As she filled the coffee brewer with water, her thoughts drifted to Carrie. She felt troubled about her friend, sensing a wound deep in Carrie's soul, a wound that wasn't healing.

Mattie knew that losing her father was a profound loss to Carrie. What she couldn't figure out was why Carrie married Daniel so soon after Jacob died. And why she never seemed bothered by Sol's leaving. Maybe, Mattie thought, it was because Daniel was the one Jacob had chosen for Carrie. As Mattie waited for the coffee to finish brewing, she looked outside the kitchen window and saw Eli and Daniel unhitching Old-Timer from the buggy the women had used to go into town.

Daniel treated Carrie tenderly, Mattie had often noticed. He lifted her out of the buggy as if she were made of fine china. He waited to sit at the kitchen table until Carrie sat first. He really was a fine-looking man, she thought, watching him lead the horse into the barn. Tall and broad shouldered, fair haired with sky-blue eyes rimmed by dark eyebrows. He had a cleft in his chin, still visible. His blond beard, circling his jawline, was just growing in. Mattie would have assumed he would be a younger version of his father Eli, slim and wiry and worried. Daniel was nearly as handsome as Sol.

As Mattie opened up the cupboard to find the coffee mugs, Daniel came into the kitchen. "Wu is sie?" he asked gruffly. *Where is she?*

"Carrie's upstairs." Just as Mattie was about to ask him if he wanted coffee, Carrie came downstairs with the box of patterns in her arms.

"Was is letz?" Carrie asked, seeing the look on Daniel's face. *What's wrong?*

He slapped an English newspaper on the kitchen table, open to the sports section with a large headline: "Amish Sol Pitches a No-Hitter." He kept his eyes fixed on Carrie, brows furrowed. Carrie kept her eyes on the newspaper.

The silence in the kitchen took on a prickly tension. "It's mine," Mattie blurted out at last. "I bought it in town."

Both Daniel and Carrie snapped their heads toward her, eyes wide in surprise.

"I saw the headline and wanted to read about Sol," Mattie said. As Daniel and Carrie continued to stare at her, she felt her mouth go dry. "I love Sol. I always will, no matter what he's done. He's coming back one day. I'm sure of it." Mattie's eyes started to fill with tears. She stole a glance at Carrie and saw hurt flood into her eyes.

Suddenly, Mattie understood.

Without another word, Mattie put the coffee mugs on the counter and quietly left to go home. She was almost to the street when she heard Daniel call her name as he ran up to her.

"Here," he said, handing her the newspaper.

❦

Later that night, Carrie changed into her nightgown and took the pins out of her hair, braiding the loose strands into a long rope. She slipped into bed and peered over the edge at Daniel, stretched out on the floor. "Are you asleep?"

He turned to his side, facing the window. "Nearly."

"Daniel—"

"Mattie was lying." He rolled over on his back, eyes facing the ceiling. "Just not sure what part of it she was lying about."

All afternoon, Carrie had been thinking the same thing. Mattie had *lied*! Carrie was the one who had bought that newspaper.

But was Mattie also lying about loving Sol? Carrie wasn't sure. She punched the pillow into shape and laid her head on it.

"Seems at times there are three people in this marriage," Daniel said in a low voice.

With that, Carrie's temper flared. "You're wrong." She looked over the edge of the bed at him. "There are *four*."

The words flew out of her mouth before she even thought about them. She was only making a guess. Until that moment, she didn't know for sure that the burden Daniel carried might have something to do with a woman. "I . . . I'm sorry," she said when she saw the stark pain in his eyes, as real as if she had struck him. "I shouldn't have—"

"It's all right," he said, in a voice that hurt her with its gentleness. "I'm going to take a walk."

Daniel grabbed his shirt, pants, and shoes, and went downstairs. She heard the kitchen door close behind him.

❦

The next morning, Mattie finished her chores quickly to have time to get to Carrie's. She needed to set right yesterday's conversation. She was mortified with herself for blurting out that she loved Sol. That was a secret she had guarded so well, for years now, from the moment she had first laid eyes on him. Just as she was turning the buggy into the gravel lane, she saw Daniel come out of the barn. He stopped when he saw her and waited until she came to a halt.

"Morning, Daniel," she said shyly. "Is Carrie inside?"

He shook his head. "Hanging the wash." He tipped his head in the direction of the clothesline, where Carrie was hanging laundry. He took the reins and helped her down from the buggy, then tied her horse to the post.

When Carrie saw Mattie approach, she put the wet shirts back in the basket and sat on the big rock in the sun, patting a spot in silent invitation for Mattie to come join her. "The wash should dry in no time with this Indian summer." A light breeze stirred the rows of clothes on the line. Yonnie's faded lavender churchgoing dress, hanging right beside her, tossed out a faint whiff of laundry soap.

Mattie nodded, head tucked down as she sat beside Carrie.

Carrie leaned against her elbows. "I've always loved this time of year. The work of summer is nearly done. It's warm, but not hot. Sort of a lull, waiting for winter."

Mattie nodded again, not saying a word, feeling like she had a knot in her throat.

Softly, Carrie asked, "Mattie, what made you tell a lie?"

Mattie covered her face with her hands. "It just flew out of me. I'm so ashamed. I feel terrible! But I could see that Daniel was upset about the newspaper."

Carrie watched the breeze twist and luff the white sheets, filling them like sails on a ship. "It was kind of you, standing up for me like that."

"I shouldn't have lied. It was wrong of me. But Carrie, we're friends." She said it in a tone as if that explained everything— her loyalty, her compassion, her devotion.

"I don't deserve such a friend."

Mattie shook that comment off. "You deserve so much more, Carrie. You're the strongest person I know. I know it's been hard lately."

Carrie looked away, but Mattie caught the glint of tears in her eyes. She noticed

Daniel, standing by the barn with his arms crossed against his black leather apron, listening to a neighbor who had just brought a horse by to be shod. "He's a good man, that Daniel."

Carrie's gaze followed Mattie's. "Why didn't you ever tell me about how you felt about Sol?"

Mattie bent down and uncoiled a shirt from the basket, shook it twice, then stood to pin it to the line. She had diverted herself on purpose to give herself time to answer carefully. "I could never help my feelings for Sol. I've loved him for as long as I can remember. But you know what a flirt he is. You know how he was with all the girls, taking a different girl home from every singing." Nearly every girl but her, Mattie thought, pausing to pick up another shirt. The truth was that Sol did not know Mattie existed for much of the time they had lived in the same town. She was far too quiet, too plain, to attract his attention.

She looked across the clothesline at Carrie. "But then, he started taking you home from Sunday singings regularly, and you didn't seem to mind." She fixed her eyes on the clothespin in her hand. "I just couldn't tell you, Carrie. I just couldn't. It's not our way."

Carrie nodded. Courting couples avoided teasing at all costs. "You're pretty good at keeping secrets, Mattie. I never would have guessed how you felt about Sol. Not ever."

Mattie smiled shyly at her.

"You must have felt some envy toward me."

"No, Carrie. Never that." Mattie meant that sincerely. She would never have let jealousy take root in her heart. "You must believe that."

Carrie grabbed the last piece of wet clothing in the basket, then hung it on the line. "Mattie, you're too good for Solomon Riehl. He has no *Demut*, no humility. He'll never return to the church."

"Don't say that," Mattie said sharply. Then she dropped her eyes to the ground. "No one is ever beyond help."

Carrie tilted her head, watching her friend. "I guess it all depends if he wants the help." She picked up the empty laundry basket and rested it on her hip. "Mattie, can I give you a piece of advice? Don't expect anything from Solomon Riehl. Then you won't be disappointed."

❦

Sunday felt different from any other day. A day set apart. Carrie had always loved church gatherings. Even as a child, there was a quiet excitement in the air. The preaching and hymn singing started early in the morning and lasted three hours, topped off with a fellowship meal, brought by the womenfolk.

Glancing across to the men's side of the room, she could see Eli, sitting ramrod straight, a somber look on his serious face. Seated next to him was Daniel. She saw Daniel's eyes lift quickly to the ceiling, as if he didn't want to be caught looking at her. It made Carrie smile, to think he was watching her. Next to Daniel sat Andy, angry and sullen.

Andy had been trying to memorize the *Lob Lied*, the hymn of praise sung at every Amish church gathering, before his ninth birthday. He had been itching to sit with the big boys in the church service, but it was tradition to wait until an Amish boy turned nine. Andy's birthday was coming up and he was determined to go in now. Before breakfast this morning, he had recited the verses one more time. When he missed the last verse, he clapped his hands on his cheeks. "Aw, Carrie, let me go in. Everyone knows I'm almost nine. They'll call me a baby."

Carrie shook her head. "No shortcuts."

"Come on!" Andy pleaded. He was near tears. "Dad would let me!"

"Go upstairs and get ready," Carrie told him. "We need to leave in a few minutes so we won't be late."

Andy bolted up the stairs, almost knocking into Daniel as he was coming down the stairs. Daniel's eyes met Carrie's briefly, then he dropped his gaze. "Is knowing that hymn so important?"

Discouraged, Carrie turned to the sink to finish the breakfast dishes. "I'm trying to make things normal for him. Trying to do what my father would want me to do with him." She scrubbed a dish. "Besides, the bishop will be watching Andy."

"Don't blame it on the bishop," Daniel said as he plucked his hat and coat off the peg. "It's Esther you're worried about. She's the one who will be watching Andy." He put his hand on the kitchen doorjamb.

"There's no such thing as normal for a grieving boy."

Through the kitchen window, Carrie watched Daniel head to the barn, thinking over what he said. It was the longest paragraph he'd uttered. Still, it amazed her that Daniel had only spent a summer in her father's home and seemed to have a better understanding of the family than she did. He was right. So was Andy. Her father wouldn't have cared about those verses. She was worried about Esther. Esther had brittle requirements for everyone, especially for Jacob's children.

Carrie threw the dish towel down, more confused than ever. She wasn't ready to be a parent, but she was thrust into that role when her father died. She decided this must be what it felt like to tuck an octopus into bed. An arm or two kept popping out.

❧

The focus of the bishop's sermon that morning was on the sinful nature of man. He was very effective. Everyone finished the morning feeling especially convicted of their wickedness. Afterward, the benches were moved and the tables set up, and the women served a soup and sandwich lunch. Carrie joined several other young women as they brought the food to the men. After the men finished eating, the women and children took their turn. When the meal was over and everything had been cleaned up, adults usually gathered in small groups to visit as children played or napped.

Today, though, folks seemed quiet, subdued. Eli herded the family into the buggy for a silent ride home. Daniel sat down on Eli's right side and picked up the reins, clucking to the horse to get it trotting. Carrie and Yonnie sat in the backseat, Andy between them. The trip home seemed to last forever, and the cramped quarters in the buggy didn't help much, either. Finally, Yonnie broke the quiet. "I think that bishop is needing a little more fiber in his diet. Maybe I'll mix up some of my special prune tea for him. Helps when the plumbing gets backed up."

Turning to look back at her, Eli scolded, "Mother! You are speaking of a bishop! Of a man chosen by God!"

"And that man is older than Moses," Yonnie muttered under her breath.

Carrie let her own smile come out in a

quick curve of her lips and a downward tuck of her chin. She avoided Andy's eyes. She knew she needed to be a good example, but sometimes she missed just being a sister, one who could share a private joke, the way they used to.

Later that day, Carrie finished feeding Hope and was leading the cow into a stall when she heard Daniel and Eli come into the barn. Through a crack between the boards she watched Daniel sit on a bale of hay, hands on his knees, chin to his chest, defeated.

Eli came over to him and put a hand on his shoulder. "You have a chance to make a new life here, a fresh start with Carrie. I knew she'd be good for you. She's a strong woman."

Carrie ducked down low by Hope's wooden wall, unnoticed. She felt as nosy as Emma, listening to people's private conversations, but from the serious way they were talking, she decided it would be worse to interrupt them.

Daniel lifted his head and said, "Didn't you hear the bishop today? Heaven's deaf to the cries of a sinner." He stood and walked to the barn door, then turned back to his father. "There's really no such thing as a fresh start. Our past doesn't let us go."

After he left, Eli sat down on the hay bale where Daniel had been. Carrie's heart nearly broke as she saw him start to shake, then hold his head in his hands as he wept. Quietly, she slipped out the back door to give him privacy.

The next morning, the weather turned cold. Carrie took some coffee to Daniel down by the barn. She watched him for a moment. Concentrating intently, he pumped the bellows to blow on the fire, then grasped a horseshoe with the tongs and thrust it into the burning coals. He looked up when he saw Carrie and gave a brief nod when his eyes rested on the hot drink. She watched him pick up the poker-hot horseshoe and plunge it into the trough of water, releasing a hiss and plume of steam.

"Every now and then, the bishop likes to remind us of our sinfulness, Daniel."

He put the tongs down and took the coffee mug from her.

"He's not usually so grim. He's really quite kind. And the ministers aren't grim. The deacon, Abraham, isn't a bit grim."

She leaned against the workbench. "Yesterday, Mattie said that maybe the bishop has been reading too much of the Old Testament lately and not enough of the New Testament." She picked up a tool, studying it. "She says that the New Testament tells us our sins are wiped clean."

Daniel took a sip of coffee but kept his eyes fixed on her.

"Whiter than snow, Mattie says. I'm not exactly sure where in the Bible it says that, but Mattie is usually right about that kind of thing. If she were born a man, the Lord would choose to give her the lot so she'd be a minister one day. I'm certain of it. Mattie's grandfather was a bishop. Caleb Zook was his name. One of the finest bishops there ever was. Everybody loved Caleb Zook. Even Esther. He passed, just a few years ago." Her words fell into an empty silence. After an awkward moment, she put down the tool and turned to go when she heard him say her name.

"Carrie?" he asked.

She spun around to face him. Daniel's eyes met hers, wide and sea blue. She could see his heart in his eyes, a heart beating with hope and hurt. She saw all of his sadness wanting to pour out so he could be freed from it. But he kept hesitating, and then the moment passed, like a cloud swallowing up the sun.

All that he said was, "Denki." He tipped his head toward the coffee cup in his hand.

"Bitte."

It was a start, she hoped.

❦

Mattie was riding her scooter down the road one afternoon when she spotted something peculiar moving in a tree. She pulled over on the scooter to examine what it was. As soon as she saw the sandy blond head, she knew. She slid off the scooter and walked to the tree. "Andy Weaver! What do you think you're doing up there?"

Startled, Andy looked down at her, eyes wide. "I'm trying to feed the baby birds. Those rotten English boys killed their mother and they're awful hungry." He put one hand in his pocket and pulled out a handful of wiggling worms. "I dug up some food for them. See?" One of the worms dropped from his hand and landed on Mattie's head.

"I'm going to the cafeteria to get Andy something to eat."

Dr. Zimmerman gave instructions to the nurse to get the IV drip for Factor IX set up for Andy, then he opened the cupboard to get the supplies for the cast. "Let's see if I can remember what they taught me in medical school." He looked at the supplies as if he'd never seen them before.

"So you're new at doctoring?" Andy asked, a little worried.

"Well, I think a day-old degree is good enough, don't you?" Dr. Zimmerman answered, eyes snapping with good humor. Andy's eyes, as wide as saucers, made Dr. Zimmerman burst into laughter at his own joke. He started unwrapping the gauze. "What color cast do you want?" he asked Andy. "Neon green would make the school kids think you're a super action figure."

"White," Carrie interrupted.

Andy groaned.

The doctor looked at Carrie with a question.

"We don't like things showy or loud," she said. "We don't want anything that draws attention."

"What's so wrong with drawing attention to yourself?" the doctor asked.

Carrie wrinkled her brow. "What's so right about it?"

The doctor shrugged. "Good point." He turned to Andy. "White would be my choice too." He lowered his voice to a whisper. "That way, you can tell kids that it's really leprosy."

"What's leprosy?" Andy asked.

"It's a highly contagious disease that eats away at your skin," he said, mixing up the plaster to spread over the gauze. "Looks pretty disgusting. Very effective way to gross out your friends."

Watching him with fascination, Andy brightened considerably at that news.

❧

After an hour's wait in the waiting room, Solomon Riehl had just been admitted into the Emergency Room. His shoulder was throbbing and he wasn't sure what was wrong with it. It had been bothering him for a few weeks now, but aspirin usually took the edge off of the pain. Not today, though. He didn't want to talk to the team's trainer; if he did, it would be noted on his records. That could tip off the pitching

coach to a problem. The coach was con-
servative like that. Sol just had to get
through another few weeks, then he could
give his shoulder a good long rest. He was
hoping he could get a cortisone shot or
something, like the other guys on the team
did.

On the far side of the room, past the
nurse's station, the silhouette of an Amish
woman caught his eye. He put his things
down on the bed, then looked closer to see
if he might know who she was. He knew
most of the Amish in Stoney Ridge. The
woman had her back to him, facing the
doctor. The doctor had put the blood pressure cuff around his own head and started
to pump, making the boy on the bed start to
giggle, then to guffaw out loud. Sol's heart
started to pound. He knew that laugh. That
was Andy's laugh. And if that was Andy,
then the Amish woman was Carrie. He
hadn't seen her since the day he had left. It
still made his insides twist up, every single
day, what he had done to her.

Sol watched as the doctor high-fived
Andy's good hand before he left. The nurse
started an IV on Andy. Sol figured it was
that hemophilia stuff he needed. After the

nurse left, Sol jumped off the bed and grabbed his jacket. In that instant, an Amish man arrived, hat in hand, and stood by the door, scanning the room until his eyes rested on Carrie. In a few quick strides, the man reached her side and stood close to her. She leaned in against him, to tell him something. Sol drew back, as if touching a hot stove.

After a while, Sol saw the man head out the door into the hallway and decided to follow him. He slipped into the hallway and saw the cafeteria doors swing shut. Sol peered through the small window of the door and noticed the man, standing in front of the coffee vending machine, feeding the machine with coins.

Sol pushed open the cafeteria door. "She likes her coffee black," he said, walking up to the man.

Daniel looked at Sol, puzzled.

"Carrie," Sol said. "She likes it black because that's how her father liked his coffee."

Recognition dawned in Daniel's eyes. "Solomon Riehl," he stated, a fact.

"I am," Sol said. "And you're Daniel Miller."

Sol and Daniel stood looking at each

other for a long moment, sizing each other up.

Daniel turned back to the coffee machine and punched the buttons for cream and sugar. After the cup filled, he turned to go.

Sol blocked his path. "She loves me, you know. She'll always love me."

Daniel swirled the coffee in his hand, watching the warm shades of brown and cream blend together.

"I happened to be in Ohio awhile back, playing a scrimmage." Sol watched Daniel carefully to see if there was any reaction, but he could have been describing the weather. Daniel's face was hugely unreadable. "Met a few Amish guys who came to watch me play. Guess they had heard about me."

Daniel lifted his head to look Sol straight in the eyes.

"They told me an interesting story about you and your cousin. About why you left Ohio."

Daniel's eyebrows lifted.

"Made me wonder how much Carrie knows. About you, I mean."

Sol thought he caught a flash of

something in Daniel's eyes, then there was nothing.

Daniel lifted the coffee cup. "She likes it with cream and sugar because that's the way her mother drank it." He opened the door to leave, tossing over his shoulder, "My Carrie is waiting for me."

Sol stood there for a moment, watching the doors swing shut. It was common for the Amish to call each other "my" or "our"; it was part of belonging. But that wasn't how he meant it, Sol thought. Daniel Miller said "my Carrie" like a claim.

A young woman's soft and soothing voice came from behind him. "Hello, Solomon."

Sol spun around to see who was talking to him. There, smiling ear to ear, stood little Mattie Zook.

❧❧

On the way home, Daniel stopped the buggy at the tree where Andy had been climbing when he fell. Andy had begged him to save the birds and bring the nest home.

Daniel shimmied up the tree and peered in the nest. "They're Cooper's hawks!"

"So?" Andy yelled.

Daniel looked down at him. "They're predators. They steal other bird eggs. And go after small animals too."

"You said that every creature has a purpose, Daniel," Andy yelled back. "You told me that."

Daniel gave an exaggerated sigh. "So I did."

"Them birds need our help!"

Daniel untangled the nest from its crook. He tucked it under his arm and shimmied back down the tree. There were three baby birds in the nest, already near death's door, panting and gasping, hardly moving. Andy reached into his pocket with his good hand and pulled out what was left of the worms he had caught that morning. He cradled the nest in his lap and tried to jam bits of worm into the birds' beaks.

"They need water," Daniel said.

"Yonnie might have an eye dropper in her medicine chest," Carrie said. "You can try that." But the feeble condition of those baby birds worried her. Andy was just barely getting over their father's death, if such a thing were possible, she thought. She wasn't really sure she'd ever feel the same way she did before Jacob died. The pain wasn't as severe as it had been a few months ago, though it would catch her off guard sometimes. Just yesterday, she found a list with Jacob's handwriting on it and tears flooded her eyes. Most days, though, grief wasn't at the forefront anymore.

Still, neither was happiness.

By the next afternoon, with Andy's vigilant care, the baby birds made a complete turnaround. They were noisy and demanding houseguests. Smelly too. Carrie insisted that the nest be moved out of the warm kitchen and into the barn. Andy objected, certain they would freeze to death.

"They'll be fine, Andy," Carrie said reassuringly. "The barn is protected." She pointed to the barn. "Go."

Just as soon as Andy disappeared into the barn with the nest, Mattie came to the door bringing a box wrapped up in warm scarves. She unwrapped the box on the kitchen table. Inside were five creamy white eggs. "They're Canada geese eggs. Dad ordered a batch to restock the pond. You'll need to keep them incubated for about a month. I thought, in case the hawk babies don't make it, well, this way he'd have something else to take care of."

Mattie packed the eggs up again to keep them warm.

Daniel took the box out of her arms to take to the barn. Solemnly, he looked at her and said, "You have a good heart, Mattie Zook."

5

It was just about a year ago, Carrie realized, on a beautiful fall day just like today—crisp and cold, with leaves on the trees in shades from red to yellow—that she had made her last batch of sweet cider with her father. She had watched Jacob closely as he mixed juices from different varieties of apples to make his sweet cider. He was very particular about his cider.

"Folks count on my cider, Carrie girl, to help them get through the long winter, so we got to make it just right."

Together, they sampled blends before deciding on the perfect combination. "Thirty-six apples, not one more or one less, make a gallon of cider," he had said, counting them out.

Even then, she felt a shiver of precognition, to seal that memory—a perfect moment, a perfect day.

After Daniel sold the fancy-grade apples from this year's harvest to a packing house, Carrie decided to use the leftover apples to re-create her father's cider. In the carriage house, Daniel had found an old cider press and cleaned it up for her. All week, she had been trying to match the taste of her father's cider—sweet and tart. Carrie didn't think the taste of her cider rivaled Jacob's—her apple varieties differed from his—but it was close enough for the neighbors. At church on Sunday, Carrie told one person, the right person— Emma—that she was making Jacob's cider, and by Monday morning, neighbors were lined up at the farmhouse with empty plastic gallon milk jugs.

One of the first customers was Annie Zook, a school friend of Carrie's who married one of Mattie's cousins and was pregnant with twins.

"That girl is about ready to pop," Emma

said, waving to Annie as she drove off in the buggy. Emma had come for the day, to help, she said, but she spent her time talking with visiting neighbors. She glanced curiously at Carrie's flat midriff. "Seems like we should be getting an announcement pretty soon, doesn't it?" Then she frowned. "Though Mother said that you might take after your own mother, who had trouble having babies. She said your mother was a frail and sickly thing. She said your mother was a carrier of hemophilia and that's why it was a double whammy with Jacob being a bleeder and Andy being a bleeder. She wondered if you might have trouble too."

Carrie stiffened but wasn't surprised. The Plain had a saying: a new baby every spring. "If Esther seems to know so much about me," she asked Emma, "why don't you just ask her?"

These days, Esther barely said more than a few words to Carrie other than to point out Andy's shortcomings. Yesterday at church, Esther had picked up Andy by the back of the collar, like a coat on a peg, and told Carrie that he needed a haircut.

Emma planted her hands on her hips.

"There's no need to get huffy. I just figured you'd be—"

"Cinnamon rolls are burning, Emma," Daniel interrupted, passing the women on his way to the barn.

"Himmel! No! I told Yonnie to take them out thirty minutes ago . . ." Emma hurried to the kitchen, her legs pumping hard as if she were being chased by a swarm of yellow jackets.

Carrie turned to Daniel. "I saw Yonnie take those rolls out of the oven awhile ago."

His eyes crinkled at the corners. "Ach? Ich bin letz." *Oh? My mistake.* Into his mouth he popped the last bite of a cinnamon roll he had hidden behind his black leather apron. A smile flickered over Daniel's lips, so quick, so faint, that Carrie thought she might have imagined it.

❧❦

The first snowfall of winter dusted Stoney Ridge on Christmas. Before dawn, Daniel woke Andy to show him the sight of moonlight casting shadows on the white earth. Afterward, the two went into the barn to feed the animals. Andy flew out of the barn and let out a thunderbuster bellow that shook the air. Carrie rushed down,

thinking something terrible must have happened.

Instead, it was something wonderful.

Daniel had surprised Andy with a pony,
Strawberry, and a cart of his own. When
Carrie saw the look on Andy's face as he
stroked the roan-colored pony in the stall,
her eyes filled with tears.

"Aw, it's not so much, Carrie," Daniel
said, but he looked pleased. "Just a way to
get him to school and back."

The Zooks had invited Carrie's family
over to share Christmas dinner, so later that
day Eli readied the buggy. Carrie looked
forward to being with Mattie, but she worried about the turn of weather. The day had
grown dark and cold, and snow was starting to pile up. Carrie fussed over Yonnie in
the buggy, covering her with blankets
warmed by the kitchen stove. Daniel wanted
to train Andy to manage Strawberry, so
they followed behind in the cart. Carrie
peered through the back window of Eli's
buggy at the sight of them. Daniel stood
with his arms wrapped around Andy, partly
to block the wind and partly to help him
control the reins. Andy's hat had blown off,
his coat was open, his red cheeks looked

windchapped. But the look of pure joy on his face warmed Carrie's heart like a summer day.

⁕⁕

Winter storms hit twice in January, just enough to keep things interesting, Eli said, without making life too difficult. In the middle of the month, the skies were blue, but a cold snap kept the ground frozen solid, so Eli and Daniel decided the time was right to prune the orchards. If the weather turned too warm, the slushy snow would turn to mud, slowing them down.

Midmorning and midafternoon, Carrie brought a warm drink and snack out to Daniel and Eli in the orchards to keep them fortified. As they finished pruning the last few acres of apple trees, she noticed that Eli had to stop frequently. He had trouble catching his breath, like he was at the top of a mountain and couldn't get enough air. She thought he was just having a hard time climbing up and down the ramp, dragging heavy saws, but she could see that Daniel was concerned.

One day at lunch, Eli felt so worn out that he decided to lie down in his room for a few minutes. After watching Eli slowly make his way up the stairs, Daniel asked her if she knew of any heart doctors in town, but she only knew of blood doctors.

"Has your father had trouble with his heart?" Carrie asked.

Daniel didn't answer right away, so Yonnie filled in. "Terrible trouble. He has a bad heart. Doctor had to open him up. Doctor said it was like . . . like fixing a leaky sprinkler."

Daniel rolled his eyes. "Surgery to fix a valve."

"I'll ask around and see if someone knows of a heart doctor to recommend," Carrie said.

"Doctor can't fix it," Yonnie said sadly. "His heart is just broken to pieces."

Slowly, like a weathervane, Daniel turned and stared at her. All the world's sorrow, all the world's pain, filled those troubled blue eyes.

"Oh Daniel, I didn't mean . . ." Yonnie's hands flew up to her mouth, as if trying to stop the flow of words.

He dropped his head, then lifted it. When he turned to Carrie, his blue eyes went still again. She'd never seen a person's face change so fast.

"Tell Eli I'll wait for him in the workshop," he told her, plucking his broadbrim off the wall peg before heading outside.

Carrie wondered what had just been said between Yonnie and Daniel. Or not said, as seemed to be Daniel's way. She closed the kitchen door, watching him. She couldn't crack that man open with a sledgehammer.

Suddenly, Yonnie's fork clattered on the floor as she clapped her hands together and started whispering, "Gottes wille. Gottes wille."

Not a moment later, a loud tumbling sound came from overhead. It was followed by an eerie silence.

Carrie ran to the kitchen door and called out to Daniel. Nearly at the barn, he spun around and bolted to the house, almost as if he had been expecting Carrie's call. He burst into the kitchen and flew up the stairs, two at a time, and threw open the door to his father's room. By the time Carrie reached them, she found Daniel cradling his father in his arms, a stricken look on his face as he called out, "Dad! Dad!" Eli's mouth moved silently, like a fish out of water. His hands were gripping his shirt, in great pain. Then he went still.

Daniel looked up at Carrie with a horrified look. "Er is nimmi am scharfe." *He's gone.*

⁂

Carrie was grateful Andy wasn't home when Eli passed. She thought she would meet him at school to prepare him for the sight of Eli's body, laid out in the front room.

As she took her bonnet off of the peg, Daniel stopped her. "I'll go. Need the fresh air."

Carrie's heart felt heavy as she saw Daniel walk down the driveway, hands jammed in his pockets, head dropped low. He seemed so alone. The deeper the feelings, she was discovering about him, the more he withdrew into himself. She didn't know how to help him.

No sooner had Daniel disappeared down the street but Veronica McCall arrived, banging on the front door as if Carrie were deaf as a fencepost. When Carrie opened the door, Veronica squeezed past her to enter the house. When Veronica's eyes rested on Yonnie's quilts, stacked up in the corner of the front room, she gasped. She rushed over to the quilts, pulling them out to admire them.

"These are masterpieces! They're stunning! They should be hanging in a museum!" She yanked them open as if they were sheets for a bed. "Did you make these, Carrie?"

"No. Daniel's grandmother made them. She's upstairs, resting—"

"Well, you just hop upstairs and wake her up! I have a proposition to make her."

"This isn't a good time for a visit—"

"Carrie, I want these quilts for the inn when it reopens! Name your price!"

Carrie sighed. "They're not for sale. Yonnie makes the quilts for her family to use. There are other quilters in Stoney Ridge who want to sell quilts."

"I know. I've been looking. But there are none like these. I've never seen any like these." Veronica McCall planted her hands on her hips and tilted her head at Carrie. "For an Amish woman, you drive a hard bargain."

"But I'm not *trying* to bargain."

"*Everyone* has a price, Carrie. Everyone can be bought. Even you."

Carrie was losing patience. "It's not *our* way," she said firmly, hoping to end the discussion.

Suddenly, Veronica McCall's eyes grew as large as dinner plates. She had just noticed Eli's still body lying on the table behind Carrie.

"Um, uh," Veronica McCall sputtered, at a rare loss for words. "Perhaps this isn't the best time for a visit." She handed Carrie a business card. "Call me later."

Carrie lacked the energy to explain to her that there was no phone so there would be no call. But she did ask her for one favor: to drive to Esther's farm and tell her and Emma that Eli had passed. She tried to explain the way to find the farmhouse, describing landmarks, as was the Amish custom in giving directions. But Veronica grew impatient, tapping her toes and frowning. She wanted specifics—street names and house numbers.

Mattie appeared at the open front door, somehow knowing they needed her. For a moment she stood listening, observing Veronica's growing frustration. "The Lord will guide you there," she said at last, steering Veronica out to her car.

❀

Daniel grew even quieter in the weeks after Eli passed. Carrie would catch him deep in thought at odd moments, his mind a million miles away, like the time he stood on a ramp in the barn leading up to the hayloft, hayfork in his hands, just staring off into the distance. Or when she found him standing beside his horse Schtarm, holding the harness, forehead bowed against the gelding's big neck. Either way, it seemed as though he was living in a world she couldn't reach.

One night in mid-March, Carrie woke suddenly. Something was wrong. Daniel's bed was empty. She heard Hope's bellow, calling from the barn, in great pain. This yearling heifer, given to Andy by Jacob when he turned eight, was not just an animal to them. She was an extension of the family. Hope was the first of the herd on their farm. *I'm counting on her, just like she is counting on me*, Carrie thought as she quickly threw on warm clothes, wrapped a shawl around her head, and hurried out to the barn.

When Carrie slid the barn door open, she saw Daniel in Hope's stall.

He looked up at her, surprised. "How'd you hear her with that wind howling?"

Carrie shrugged, her eyes fixed on Hope.

She was in trouble. A tiny hoof stuck out between her hind legs. Swiftly, she reached for the thin chain hanging on the wall.

"No. Let me," Daniel said, taking it out of her hands.

He reached a gloved hand into Hope, catching the little hoof with the chain, before a contraction started that nearly squeezed his arm off. Carrie gasped when she saw his face contort, matching Hope's pain.

When the contraction subsided, he asked her to crank the chain as he gently tugged.

"Careful, Daniel, careful."

Carrie cranked, Daniel tugged, Hope pushed and bellowed. Slowly the calf began to ease out of the canal. Daniel motioned to have Carrie come next to him. He gently guided her hands into Hope's canal, under the calf's warm and slimy body.

"You make the delivery," he said.

So Carrie began to tug and tug, and ever so gently the calf began to come out. First the hoofs, then the shoulders. Then the neck. Before she knew it, a miniature white face emerged. Then the entire body slipped out, like shooting down a waterslide. Carrie collapsed to the hay-covered floor, the calf half in her lap and half on the floor.

"A girl!" Carrie said, relieved. Had it been a male, she would have to sell it soon to a farmer who raised steers.

Daniel and Carrie watched with wonder as the little white nose wrinkled, sneezed, and took in her first breath. Hope turned and began to rasp her rough tongue along the wet whorls of her baby's hide. With this stimulation, the calf began to struggle to get to her feet, wobbling toward her mother. They touched noses, a first meeting. Then the calf nuzzled to nurse as Hope continued cleaning up her newborn.

It was that quiet time of a new day, when the earth seemed to be holding its breath, gently turning from darkness to daylight. "The circle of life, once again completed," Carrie said softly.

Hope swung her heavy head at Carrie with big, soulful brown eyes, blinking her long white eyelashes as if in agreement with the assessment.

Carrie laughed and hooked her arm through Daniel's. "It's a sign, Daniel. Everything's going to be fine."

"Think so?"

"I do. I'm sure of it," she answered, sounding more confident than she felt.

He gave her a soft, slow smile. They looked at each other, sharing a mutual thought, a fragile hope. Gently, he leaned over to kiss her, grazing her lips with his. Then his arms slid around her waist and he pulled her to him, pressing his lips against hers as if a kiss could tell her what words would not.

That first kiss from Daniel made Carrie think about the last kiss Sol had given her. About how different they were. A beginning and an end.

❄❄

As Carrie thought about Hope's new calf and the way Daniel had held on to her, as if he was a drowning man and she was throwing him a long branch to drag him to shore, she made a decision.

Ready or not, it was time that Daniel got off of that cold floor. He had never complained, but she knew he would jump at the chance if she invited him into her bed. More than once, she caught the hungry look on his face, watching her as she got ready for bed, combing out her hair. Not long ago, she had even put aside her modesty and talked it over with Mattie. Her response jolted Carrie. "Daniel is a man, not a saint. What are you waiting for?" Mattie told her, sounding like a seasoned woman of the world.

So what was Carrie waiting for?

It wasn't love. She was practical enough to know that she would never feel for Daniel what she had felt for Sol. She hadn't married Daniel with any schoolgirl notions. Still, she was growing fond of Daniel and his quiet, kind ways. She appreciated how patient he was with her brother, how tender he was with his grandmother, how thoughtful and caring he was to her.

So what was she waiting for?

After giving that question some serious thought, she realized she was waiting to feel as if she knew Daniel, really knew him. She remembered how she used to hear her mother and father talk with each other at the kitchen table after she had gone to bed. That's what she hoped for in a marriage, that kind of closeness. In that way, she wanted Bund. *Intimacy. A bond.*

But sometimes, she thought Daniel would never really let her know him any better than she did. He seemed so closed up, so private. He rarely spoke more than a few words at a time—even his sentences seemed economized.

Later that afternoon, Daniel and Andy went to the feed store in town to buy bird food for the Cooper's hawk babies. At the last minute, Yonnie decided to go too. Carrie put some hot water in empty milk jugs to keep Yonnie warm, and covered her with extra blankets in the buggy.

After they had left, Carrie went out to the barn to check on Hope and the new calf. She sat on the milking stool beside Hope, milking her for the first time. This first milking, filled with colostrum, would be put in a bottle for the calf's first meal.

She rubbed the indented spot between Hope's two ears. "Thank you, sweet girl."

Hope licked and huffed and looked at her with large, peaceful eyes. As Carrie bent over to pick up the bucket, she heard the barn door slide open and fill the room with afternoon sunlight. Carrie looked up to see who it was, but the sun, behind the barn's door in a blaze of glory, dazzled her eyes so that all she saw was a black silhouette.

"Hello, Carrie," a man said.

At the sound of that deep voice, Carrie's heart started pounding so loud she was sure Solomon Riehl could hear it.

"I didn't mean to frighten you," Sol said, taking a few strides into the barn. "I just want to talk to you, face-to-face."

As her eyes adjusted to the light, she took in the changes in Sol. His hair was shingled and short, like an English man. His face seemed a little older, tired. He had dark circles under his eyes as if he hadn't rested well.

"We have nothing to talk about." Her words came out harsh, coming from an old and festering anger that she still felt.

"Carrie," he said, coming closer, "I made a mistake."

He was close enough now that she could smell him. It was a familiar smell to her, a smell she had once loved. She took a step back, nearly knocking over the milk bucket.

"I had to give baseball a try. When your father died so unexpectedly, and you wouldn't come with me, I panicked. I never should have left without you. I never should have left without telling you I was going. That I'd be back for you."

He smiled at her, but she didn't smile back. She crossed her arms and looked away, just to avoid his gaze. She was afraid if she looked at him, she'd be drawn in, unable to resist him. She wasn't even sure she could get any words around the knot in her throat, a knot made of tangled threads of anger and hurt.

He took a step closer to her. His voice dropped to a whisper. "But how could you have married him? Why couldn't you have waited for me? You knew I loved you. You knew I'd be coming for you."

Her chin lifted a notch. Defiance surged through her. "You gave me no reason to think you'd be back."

He put his hands on her arms. "Carrie, we can still be together. It's not too late. And you can bring Andy. I'll take care of both of you."

She jerked his hands off of her. "I was baptized into the church. And I'm . . . I'm married now."

He gave a slight shrug, but he kept his eyes lowered to the ground. "People leave. They leave all the time."

He didn't really believe that, she thought.

He couldn't be so far removed from their ways that he would think she would leave. "You made your choice, Sol. I made mine."

"But that's what I'm saying, Carrie. I made a mistake." He reached out for her hands and tangled his fingers with hers, the way he used to. "It doesn't have to fashion into a crisis."

"It's not a crisis. But it is decided."

"You just married him to spite me."

Carrie gave a short laugh. "You don't have any idea why I married Daniel."

Sol released her hands. "Carrie, you don't really know him."

"And you do?"

"I know things you don't know. He hasn't been honest with you. There's something in his past—"

She raised her hands to stop him.

"Carrie, listen to me."

"No. I stopped listening to you at my father's funeral." Anger spilling over, she took a step closer to him. "You want to know why I married Daniel?" she asked, her voice shaking. "Because he was there."

And you were not, echoed silently through the barn.

She picked up the milk bucket. "And you wouldn't be here today if you had a baseball game to play."

Sol blocked her path. "I'm here today because of you. I have never stopped loving you. Not ever. I have regretted leaving without you every single day. It was the stupidest thing I've ever done. I'm here to make it right. Carrie, I want you more than baseball. It's *nothing* without you by my side."

She stepped around him to leave, but he blocked her path again.

"At least read this. Then you'll know more. About him." He thrust a paper into her hands.

She left the barn and broke into a run, despite sloshing milk all around her, so that he wouldn't see the tears splashing onto her cheeks.

❦

Carrie didn't say anything to Daniel during supper, but after they'd eaten and she'd cleaned up the dishes, she went out to the barn to find him. Daniel always went out to check on the animals one last time before evening prayers.

When she slid open the door of the barn, Daniel glanced at her from one of killed." He took a deep breath. "A man and . . . ," his voice broke on the word, ". . . and a child."

"Daniel—"

"Abel didn't cause the fires that killed them, Carrie." He held up the paper, a copy of a newspaper clipping. "It seems that way from this article, but the truth is that Abel was innocent. I caused the fires. I did it." He lowered his head. "Abel went to jail in my place. But I'm responsible for the fires. For the deaths. I'm the one."

She felt all fuzzy headed as if her head was wrapped in her wooly shawl and she couldn't hear him clearly. As understanding started to dawn, a panic rose within Carrie. She suddenly felt as if this man whom she thought was safe wasn't safe at all. She didn't really know Daniel. Or what he was capable of doing.

Carrie knew what she should do. She should stay. She should get Daniel to tell her the whole story.

Instead, she turned and ran.

❦❦

Carrie didn't return home for hours. When she walked up the kitchen steps, Yonnie was waiting by the door.

the horse's stalls. He had been filling bucket with water, but put it down when saw her. He closed the horse's stall, turn the latch, and approached her, a questic in his eyes.

She handed him the paper that Sol ha given her. "It's about your cousin Abe Daniel. I know he caused a fire that killed some people. I know he's in jail."

Daniel unfolded the paper and quickly scanned it.

Softly, she asked, "Was she the girl you loved, Daniel? Is she the reason you carry such a burden?"

He didn't say anything.

"It hurts that you felt you had to keep this secret, instead of telling me. I would have understood."

He closed his eyes. He seemed to be searching for words. Then he lifted his head and quietly said, "The two women who were killed in that fire were Katie Yoder and my mother." He looked past her, out the open barn door. "Katie and I were to be married."

"That's what I—"

Daniel put up a hand to stop her. "There was another fire. Two other people were

"What are you doing up?" Carrie asked, as she hung her shawl up on the wooden peg.

"We were worried about you," Yonnie said.

"I'm sorry to cause you concern. I was over at Mattie's." Carrie had spilled everything out to Mattie, about Sol showing up and the newspaper article, about what Daniel had said. Mattie listened carefully, then told Carrie to stop making up her mind ahead of the facts. She told her to go home and *ask* Daniel about the fires, to give him the benefit of the doubt, to trust what she knew to be true about him.

Yonnie glanced at the grandfather clock. "Is Daniel still in the barn?"

"No. Isn't he asleep?"

Yonnie's chin jerked up. "No! He went looking for you about an hour ago. He took Schtarm because Old-Timer has a sore leg."

"Schtarm? He used Schtarm in the buggy?" At an auction last fall, Daniel bought Schtarm, a young racehorse that didn't cut it on the tracks. He wasn't buggy broke yet and had such a skittish nature that Carrie doubted he would ever be a good buggy horse, but Daniel had confidence in him. She glanced out the kitchen window. "I wasn't on the road. I cut through the orchard. We must have missed each other."

All of a sudden Yonnie clasped her hands together and started her chanting, "Gottes willes. Gottes willes."

Not a minute later, Schtarm galloped into the gravel driveway, skidding to a halt at the barn. Carrie ran outside and saw that he was lathered up, buggy traces hanging by his side. His eyes looked wild and she had trouble getting close to him. She spoke calmly to him and was able to grasp one rein, just as a police car turned into the driveway. Mattie was in the backseat. She opened the door and ran over to Carrie, throwing her arms around her. For a split second, Carrie thought that Mattie seemed as frantic and wild-eyed as Schtarm. She looked over Mattie's shoulder at the police car, expecting Daniel to come out the other door. Instead, it was a police officer. He approached Carrie and Mattie, standing a few feet back.

"I'm Chief Beamer. Are you the wife of Daniel Miller?"

Carrie looked curiously at the policeman. Why was he here? Mattie released
her grip on Carrie. "Oh Carrie! There's
been an accident. The buggy. A car."

"Slow down, Mattie. Take a deep breath
and tell me what happened."

"Daniel's buggy was turning left into my
driveway when a speeding car passed by
him."

Carrie took a deep breath and squeezed
her eyes shut. When buggies and cars col-
lided, the buggies always lost. She glanced
at Schtarm, grateful he wasn't hurt.

"You're going to need to come with me,
Mrs. Miller," Chief Beamer said.

"Where's Daniel?" Carrie glanced at the
police car. "Isn't he in the car?"

"No, Carrie," Mattie said, her voice breaking on the word. "He's not." She started to
cry.

Carrie looked at Mattie and the officer.
She tilted her head, trying to understand
what Mattie meant. Her mind wasn't working right. She had been up so early with
Hope's new calf, then Sol's visit, and then
finding out about Daniel and his cousin
Abel. The fatigue of the long day suddenly
hit her.

Mattie braced Carrie's shoulders to make her look at her. "He's dead, Carrie. Daniel was thrown from the buggy and killed instantly."

Carrie tried to concentrate on Mattie's moving mouth, but she didn't think Mattie made any sense. *Poor Mattie. She looks so troubled.* Carrie felt like she might be getting a fever, all shaky and sweaty and cold inside. Her leg muscles felt wobbly and she kept forgetting to breathe. *I must breathe. I must.* Everything started to swirl around her before it all became fuzzy and blended together. She didn't even remember falling, but the next thing she heard was Chief Beamer's deep voice, hovering over her.

"She's fainted. Dropped like a stone. Does someone have a blanket?"

6

Over the next few days, Carrie took comfort in the long-established rituals and traditions of burying a family member, as they gave anchor to her churned-up feelings. The day before Daniel's funeral, the bench wagon was delivered by two men. They helped move out all the downstairs furniture to store in the barn. Then they set up the benches in the empty house. Neighbors stopped by all throughout the day, bearing dishes of food for the shared meal after the burial.

As long as Carrie stayed busy, she was able to push away troubling, stray thoughts.

Just like when her father died and Sol left, she found that the sun rose and set and the days would come and go, and there was the washing and the cooking and the gardens to care for. One couldn't live on the crest of grief every single moment.

The day after the accident, the undertaker returned Daniel's embalmed body to the farmhouse for the viewing. Tears streaming down her face, Yonnie held the Crazy Quilt in her arms that she had given Carrie for a wedding gift.

"Do you mind, Carrie?" she asked her as they tended to Daniel's body, just as they had tended to Eli's only weeks before. "I know it's custom to use a white quilt to bury him, but I want to wrap him in the quilt he loved best."

"Of course not," Carrie said. "I think he would be comforted by being wrapped in the quilt you had made for him." She felt numb, exhausted to the bone, worried.

The police had taken her to the city morgue to identify Daniel's body. Mattie came too. It was nearly dawn by the time they returned to the farmhouse. When Andy woke, Carrie told him about the accident. What worried her most was that Andy didn't cry. He became quiet and still, like a candlelight right before it's snuffed out. Andy spent the day in the barn, playing with the Cooper's hawk babies, avoiding the steady stream of neighbors who heard the news and wanted to pay their respect.

At the end of the day, a car turned into the driveway. Mattie climbed out of the backseat, but the other people, clearly English, remained in the car. Carrie met Mattie at the kitchen door.

"Carrie, the girl who hit Daniel's buggy is in the car," Mattie said. "She's with her mother. She wants to ask you to forgive her."

Carrie braced her hand against the doorjamb as if she needed it to hold herself upright. "Oh Mattie, I can't. I just can't."

"Yes, you can," Mattie said, firm but kind. "Her name is Grace Patterson. She's only seventeen. She works part-time over at Honor Mansion. She needs your forgiveness. You need to give it to her for your own sake."

Closing her eyes for a moment against the pain and loss, Carrie asked quietly, "And what if I don't feel any forgiveness for her?"

Softly, Mattie whispered, "Feelings follow intention." Mattie took Carrie's hand and led her out to the car.

An elderly woman got out of the car first, her face solemn and sad. Then the girl got out. Carrie had to force herself to look at her. She was so young. Her eyes were swollen with crying. Her face was red and blotchy. Carrie recognized that kind of misery and despair; she felt it when her father died.

Without thinking, she opened wide her arms. The girl looked at Carrie as if she couldn't believe what she was offering to her. Then she rushed into Carrie's arms, breaking into big, heaving sobs.

❧❦

When Carrie finally went upstairs that night, she saw that Yonnie had replaced the Crazy Quilt on her bed with another quilt. The cold March wind seeped through the windowsills, and she shivered as she undressed. She wore two pairs of woolen socks and a sweater over her nightgown and still couldn't get warm. She wasn't sure she had ever felt quite so alone as she did that night, slipping under the covers. Never had so many changes come upon her in so little time. It was as if she had left her old life and stepped into someone else's life. The last thought she had before falling asleep was: *And now I am a widow.*

❦❦

The sun shone brightly on the day of Daniel's funeral, but the wind still had winter's bite to it. At the graveside, four young men shoveled dirt on top of Daniel's coffin. Carrie heard no other sound other than that—*whoosh-whump . . . whoosh-whump.* No airplanes flying overhead, no cars driving past, no squawking jaybirds, just the silence of grief. A cold breeze blew the strings of her prayer cap across her face. She must have flinched as the clods of dirt hit the pine box, because Mattie quietly linked an arm through hers, as if to say, "You're not alone."

Afterward, back at the house, as they cleaned up the kitchen, Emma asked Carrie, "Want me to stay? I could ask Mother to stay too."

Carrie shook her head. She was in no mood for more of Esther's advice. Her only word of solace to Carrie had been, "Folks should not overgrieve much, for that is a complaint against the Lord."

Throughout the long day, Esther made broad hints to Carrie about the bishop's grandson, John Graber. She had picked him for Carrie's husband years ago, often inviting him over for supper and family gatherings. Carrie had no interest in him; she thought John Graber was odd.

Carrie had enough to worry about right now. Ever since Eli had passed, the job of bill paying had fallen to her. The second installment of the property tax bill, still in Eli's name, sat on Daniel's desk, and she didn't have the money to pay it.

Just two weeks ago, she had shown the tax bill to Daniel after they had accepted help from the church to pay the last of Andy's emergency room bill. Carrie offered to go back to work at Central Market, but Daniel objected, saying Yonnie needed minding. The older woman had fallen recently after losing her balance. She wasn't hurt, but she couldn't get herself back up. Daniel had told Carrie not to worry, that he would pay the tax bill by doing extra smithy work.

But now that was over.

Deacon Abraham, a kind man with a smiling face, ruddy as a bright apple, and a great booming laugh that jiggled his big belly, brought over a spare buggy to use since Carrie's had been destroyed in the accident. He also asked to buy Daniel's blacksmithing tools. He insisted he needed them, and then offered her three times what they were worth, refusing to pay less. Still, it didn't come close to the amount due for taxes. And it wasn't just this tax bill that worried her, it was the one after that, and the one after that. How was she ever going to be able to make ends meet? These were all new worries for her, ones she had never known before.

After Emma and Esther left, Carrie got ready to go to bed, exhausted. Andy and Yonnie were already asleep. As she leaned over to turn off the gas lamp in the living room, Yonnie's stack of quilts caught her eye in the flickering light. She spread her hand over a quilt, admiring again the tiny, even rows of stitches, the even binding, the splashes of yellows, purples, and deep blues that Yonnie coordinated so skillfully.

Carrie's heart almost slammed into her chest. She would have to talk to Yonnie in the morning, but it was just possible that she had found the means to hold on to the orchards. At least for the foreseeable future.

⁂

"I don't mind a bit," Yonnie said the next morning, when Carrie explained to her the idea of selling a quilt to Veronica McCall. "I made those quilts for my family to use. This is just one more way the quilts can be of use." Yonnie went over to the quilts and pulled them out and spread them on the kitchen table. She was trying to decide which one to sell.

Carrie's heart ached as she watched her. She knew those quilts told the story of her life.

Yonnie pulled out a red and yellow quilt she called "Ray of Light." "Think that fancy redheaded gal would like this one? She seems flashy."

Carrie nodded. "I think it's perfect, Yonnie."

As soon as the skies cleared after a soaking rain, Carrie hitched Old-Timer to the buggy. The sun shone on Carrie's face, relaxing her a little, as she prepared herself during the ride for this visit to Honor Mansion. She hooked Old-Timer to a post at the hotel, stroked his face, and ran her hand down the length of his sore leg. He seemed fine today. The buggy looked glaringly out of place in the parking lot filled with construction workers' trucks and Veronica McCall's red convertible. She gathered the quilt that Yonnie had carefully wrapped up in paper and knocked timidly on the door of the hotel.

When the door opened, Carrie inhaled sharply. Grace Patterson stood at the threshold, looking just as shocked to see Carrie.

"Hello, Grace," Carrie said. A surprising wave of tenderness filled Carrie as she looked at Grace. She took in Grace's appearance. Her hair was short and spiked, a funny color, and her eyes were traced with a thick black liner. But she wasn't as tough as she looked, Carrie thought. She really didn't know much about this girl other than she thought Grace seemed like a fragile teacup.

Grace's eyes went wide. "Did you come to see me?"

"No. I'm here to see Veronica McCall." Carrie tilted her head. "Is your hair . . . were you born with that color?"

Grace ran a hand through her hair.

"Oh no! I dyed it. It's called Manic Panic red."

"Well, it is really . . . bright." She tried to sound positive. "Thank you for coming to Daniel's viewing. I know that was hard. Please thank your mother too."

"Mrs. Gingerich? She's not my mother. She's my foster mother. More like a foster grandma, actually. She's pretty ancient." Grace came outside on the porch and closed the door behind her. "But she's cool. I mean, like, her viewing habits totally bite, but other than that, she's okay."

Carrie didn't understand what Grace meant. She answered with silence.

"And she eats weird stuff. She only buys organic and won't eat glutens and . . . what is a gluten anyway? I don't have a clue but it's all anybody talks about anymore."

Carrie was mesmerized for a moment, watching Grace carry on a conversation by herself. There was something very earnest about her, something sweet and likable.

"It sounds so lame," Grace rolled her eyes, "but I thought the Amish people

might bring shotguns and try to off me."
She shook her head. "But everyone was
so kind."

"My people?" Carrie asked. "You thought
my people would shoot you?"

"Yes. I've lived in Lancaster County
most of my life, but I really don't know
squat about the Amish."

Carrie smiled. "You could probably say
the same thing about how little we understand the English."

"So, um, I have to go before the judge in
a few months. To see if . . . I might be
charged . . ." Her voice trailed off as she
looked out at the street.

Carrie's heart felt a tug of pity. Grace
was so young to carry such a yoke. "Perhaps I can help in some way. I could write
letters to the judge asking for mercy."

Grace's head snapped back at Carrie in
astonishment. "Would you? Would you really do that for me?" She crossed her arms
tightly against her chest and her eyes filled
with tears. "But why? It's my fault that your
husband is . . . dead. I don't deserve that.
I don't deserve mercy."

For some reason, Carrie thought of

Mattie. She knew just what Mattie would say and found herself echoing it. "None of us do, Grace."

�֍֍

Grace pointed down the hall to Veronica McCall's office and went back upstairs. Before Carrie knocked on the door, she noticed a reflection of herself in a hall mirror. She hadn't looked in a mirror since she had left Esther's home. She walked up to it, slowly, unsure of what to make of what she saw. There stood a woman, not very tall and a little too thin, in a black mourning dress and apron and cape. Her cheeks were flushed pink, for it was a cool spring day. What surprised her most was that she didn't look like a girl anymore. She thought of herself as barely old enough to be a wife, let alone a widow.

But her eyes, they showed her youth. They looked a little frightened, like a cottontail caught in a flashlight's glare.

Veronica was typing furiously at a computer and looked up when Carrie knocked, stunned, as if she wasn't sure who she was. "Carrie? Sit down, sit down." She moved some papers from a chair and pointed to it. "Listen, if you're here about Grace, I can assure you that Honor Mansion can't be held liable for the accident. First of all, she's only part-time, and secondly, she was off-duty and had left the property—"

"No." Carrie waved a hand to stop her. "No. I'm not here to discuss that . . . with you."

A wide smile spread across Veronica's face. "So, you're ready to sell."

"Not the property." Carrie put the quilt on her desk top and carefully unwrapped the paper. "But a quilt."

Veronica McCall leaned back in her chair. "It's beautiful." She spread it out and looked it up and down. "It almost looks as if it were done by hand."

"It was. Even the pieces are sewed together by hand, not on a machine. It took Yonnie thousands of hours to make it."

Veronica McCall's eyebrows shot up. "How much?" she asked, narrowing her eyes at her.

Carrie took a deep breath. Bargaining was new to her, but she had given the price a great deal of thought. "One thousand dollars."

"Five hundred," Veronica volleyed back. She smiled, but her eyes stayed cold.

She enjoys this, Carrie thought. "One thousand dollars."

"There are plenty of other quilts out there."

"Yes. There are many fine quilters in Lancaster County. None quite like Yonnie, though." *But Veronica knows that.*

One thinly plucked eyebrow raised up. "You drive a hard bargain."

"But I don't bargain, Veronica McCall. I've told you that before. It's not our way. One thousand dollars is a fair value for the quilt."

"Seven fifty."

Carrie started to pack up the quilt. She wasn't sure where she would go next, but she wasn't going to accept less for Yonnie's handiwork.

"Fine! Fine," Veronica McCall said, laughing. She pulled out a checkbook from her desk drawer.

"Would you mind giving me cash?" Carrie asked her. "I don't have a bank account." It was one of the things on Carrie's to-do list, under the heading, "Things to figure out now that I am a widow."

Veronica's eyes narrowed, as if she thought Carrie didn't trust her. She left the room for a moment and came back with the cash, counting it out in her hand.

As Carrie stood up to leave, Veronica said with a smug smile, "Nice doing business with you. I would have gone as high as fifteen hundred."

"But the fair value is one thousand dollars."

"Well, all's fair in love and war."

Carrie cocked her head at her and wondered why the English spoke in riddles. Her gaze shifted to the computer on Veronica's desk. "Do you use that often?"

"Oh, yes." Veronica gave a confident nod. "I'm a computer whiz."

"Someone told me that it's like a library." It was something Sol had told her once. He loved computers. He used to go to a coffee shop where he could "surf the internet." He tried to teach Carrie, but she had felt guilty for a week and could hardly look her father in the eye. She knew her father felt that the internet was a gateway to evil, just like television. It was one of those areas she had felt conflicted about, because through Sol's eyes she could see the good in those worldly things too.

"Sure is! I can google anything."

Carrie was nonplussed. It almost sounded like Veronica was trying to speak their dialect. "You can ferhoodle anything?"

"No! Google. It's a search engine." Veronica read the confused look on Carrie's face and waved away an explanation. "Never mind. Is there something you want me to look up?"

Carrie wasn't entirely sure she was doing the right thing, but Daniel's untimely death left her with missing pieces of a story. She felt as if she needed to know the truth about those fires in Ohio, and Yonnie couldn't or wouldn't discuss them. Just yesterday, Carrie tried asking her, straight out, but Yonnie went pale and started to tremble, then went upstairs to lie down. "I'm looking for some information about two fires in Holmes County, Ohio, that caused the death of two women, a man and his son, a few years back."

She gave Veronica McCall the few details that she remembered from the copy of the newspaper clipping Sol had given her. Veronica pecked at the buttons on the computer, stared at the screen for a long while, asked a few more questions, then typed more buttons.

Suddenly, Veronica let out a yelp. "Voilà! Found it." She gave a satisfied smile to Carrie. "I can find anything." She pressed a button and another machine spit out a paper. "Here's what you're looking for, Carrie." She reached over, grabbed the paper from the printer, and handed it to her.

Carrie folded it up, quickly, so Veronica wouldn't read it. Then she thanked her and left with the quilt money and the information about Abel Miller. Just as she closed the door, she heard the printer click into action a second time. Carrie's heart rose in her throat. *Veronica McCall wouldn't have made a copy for herself, would she? No, of course not. Why would she bother?*

About halfway home, Carrie pulled Old-Timer off to the side and read the paper. It was a report from a newspaper article, with a grainy picture of Abel Miller on it. She started to read the article: "Amish Man Fined and Sentenced to Prison."

Abel Miller, 21, was sentenced today to three years in prison and fined $250,000. He pled guilty to two acts of negligence that resulted in involuntary homicides. Miller had a business supplying kerosene fuel to local Amish farmers. Last November, gasoline had contaminated the containers, causing explosions in two Amish homes that resulted in the death of two women, forty-eight-year-old Lena Miller, a relative of the defendant, nineteen-year-old Katie Yoder, thirty-two-year-old Elam Lapp and his seven-year-old son, Benjamin Lapp. Against advice of counsel, Miller refused to appeal the conviction.

Carrie sighed. The story only raised more questions than it answered. She re-read it, looked again at Abel Miller's photograph and stared at it for a long while. Her heart felt a pity for this Abel. How humiliating for an Amish man to have his photograph taken and printed in such a way. For the first time, Abel seemed real to her. Not just a shadowy figure in the Miller family, but a real man.

She wondered why Abel took Daniel's place in jail. More importantly, why had Daniel let him?

She folded the paper up carefully and placed it in her apron pocket. She didn't want Yonnie to come across this, adding to her suffering. Yonnie carried on bravely, but Carrie knew she was grieving deeply over Eli and Daniel.

❦

One evening, Carrie went through Eli's accounting books to see what kind of expenses she would be facing. She knew there would be feed bills, a propane gas bill, and in a few months, yet another tax bill to pay. She knew they needed to sell another quilt or two to pay for expenses until the harvest, but it pained her to ask Yonnie.

Carrie was doing her best to keep the farm up, but it was already looking like the weary efforts of two women and a boy, not the pristine condition that Eli and Daniel had kept it in. Every few days, a kind neighbor or two stopped by to lend a hand with a chore or two, but they had families and farms of their own to care for. Thankfully, Daniel had finished pruning the trees in January and had returned the beehives to the orchards in early March, but her vegetable garden—food that she counted on for summer canning and for roadside stand sales—looked limp.

As Carrie closed Eli's accounting book, she suddenly felt a weariness that settled and went bone deep. She felt anxious about the future, and then anxious about being anxious. She put her head in her hands and squeezed her eyes shut.

Yonnie came up behind her, rested her hands on her shoulders and said, "Try not to worry. The Lord God hears our prayers."

Carrie patted Yonnie's hands and told her she was right, of course. But a part of her mind told her that maybe Daniel was right. Heaven had gone deaf.

As Carrie said goodnight to Andy, he asked her if they were going to lose the farm.

"What makes you think that?" she asked.

"I heard you and Yonnie talking. I saw you scribbling down numbers on a pad of paper." He climbed under the quilt covers. "Maybe I should quit school and stay home. I could do stuff. I could make money choring for people."

Carrie smiled at him and tousled his hair. "Your job is to stay in school and learn all you can. Someday, these apple orchards will be yours. You'll need to know all about numbers." She stroked his hair.

"I know plenty already. More than that ol' teacher. Bags of fat on her arms bounce when she writes on the board!" He lifted a skinny arm and pinched it, trying to mimic his teacher.

Carrie tried to frown at him but broke into a grin. "Enough of that talk. Like I said, you do your part by doing well in school. It's my part to think about making ends meet." She reached over and turned off the gas lamp. "Night, little brother."

"Night, Carrie."

Before she closed the door, she asked, "Are those English boys still bothering you?"

"Nope."

"Daniel was right, then. He said they would lose interest."

Andy didn't respond. He just rolled over on his side.

"Andy, do you miss Daniel?"

"Nope."

Carrie leaned on the doorjamb and watched him for a moment. She worried about him, her Andy. She knew he must be hurting. She wondered how he really felt about Daniel's death. He didn't show any emotion during the viewing and funeral. He didn't really show much emotion about anything, she realized, except for caring for the baby Cooper's hawks and Mattie's hatched goslings.

Those downy goslings looked like yellow balls of cotton that followed Andy around like he was their mother. It was incredible how quickly they grew; in just a few weeks, they were the size of leghorn chickens. Carrie and Andy made a makeshift cage for them in the barn. She was grateful that these creatures hadn't died. It made her sad to think Andy had grown calloused to death, at the tender age of nine.

She had to admit, she wasn't really sure how she felt about Daniel's death, either. She pushed thoughts of him off to the side before they could settle in for a stay, just like she did with Sol.

❧❦

Spring training was under way. Sol thought he might be able to add a little more speed on his fastball after the weight training he'd done in the Clipper Magazine Stadium workout room all winter. The manager had even used him as an example to the other players.

"If the rest of you players would work as hard as this guy," he patted Sol on the back during the team meeting, "you'd have a chance for making the All-Star game this fall."

The way the manager said it, it seemed as if he was hinting that Sol had a chance for a pitcher's spot on the All-Star team. Just thinking about it made Sol all the more determined to speed up his pitch. It was all so close to him, within his grasp, this dream of making something of himself, he could practically see himself in the All-Star uniform, jogging out to the mound in Newark or Camden or Long Island, wherever the games were going to be held.

The only thing missing was no one would be there to watch him.

But then he got to thinking, with Daniel Miller gone—and it shamed him to admit it but when he heard the news from his mother he was elated—he and Carrie were given a second chance to get it right. Maybe by fall, she'd be at that All-Star game, watching him.

❧

Late one afternoon, Veronica McCall walked right into Carrie's farmhouse. "Hello? Hello? Is anybody here?" she called out, before spotting Carrie by the far window in the living room, letting down the hem on Andy's trousers. "There you are! I knew someone would be home." She blinked her eyes. "Why is it always so dark in here?"

"We use the sun's light. And it's a cloudy day." Carrie put down the trousers and stood to meet her guest. "Is something wrong?" She could tell Veronica McCall seemed more on edge than usual today.

"There's a flaw in this quilt of Yonnie's." Veronica threw the quilt on the kitchen table, searching it over. "There! There it is! See?" She pointed to a corner piece in which a mismatched fabric was sewn in, disrupting the pattern.

"I do see," Carrie answered calmly.

"So she needs to fix it."

"No. It's meant to be there."

Veronica McCall looked at Carrie as if she were a dense child. "I can't have a flawed quilt. She'll have to fix it."

Carrie smoothed a hand over the red and yellow quilt. "Yonnie's quilts have a mark of humility."

"A what?"

"It's a sign of imperfection. Man will never achieve perfection, and we don't want to be prideful in even trying to achieve it. So many Amish quilts are made with an intentional flaw."

g lies. He insisted that they weren't
he just didn't volunteer the truth.

nd the part about the leprosy?" Carrie
d, one eyebrow raised. "Your cast has
off for months now."

ell, the doctor said it *looked* like lep-
' he told her solemnly. "And my skin
ook gross when the doctor took off
ast. All wrinkled and white."

e tried to make him understand that
elling the truth *was* an untruth, that
tart with a seed of untruth that quickly
s into vines—jungles—of deceit. She
tell she wasn't making much of an
ct. What he really needed was his fa-
She couldn't do anything about that,
he could make sure he finished out
chool year, like it or not.

"Every one?"

"Not all, I suppose." Carrie folded the
quilt gently. It pained her still, to have sold
Yonnie's quilt.

"Well, that's . . . interesting, I guess."
Veronica tapped her chin. "Hmmm . . . I
wonder if I could spin it? Maybe I could
even point customers to the flaw, to prove
it isn't machine made . . . oh, this could be
good!" She clapped her hands together,
delighted. "Bet I could charge more too."
She scooped the quilt out of Carrie's arms
and left, nearly knocking Andy over as he
came in from school. "Toodles!" she called
out, banging the kitchen door behind her.

Just an hour later, Andy sat at the kitchen
table eating a snack while Carrie was making dinner. Suddenly, he spotted something
out the window and flew out the door, tossing over his shoulder, "Gotta check on my
birds!" Instead of going straight to the barn
like he always did, he slipped around the
side of the house and behind the vegetable
garden, out of sight. Carrie saw a young
Amish woman walk up the path to the
kitchen door. When she reached the house,
Carrie could see it was Andy's teacher, Rebecca King.

She started the teapot to boil as Rebecca took off her cape and bonnet. "What a nice surprise, Rebecca! On such a cold spring day too." Carrie took two teacups down from the cupboard and filled them with hot water from the kettle. "Seems as if we should be getting warm weather by now."

Rebecca's round cheeks were bright red with cold. She wrapped her hands around the cup to warm them. "I wish I could say that the reason for my visit was just because we're overdue, Carrie, but . . . ." She glanced at Yonnie, quilting in the other room.

"Something about Andy?" Carrie straightened. "He's not giving you trouble, is he?" She had a sinking feeling in the pit of her stomach, like something terrible was coming.

"No, I wouldn't say that," Rebecca said. She took a sip of tea. "You see, he's not at school. Ever since . . . your Daniel passed . . . he hasn't been to school."

"But that's been weeks now!" Carrie said, shocked. "Where has he been all day?"

"I don't know. All I know is that he told the kids he was very sick. He said it was

extremely contagious. I ca exactly what the disease wa

Carrie looked out at the leprosy, by any chance?"

"Yes! That's it!" Then her f ried. "Does he really have it'

Slowly, Carrie shook her f

"I didn't think so." Rebecc tea and picked up her cape "I'd better get home. You'll s about returning to school?"

"Yes. He'll be at school to rie said, walking Rebecca to can count on it."

For the next few weeks, u term ended, Carrie rode the side Andy to school every even waited to leave until the bell and she knew he v one-room schoolhouse. Car get Andy to confess where spending his days; out by Bl birding, most likely. Once Da him to birding, he preferred v to watching Rebecca's jiggl on the blackboard. But it b to discover that Andy was s

tellin
lies,
"A
aske
beer
"V
rosy
did
the c
S
not
lies :
grow
coul
impa
ther.
but s
the s

7

Spring inched to summer and the apple blossoms in Carrie's orchards faded and died, leaving in their place the promise of a crop to harvest, come autumn.

One August afternoon, the sun burned the back of Carrie's neck as she drove the wagon over to the Stoltzfuses' roadside stand to deliver tomatoes to sell. She stayed too long for a visit with Ada Stoltzfus, a woman known to be blessed with the gift of conversation. Carrie ran a few errands in town but was later than she wanted to be as she returned to the farm. Angry, dark clouds had choked out the sun, the air was gummy and heavy, foreboding a downpour, and the wind whipped fiercely against the trees. A summer storm was coming and she wanted to get home as fast as she could.

As the wagon clattered into the covered bridge, Old-Timer balked. Carrie snapped the reins but he wouldn't budge. Government workers had been reconditioning the covered bridge and had placed sawhorses with blinking lights so people would stay clear of their equipment. She got out of the wagon and tried to lead Old-Timer, but the horse would not move forward. He was frightened by the white cuts of lightning that lit the sky, making strange shadows in the bridge.

"You old fool," she said to Old-Timer. "Now what am I going to do?"

Out of nowhere, Carrie heard a young man's voice. "If you trust me, ma'am, I think I can help you." He had a gentle voice, soft-spoken, polite.

She whipped her head around to see where the man was standing. She couldn't make him out in the darkness, only his profile, but she could tell he was English. The stranger told Carrie to hop back on the wagon. He took off his coat and covered Old-Timer's head with it, talking to him softly. Old-Timer took a tentative step forward, then another, and finally made it through to the other side. The stranger removed his jacket and gently stroked Old-Timer's head.

"See?" he said with a grin. "It's as simple as that."

"Thank you for your help," she said. "Can I be offering a ride to you? This weather is turning bad." She looked up at the bruised, dark sky.

"I'm looking for the Miller home," he said.

Carrie felt a smile tug at the corners of her mouth. "Millers abound among the Amish. Any idea which Miller?"

"I'm looking for the home of Daniel Miller. Moved here from Ohio last summer. Father's name was Eli."

She snapped her head up to look at the man for a second time. Her heart started pounding so loudly that she heard it in her ears. She recognized the man from the article printed out by Veronica McCall's computer.

This man is Abel Miller.

❄❄

Carrie shouldn't have been surprised by now that Yonnie seemed to be expecting Abel—the woman had an uncanny sense of knowing these things. She was standing outside on the kitchen steps as the wagon wheels rolled into the driveway. Abel jumped off the wagon and ran to her, hugging her little elderly body tightly to his, tears flowing down both of their faces. Carrie thought it was pure sweetness to watch. It felt good to see Yonnie happy. At times she was amazed at how Yonnie carried on, despite so much sadness in the last few years. It almost seemed as if she poured her feelings into her quilts, and that's why the colors were so dramatic and bold. Carrie left the two of them alone and went in to get dinner started.

On the ride to the house, Abel had told Carrie he had received a letter about Daniel's passing. He didn't say from whom and Carrie didn't ask. He said it was hard for him to get his mind around the fact of losing his cousin. His uncle too. "I needed to see Yonnie, as soon as I could," he said. "She's all I have left."

Yonnie was practically glowing as she joined Carrie in the kitchen. "Abel is un-hooking Old-Timer from the wagon and said he'd brush him down." She smiled. "A good Amish man takes care of the buggy horse first."

Carrie glanced sideways over at Yonnie as she peeled the carrots for dinner. *Was* Abel an Amish man? He was dressed in English clothing, his hair was shingled. Maybe he was wearing clothes he had been given when he left prison, Carrie reasoned. But another curiosity: Yonnie spoke English to him, not Deitsch.

By the time Abel came in from the barn, Carrie had supper in the oven.

"I filled your horses' water buckets and gave them all two flakes of hay. But your cow looks like she's about to burst. If you'll give me a milk bucket, I'll take care of her," he said.

Abel Miller was no stranger around horses, she decided, gathering clues about him. Maybe he was a smithy too.

"Thank you," Carrie said, "but my brother

should be home by now and that's his chore."

As if on cue, Andy burst in the door, doffed his hat, reached a hand into the cookie jar, but froze in motion as his eyes landed on Abel.

"Andy," Carrie said, pulling his hand out of the cookie jar, "where did you disappear to? You were supposed to weed the garden. We're just about to eat. Hope needs milking, first." She led him by the shoulders to meet Abel. "This is Daniel's cousin, Abel. He's come for a visit."

Andy looked Abel up and down. "Ich gleich sei Guck net." *I don't like his looks.*

Carrie squeezed his shoulders in warning. "Andy! Was in der Welt is letz?" *What in the world is wrong with you?* She turned to Abel. "Kannscht du Pennsilfaanisch Deitsch schwetze?" *Can you speak Pennsylvania Dutch?*

Abel shrugged. "I'm pretty rusty."

Carrie turned to Andy. "Speak English."

Andy frowned at her. "I only said, 'You don't look like Daniel.'" A frown looked funny on such a young face.

Abel's mouth deepened at the corners, trying not to smile, yet he seemed amused.

Carrie couldn't tell if he could understand what they were saying or just found them entertaining.

"Maybe not. But he's my grandson too, Andy," Yonnie said with surprising firmness. She still hadn't stopped smiling since Abel's arrival.

Andy shrugged, grabbed the clean milk bucket off of the bench, and ran outside to milk Hope, who was lowing unhappily from the barn.

As Abel washed up, Carrie set the bowl of stewed beef, carrots, and green beans on the table and passed the bread to Yonnie to slice. As soon as Andy returned, they sat down to dinner, closed their eyes, and bowed their heads for silent prayer. Abel held his hands open as if he was receiving a gift, eyes wide open, and launched into an out-loud prayer.

"Father, thank you for all the prayers you've answered for me today. For bringing me safely here to Yonnie, Carrie, and Andy. Help us to trust you more with each day that passes. In Jesus' name we pray, Amen."

Yonnie's, Andy's, and Carrie's heads bobbed up in surprise. Carrie was appalled by the familiarity with which Abel prayed, as if the Lord God himself was sitting next to him. Abel was raised Amish, Carrie thought; he must know their ways. Why had he prayed aloud?

Abel reached a hand out to the bread basket, passed it around, then picked up the butter knife and slathered a slice. "Mmm, good!" he said, after taking a bite. "They sure didn't have food like this in the slammer."

Carrie was so startled by his blunt remark that her fork slipped out of her hand and onto the floor.

Abel didn't notice. He started asking a lot of questions about the farm—the acreage, the kinds of apple trees, the outbuildings, and the livestock, of which there was little, for now.

"Hope just had her first calf, Lulu," Carrie said, passing the bread and butter to Andy. "So we finally have fresh milk. Up to a few months ago, I've had to buy milk from the Stoltzfuses, next farm over."

"You named a cow Hope?" he asked, his eyes laughing.

"Carrie named her Hope because she has high hopes for her," Yonnie said. "Carrie likes to give things meaning with their names. Her calf's name is Hallelujah because we're so happy she was born."

Abel grinned. "Sounds fittin'."

"We always name the calf after the initial of the mother." Andy spoke in a tone of someone who was firmly in charge of this farm. "That's the way my dad did it, so that's the way we do it."

Carrie looked at Andy curiously, wondering what was running through that boy's head. That was the first flicker of interest he showed in Abel, and it sounded nearly like an accusation.

Unfazed, Abel nodded at him. "Sounds like a solid system."

"So how long were you in jail?" Andy asked, eyes narrowed, his voice cold as winter earth.

"About a year and a half."

Andy's eyes roamed up and down Abel's arms. "Any tattoos?"

"Andy!" Carrie said, frowning, but Abel only laughed and shook his head before asking Carrie more questions about the property.

As Carrie answered Abel, she surprised herself by how much she knew about the orchards. She must have picked up more from listening to Eli and Daniel than she realized. "We only have twenty acres, but the trees were planted pretty dense. About one hundred trees to an acre, give or take a few. We have two acres of Northern Spy, three of Rusty Coat, two of Newtown Pippin, three of Smokehouse, two of Golden Russet, five of Honey Cider, and three of Pumpkin Sweet."

"I've never heard of those varieties," Abel said.

"They're Mid-Atlantic heirlooms," Carrie said. "Then we made cider from the apples that didn't make fancy grade."

Abel looked confused. "Fancy grade?"

"Eating quality," Carrie said. "Crisp to the bite and good looking. Those get sold to the packing house for top dollar."

"Carrie's known for her cider," Yonnie said. "Some say it's the best cider in the county."

"It was my dad's cider recipe," Andy said, without looking at Abel. "We use five kinds of apples."

"That's right," Carrie said, eyes shining. "We called it Jacob's Cider and can't make enough of it. On cider press day, folks line up at the crack of dawn, holding their own empty milk jugs."

"Saved 'em a quarter if they brought their own jugs," Andy said, with the voice of authority.

Abel cocked his head, watching them intently as they talked. "Well, you all sound like apple experts."

"There's much still to learn about taking care of an orchard," Carrie said, more to herself than to Abel.

"That's why I'm quitting school," Andy said. "To stay home and take care of our apples."

Carrie pointed a finger at him. "You'll do no such thing."

Yonnie turned to Andy and said, "The Lord God answered our prayers, Andy. Our Abel is home to help us." She reached over to squeeze Abel's hand.

Abel seemed perplexed for a moment, as if he had something on his mind, then he smoothed out his puzzled look. "That was a fine dinner."

For a split second Carrie had a vague impression he was hiding something. But maybe not. What did she really know about this English man? She'd only known him a few hours.

After dinner, Abel surprised Carrie by taking dishes to the sink, stacking them to wash. She had never seen her father, Eli, or Daniel touch a dish unless they were eating off of it.

"Did a lot of dish washing in the joint," he said, adding soap to the hot water. He smiled at the look on her face when he mentioned prison. "Kind of silly to pretend it didn't happen, isn't it? That's where my last seventeen months, thirteen days, and two hours—or so—have been spent." He had a dimple in one cheek that gave him a slightly crooked smile, as if he was grinning about a private joke. "Not that I was keeping track."

"You don't mind talking about it?" Carrie asked as she dried a wet dish.

"Not a bit." He handed her another dish to dry. "Truth is, I met the Lord Jesus in prison. And all things considered, I consider that to be a gift."

Carrie nearly dropped the dish when she heard him say that. She stole a look at Yonnie who had stopped her chair mid-rock, leaning forward as if she wasn't sure she heard him right. Even Andy, who had crammed so many cookies into his mouth that his cheeks puffed out, looked wide-eyed at Abel's declaration.

Abel laughed at them. "Now, ladies, pick your jaws up off the ground. I'm telling you the gospel truth. I found the Lord in a jail cell. I'm mighty grateful he saved my sorry hide." He grinned at both of them. "Sort of sounds like a country song, doesn't it?"

Abel Miller was a strange one, Carrie decided.

❧

Abel insisted on sleeping out in the barn instead of in the house. The storm had passed mostly by, leaving the air fresh and sweet smelling. Abel carried a lantern, lighting the path ahead of Carrie. When she nearly slipped, he insisted on holding her elbow to steady her. In her arms were a stack of Yonnie's quilts, topped with a pillow for him.

"I'd forgotten how dark it can be in the country," he said, looking up at the heavens. The sky was a thick, cloudy soup. The only visible light came from a tiny slice of moon.

Carrie showed him where the workshop was, at the back of the barn, and the cot he could sleep on, and how to get the wood-stove started. One of the horses whinnied from his stall.

"That's Schtarm, saying hello," she said, handing a pillow to Abel.

"You named him Storm?" Abel asked.

Carrie nodded. "Daniel named him. His name suits him. He's a retired racehorse that Daniel bought at an auction. A little high-spirited. He's too much for me to han-dle, but Daniel was trying to gentle him for the buggy when he . . ." She found she didn't know quite what to call it. Had an accident? Before he died? She pointed to the other horse's stall. "I use Old-Timer for the buggy. He's old, very, very old. Some-times I think if he went any slower we'd be going backward, but at least he doesn't shirk in his traces like Schtarm."

Abel smiled. "Daniel had a keen eye for horseflesh." He took the quilts out of her arms. "Folks in Ohio used to ask him to go to horse auctions, just to offer his opinion."

Carrie wondered what magic those Ohio folks had used to pull an opinion out of Daniel. "In the far stall is Strawberry. Daniel bought her, along with a pony cart, for Andy last Christmas." She spread some sheets on the cot and tucked in the edges. "Andy hasn't ridden her since . . . Daniel passed."

Abel turned his head slowly and gave Carrie a long, steady stare.

"Tomorrow I'll take you out to where they—Eli and Daniel—are buried." She shuddered when a clap of thunder, lingering from the storm, sounded close to the house. "I hope the lightning doesn't hit the house or barn."

"I noticed you have lightning rods on the house," Abel said. "But not on the barn?"

"Leftover from the English owner. He didn't keep any livestock in this old barn so he didn't have lightning rods on it. We haven't taken them down yet from the house. Been too busy with . . ." With funerals, Carrie realized. She changed the subject. "Sure this will suit you?" she asked, looking around the room. "It's not much more than a workshop."

"A big improvement to my former surroundings," he said with that crooked grin of his. Something about his smile made it impossible not to smile back.

She watched him for a moment as he cracked some kindling over his knee to spread on top of the fire he had started. She would never have known he and Daniel were related. If a man could be called beautiful, that would have been the way to describe Daniel. Abel wasn't as fine boned and handsome as Daniel, but he moved with a confidence and assurance that Daniel had lacked. Abel had a toughness about him, like a boxer in a ring that she had seen once on a trip to town. And yet, Abel's eyes—as soft and warm as melted chocolate—belied his tough exterior. They gave him away.

Abel glanced at Carrie, aware she was appraising him. "Thank you, Carrie. It's good to finally meet Daniel's wife."

The way he said it made her feel funny, like he knew more about her than he let on. And, in return, she knew nothing about him. She was halfway through the door when he asked, "So, Carrie, have you made a plan?"

She swiveled around. "What do you mean?"

"I just wondered, have you thought of moving back home with your folks?"

She stepped out of the shadow and into

the light. *"This* is my home. Mine and Andy's. *That's* my only plan." She lifted her eyebrows. She suddenly realized why he had that odd look on his face at dinner, when Yonnie said he was an answer to their prayers. He wasn't planning on staying. "What about you, Abel Miller? Do you have a plan?"

They looked at each other for a moment, a standoff. Then lightning lit the sky and thunder rumbled loudly on its heels.

"Let me walk you back to the house," he said. "Don't want you slipping and hurting yourself."

He had neatly avoided her question, she noticed.

Later, after turning off the switch on the gas lamp next to her bed, Carrie peered outside from her bedroom window at the soft moonlight of the apple orchards. She saw the buttery glow of lantern light coming from the small windows of the barn. It felt strangely comforting.

※

In the pale dawn of the morning, Carrie woke, half expecting Abel to be gone, but she saw he was up, coming in and out of the barn like he'd been up for hours. When she went out to the barn, she found that he had shoveled manure out of the cows' and horses' stalls, fed them, filled the egg basket with fresh eggs, and milked Hope.

"Denki, Abel," she said when she found him sweeping out the workshop. She handed him a cup of hot coffee.

He gratefully accepted the cup and took a sip. "For what?" He looked genuinely surprised.

"For your help."

That odd look passed over Abel's face like it did last night, the same look Andy got whenever she caught him with his hand in the cookie jar. "I should be thanking you," he said. "Best sleep I've had in years. I've nearly forgotten what it was like to fall asleep to the sound of night birds instead of prison gates clanging shut. Or closing my eyes in a room that was dark. Cells are never completely dark. The lights in the hallways stay on so the guards can make their rounds."

Carrie's eyes went wide. And what could she say to that?

After breakfast, she told Abel she would take him to the cemetery as soon as she had finished hanging the laundry. He gave her a brief nod and went back out to the barn. Awhile later, she found him out in the barn, Schtarm's right front hoof up on his thigh; he was scraping caked dirt and dung out of it with a hoof pick. He straightened up as soon as he saw her.

"This horse is a beauty."

She came around to the horse's left side and patted Schtarm's velvet nose. "True, but I can't handle him," she said. "Been thinking about selling him. He has a skittish nature."

"There's usually a reason why a horse acts so nervous. He just doesn't know how to say what's troubling him," Abel said, gently rubbing his hand along Schtarm's glossy cinnamon hide. "So, he misbehaves. But the truth is he's just trying to be heard."

His gaze fell away from hers and he picked up a curry comb to brush Schtarm, running it over his neck and withers. The way Abel touched the horse gave Carrie a shiver. It was so gentle and tender. "Are you skilled at blacksmithing?"

Abel gave a hard, short laugh. "No, ma'am. I'm no horse pedicurist. Left that particular skill set to Daniel and Eli. I prefer to keep my distance from the back end of a horse." He unhooked the halter from the post and led Schtarm back into the stall.

Abel had no trouble hitching up Old-Timer, Carrie noticed. He did it in the same careful pattern as all Plain folk did, like he'd been doing it all his life. He helped her up on the buggy and took the reins without asking, holding them loosely in his hands. The sky was bright blue, washed clean from last night's rain. Large puffy clouds chased each other in the sky. Abel pointed out the different farms along the way and asked about each of her neighbors.

At the cemetery, Abel's lighthearted mood dimmed, like a cloud passing over the sun. After showing him the graves, Carrie left him alone and walked over to her father's small tombstone, identical to all of the others; a sign of humility. Carrie stood by her father's grave for a long while, remembering. Then she went back to wait in the buggy and distract herself from dwelling on loss. Esther's voice echoed in her mind, "Overgrieving is a complaint against the Lord." But it was so hard, so hard to accept the mysterious will of God.

From the buggy, Carrie watched Abel. He sat down on the damp ground in between Eli's and Daniel's graves. He held out his hand, gently running one hand over the rounded edge of the stones, the same gentle way that he had touched the curve of Schtarm's neck. She could see his lips moving, as if he was talking to them. After a long while, he wiped his face with both hands and brushed off his pants. The damp ground had soaked the knees of his pants in large dark patches. He looked a little embarrassed, but relieved too, as he climbed in the buggy.

"So glad that six feet under isn't the end of things," he said. "Their souls are with the Lord Jesus."

"That's our hope," Carrie said, automatically.

He shifted in the buggy seat to look at her. "The Bible says that when we're absent from the bodies, we're present with the Lord. Second Corinthians 5:8."

Carrie didn't want to argue with him. He knew his Bible better than she knew hers, she could see that. He spouted off a few verses last night like he had the whole thing memorized. Besides, she had another question burning inside of her. As forward as it seemed, Carrie felt she had to ask, especially once she figured he didn't seem likely to be sticking around.

She slapped the reins to get the horse moving. With her eyes fixed on Old-Timer's rhythmic back quarters, she said, "There's something I need to ask you. About Daniel."

"Ask me anything," Abel said, regarding her with inquiring eyes, his head slightly tilted.

"Daniel said he caused the fires."

Abel made a small sighing sound, as if he'd heard this story before. "Is that what he told you? That he caused them?"

She nodded. "He said he was responsible for them." Her gaze returned to the reins. "I don't understand why . . . how . . . he could ever harm someone."

"Do you know much of what happened in Ohio?"

She shook her head, her heart pounding so loudly she was sure he could hear it.

Abel was quiet for a moment, as if gathering his thoughts. He reached over and took the reins from her, then pulled Old-Timer over to a stop at the side of the road. He shifted in his seat to look at her. "A few years back, Daniel started a business of delivering kerosene to the Amish. I helped him out when Eli didn't need me in the fields. Most of the folks lived down macadam roadways, and it was easier for us to make deliveries using horse and wagon than for the delivery truck. We built a shed to keep the containers clean and dry, separate from the barn. Separate from anything that could contaminate the containers. Only thing we had in the shed was a telephone, to take orders. In Eli's district, folks were allowed a phone for business, as long as it wasn't in the house."

Carrie nodded. It was the same allowance for her district.

"You know about Katie?" he asked.

Carrie nodded again, though all she really knew was her name.

"A week before Daniel and Katie's wedding," Abel continued, "the containers became contaminated with gasoline. Kerosene and gasoline don't mix." He glanced over at a farmer's field of tall corn, yellow-brown stalks rustling in the breeze. "We still don't know how it happened. They had arrived clean as a whistle, without a trace of gasoline. Daniel signed off on them and put them in the shed. Later that day, he made the deliveries. By that evening, two households had explosions. Lena, Daniel's mother, happened to be at Katie's, preparing for the wedding, when the kerosene was lit. It exploded and killed her instantly. Katie was burned badly and died the next day. Another man and his son were killed too." He stopped for a moment, as if the words had caught in his throat. "We just don't know *how* it happened."

The air had grown thick and heavy, as before a storm, though the sky was empty of clouds. Carrie's eyes prickled with tears; she kept her eyes on her hands, folded in her lap. As he spoke the words, she knew them to be true. She had known, deep in her heart, that Daniel could never have caused harm to anyone. As the truth slipped in and pushed away any lingering doubt about Daniel, on its heels swept in an overwhelming sorrow. A single tear fell onto her lap, followed by another and another. She wiped them away with the back of her hand as quickly as they came, hoping Abel didn't notice.

From the corner of her eyes, she saw his chest move as he drew in a breath. "The police traced it back to the shed. They found small traces of gasoline on a shelf. Since it was a business, Daniel was held liable, even if it was an accident, even if Amish families would never sue him. He was still negligent. The judge gave him a stiff fine and an even stiffer prison sentence—he wanted to make an example because there have been other problems with fuel delivery companies. He knew the sentencing would make headlines and he knew the Amish would never appeal. But he didn't care who went to jail, so I told the judge it was my fault, and next thing I knew, I was a long-term houseguest of the Ohio State Penal System. Soon as I was paroled, my parole officer gave me permission to leave the state, as long as I check in with him."

He turned to her. "I guess to answer your first question, Daniel *felt* responsible, but he didn't *cause* those accidents. We'll never know how it happened, but Daniel was innocent. I know that." He gave her a gentle smile. "It's good that you asked, Carrie. You deserve the truth. The Bible says that the truth will set us free."

Well, she had the truth now, but it didn't make her feel free. It made her feel weighted down with regret. She smoothed out her apron, as if trying to push away the sadness. "Seems to me you lost over a year of your life."

"Oh no." Abel looked right at Carrie. "No, I didn't. I gained my life."

Before Carrie could even wrap her brain around that statement, a little red convertible roared past. It startled Old-Timer, who jerked the buggy off the street.

"Oh dear," she said without thinking. "We'd better get back to the house. Gschwind." *Fast.* She took back the reins from Abel and urged the horse forward.

When they arrived home, Veronica McCall's red convertible was parked by the front door.

Abel looked amused. "Who does that car belong to?"

"A woman who works at the Honor Mansion, up the road. She keeps badgering me to buy this property."

Abel gave Carrie a sharp look. Then he hopped down and helped her out of the buggy. "You go on in. I'll put away the team."

Carrie went inside and found Yonnie spreading out quilts all over the kitchen table, with Veronica McCall picking and choosing which ones she was interested in.

"Hello," Carrie said as she took off her cape and untied her bonnet strings.

Veronica McCall spun around on her high heels. "Carrie! Where have you been? Our interior designer went berserk when he saw that quilt you brought to me. Over-the-moon berserk! Now he wants Yonnie's quilts in all of the rooms at Honor Mansion!" She turned back to the quilts and started snatching them up, to make a pile. "He's using them as his focal point in every room."

Carrie searched Yonnie's face, wondering what she thought about that plan. "Perhaps we could get back to you, Veronica McCall."

Just then, Abel came through the kitchen door.

"Veronica, this is Abel Miller," Carrie said quickly, hoping to distract Veronica from piling up Yonnie's quilts. Veronica glanced quickly at him, then did a double take. It reminded Carrie of how Veronica looked when she first saw Yonnie's quilts. And how she always looked when she talked about

Carrie's property. Like a hunter who found her prey.

Carrie looked over at Abel. Jaw wide open, he was gaping at Veronica McCall as if he had never seen a woman before.

8

The next afternoon, Veronica McCall found Carrie picking cucumbers in the vegetable garden. "Yoo-hoo, Carrie! I need to talk to Abel. Where is he?"

Carrie pointed to the barn. "In the back. There's a room where he's staying."

"Thank you!" Veronica called out, spinning on her high heels as she turned to hurry to the barn.

Carrie wondered what Veronica McCall would need with Abel. Before long, she heard the car engine start up. She straightened up from bending over a cucumber bush just in time to see Veronica McCall drive off. Abel was in the seat beside her.

It was dusk when they returned. Carrie was at the kitchen sink, cutting vegetables for the stew. She saw Abel get out of the car, and Veronica McCall reach over to hand him a large manila envelope, as if he had forgotten it. He gave a sideways glance at the house before accepting it from her. For a split second, Carrie thought she saw that uncomfortable look on his face again. Then he tucked the envelope under his arm before heading to the barn.

At dinner, Abel talked and asked questions but didn't volunteer an explanation about his outing. It still surprised Carrie to have conversation at the dinner table. Silence wove itself through most of her day; even meals were quiet. At least, it had always been so at Esther's table, and Eli's too. But Carrie found herself enjoying Abel's stories. Tonight, he told about the friends he made in prison, fellows with odd names like Five and Steelhead. Andy, Carrie noticed, was trying his best to look bored. But he didn't bolt from the table as soon as they prayed a quiet prayer after the meal was over, like he had been doing since

Abel had arrived. Carrie thought Abel would make a good preacher; he seemed to have a habit of slipping Bible phrases into the conversation whenever he could, which was often.

Clearing the plates from the table, Carrie asked, "Why did his parents name him Steelhead? Was it after the trout?"

After Abel stopped laughing at Carrie, he said, "No. He actually had a steel plate put in his head after he got shot at during a botched robbery."

Her eyes went wide. Even Andy couldn't hold back a look of surprise. "Oh, he didn't have a gun," Abel said. "Steelhead would never hurt a fly. It was the store owner's gun. It went off, by accident, when Steelhead sneezed during the holdup."

Andy tilted his head. "What about Five?"

"Five went to jail for the five-finger discount." He wiggled his fingers in the air.

Andy and Carrie exchanged a confused glance.

"Shoplifting," Abel said. Realizing they still didn't understand, he added, "He stole things from stores." He leaned back in his chair, folding his hands behind his head. "Now those are two characters I will miss."

After dinner, Abel joined them in the living room. Yonnie had decided that Abel needed a quilt, so she started laying out fabric pieces on the cardboard table. She asked Abel what colors he liked and which patterns and shapes. Abel patiently answered her questions, helping her come up with a final vision for the quilt.

"When you marry," Yonnie said, "I'll make you another one. For your bride."

Abel laughed. "Don't get started yet on that one, Yonnie. I'm in no hurry to find love."

Yonnie peered at him in that knowing way she had. "But love might be in a hurry to find you."

An image of Veronica McCall bounced into Carrie's head.

When the clock struck nine, just like always, Carrie took out her father's Bible and knelt down to read a chapter.

"Carrie, do you mind if I read?" Abel asked.

"No, I don't mind at all." In fact, she was pleased. She held the Bible in her hands, thinking back to all of the moments of her childhood, kneeling in the living room, listening to her father's dear voice read from the Good Book. The sweet memory was as firmly imprinted on her heart as were the words of God in the worn old leather Bible.

She handed the Bible to Abel, but he shook his head and pulled a small book out of his coat pocket.

He opened his book, leaned back in his chair, and started reading, "'Yahweh, investigate my life; get all the facts firsthand. I'm an open book to you, even from a distance, you know what I'm thinking. You know when I leave and when I get back; I'm never out of your sight. You know everything I'm going to say before I start the first sentence. I look behind me and you're there, then up ahead and you're there, too—'"

"Abel," Carrie said. "It's time to be reading the Bible now."

"It is. This is from Psalm 139. David wrote it."

She frowned at him. "That's plain old English."

"It's a modern translation. It's called *The Message*. It's a Bible I read from in jail every day—"

Carrie's back stiffened. "Just seems you ought not to be talking to the Lord God like that." She looked to Yonnie for support, but she had nodded off to sleep, like she always did during the evening Bible reading. She glanced at Andy, but he had quietly returned to his puzzle when she and Abel started to talk.

Abel lifted his head and looked at Carrie with genuine puzzlement. "Like what?"

"Like . . . well, like . . . he's one of your odd-named friends from jail."

Abel closed the book and smiled. "But the Bible says we can talk to God like that."

Abel's talk about God made Carrie fidget in her chair, uneasy. She knew her father faithfully read Scripture, but he didn't pause and ponder any of it or ask questions of anyone about what he read. And he never would have talked to God like he was . . . a . . . fishing buddy. That was thought to be grossfiehlich. *Haughty or high-minded.*

Carrie told Andy to go to bed and followed him upstairs to make absolutely sure that's where he was headed. Just last night, she found he had crawled out his window to sit on the porch roof, searching the sky for night birds with Daniel's binoculars. While she said goodnight to Andy, she heard the buzz of low voices downstairs,

Abel and Yonnie's. She waited until she heard Yonnie climb the stairs to bed in her cautious, creaky way. Carrie figured Abel had gone to the barn so it was safe to go downstairs, but there he was, seated at the kitchen table. She wanted to turn tail and head back upstairs, but he heard her footsteps on the stairs and stood, waiting for her.

"I wanted to finish our conversation," he said.

Awkwardness covered her like a blanket. "I ought to be getting to bed. Dawn comes early." She went into the living room to turn off a gas lamp.

"Carrie, I do know the Amish ways."

She turned off one more light, then spun around in the dimly lit room to face him. "Then why don't you follow them?"

"Because I pray out loud? Or read an English Bible? Or both?"

She nodded, but the truth was, it was Abel's praying that rankled her the most. He talked to God like he was sitting up there in heaven, taking down notes so he wouldn't forget what Abel wanted. She knew God was going to do whatever he wanted to do, regardless of anyone's pleading.

"I've learned more about God in the last year or so than I ever did in Eli's home. There's so much more to God than what we've been taught."

"Like what?"

"Like, there's a difference between religion and relationship. It's all right here," he said, tapping his Bible.

"Christ came not for relationship, but for our will," Carrie said. "I've heard the bishops and ministers preach that all of my life."

"Maybe he came for both," Abel answered quietly.

Carrie wasn't sure what to say to that. She hadn't thought these things through. It occurred to her that she had always just accepted what her father had told her, what her church had told her, then what Sol had told her. As she was finding herself doing frequently around Abel, she became uncomfortable. She crossed her arms defiantly against her chest. "So, you're not planning on joining the church? You would leave your faith?"

An ill-at-ease look swept over Abel's face. He went to the kitchen table and sat down, pulling a chair out for her. Reluctantly, she sat down. He put his hands together.

"Carrie, my faith is mine. I'll never leave it. It doesn't matter what church I go to." He looked at his folded hands. "I'm just not sure I can act Amish."

"You don't 'act' Amish. You live it. You *are* it." Even as she said the words, she felt the sting of her own hypocrisy. Here she was, lecturing Abel as if she had never had doubts about bending at the knee. Not much more than a year ago, she was willing to throw it all away for Sol. "You'll turn out the kitchen light?" she asked him, waiting for his nod before she went up the stairs.

She whispered an apology to the Lord God for sounding so proud. She also hoped that God would understand that Abel Miller was a fence jumper and not blame her for bringing him into her home. Like Esther would, if she knew.

Carrie shuddered, hoping she could hold that off as long as possible.

Later that week, Mattie dropped by Carrie's house with fabric for Yonnie. Mattie's mother was hosting a comfort knotting the next Wednesday, and Yonnie had offered to help by cutting fabric into squares to be sewn into a comforter. The quilts would be sent to homeless shelters in Philadelphia.

Mattie set the box down on the table and pulled out *The Budget*, the Amish newspaper, for Yonnie. "Here you are. Just like I promised. Mom said she's done reading and you're welcome to it."

Yonnie was thrilled. She loved *The Budget*. She spent hours sitting and reading the letters sent in by the scribes all over the country. She settled into her favorite chair, basked by sunlight, and spread out the newspaper on the quilting frame in front of her. First, she always turned to the obituaries.

"Why do you like the obituaries?" Mattie asked, watching Yonnie scan the page.

"Making sure I'm not dead yet."

Smiling, Mattie came in to join Carrie in the kitchen, boiling jars and lids to fill with blackberry jam. "A hot day for hot work! How can I help?"

Carrie pointed to the box on the table. "Those are jars that need washing before I can sterilize them."

Mattie washed her hands and rolled up

her sleeves. "I always look for weddings in *The Budget* first. Then I read about the visiting." She started taking the jars out of the boxes and put them in the sink to wash. "What about you, Carrie? Don't you always look for wedding news?"

Carrie lifted the hot jars out of the boiling water and set them carefully on the countertop. "I used to. Not so much anymore." She ladled the thick, lumpy, hot purple liquid into the jars, then topped them with a metal lid.

"Oh, it won't be long before you're married again. Remember when we were girls? If we held a ripe dandelion seed head and blew three times, then the number of seeds left would tell us how many children we'd have." Mattie smiled, rinsing out the sudsy jars before handing them to Carrie to sterilize.

Carrie didn't answer at first. "I don't want to marry again." She put the jars Mattie had washed into the large pot of boiling water. Drips of sweat were streaming down her neck.

Mattie looked up at her. "You don't mean that. I thought—"

"You thought I'd be thinking about Sol?"

Carrie asked. "I'm not." Her voice sounded crosser than she intended. But it had occurred to her that Mattie might feel worried Sol would start coming around now that Daniel was gone. Carrie hadn't heard from Sol in months. That suited her just fine. She might not know how she felt about Daniel, but she knew how she felt about Sol: zannich! *Angry!*

"Did I say such a thing?" Mattie handed Carrie two jars. "I just thought you'd want to marry again. That's all."

The gentle reproach in Mattie's eyes stung. Carrie turned her eyes to the filled jars. "All I want is to be able to give these apple orchards to Andy one day. If I can hang on to them."

Mattie tilted her head. "Are you having money troubles?"

Carrie hesitated a moment, listening for the pop of the jam jars to indicate the lid suctioned into a seal. "Not troubles, exactly. Not yet." She had refused Veronica McCall's offer to buy Yonnie's quilts. She just couldn't let Yonnie part with any more of them. She was sure there had to be another way to pay the bills.

"Can't you ask Esther for help?"

Carrie winced. Esther had never truly forgiven Carrie for insisting that Andy come live with her. "Her solution would be to move back in with her."

"You could talk to the deacon. He would be able to help."

"I know. If I need to, I will." She wiped the counter with a clean rag. "For now, we're all right. It's looking like this will be a good apple year." She took the jars out of the water and set them down. Mattie ladled the jam into the clean jars and put a lid on each one. "So if keeping the orchards is what you want for Andy, what do you want for yourself?"

Carrie shrugged a shoulder carelessly. "We don't get everything we want, Mattie."

Mattie bent an ear down to hear the *pop! pop!* of the lids. When she heard them, she smiled, satisfied. "No, maybe not, but the Lord promises us everything we need."

⚜

A few days later, Carrie made hotcakes with apple butter for breakfast. She was pouring Yonnie a cup of coffee as Abel came in from the barn.

"Mmmm! They smell delicious." Abel grabbed a plate and forked a few steaming hotcakes onto it, spooning apple butter on top.

"Daniel loved Carrie's hotcakes too," Yonnie said.

"Only time I ever saw him give an all-the-way-to-the-toes smile," Carrie said.

The words flew out of her mouth before she caught them. She clamped her lips shut as Abel's chin snapped up. He looked straight at Carrie, but she kept her eyes lowered to her plate.

The morning was already so hot that Carrie went down to the barn to make sure the animals' water buckets were filled. Abel came in from the workshop when he heard her.

"Got a minute?" he asked.

She finished pouring water into Lulu's bucket, then straightened. "No. I've got an apple snitz in the oven."

"I was pulling off some rotted boards on the barn to replace them and got a nasty splinter in my hand." He held up his hand to show her.

"Come over to the window."

He held out the hand with the wood splinter. As she tried to pull it without breaking it off, he said, "Those Cooper's hawks

need to be set free. They're nearly grown."
The hawks were squawking a raucous call
at them from the cage Andy had made for
them by converting a horse stall.

She nodded.

"They're wild creatures. Keeping them
in a barn is no place for them."

"I've said as much to Andy, but he won't
part with them. I think it's the last link he
had to Daniel."

In a voice low and kind, Abel asked,
"Carrie, was Daniel good to you?"

She dropped his hand as if it was a hot
coal. Abel's gaze was steady—he looked
at her with brown eyes that were warm and
concerned. He made her uneasy, though,
asking her questions that no one ever asked.
Sometimes she couldn't believe he and
Daniel were related. He must have been a
perfect complement to Daniel. Abel liked
to talk. He probably filled in the emptiness
of Daniel's silences, she decided, turning
her attention back to the splinter, ignoring
his question.

"Done," she said. "Best to put a bandage on that." She turned away quickly.

Abel put his hand on her forearm. "Was
he good to you, Carrie?"

Her gaze shifted to the birds in the stall, staring at her with their beady black eyes.

Abel waited. And waited. The silence in the barn took on a prickly tension. Carrie knew he expected her to pour out all the grief and sorrow she had stored up for so long. She felt close to tears and she didn't know why. How could she admit to him that the sadness she felt whenever she thought of Daniel was caused by guilt, not grief?

Keeping her eyes averted, she answered, "Daniel was always good to me. Very, very good to me."

Walking back to the farmhouse, she realized she had spoken the truth. Daniel had been good to her. Still, her feelings about Daniel were a tangled mess. She felt terrible about how things had been left between them. She felt a deep guilt that shadowed her, the way Daniel's burden had shadowed him. But most of all, she felt a sorrow that things were left unfinished between them.

※

The following day, Veronica McCall came to Carrie's house and walked right into the kitchen without knocking. She didn't close the door tight, so Carrie hurried past her to shut it before hot sticky air could rush in.

"Where's Abel?" she asked.

"I heard him nailing some boards on the back side of the barn," Carrie said. "That barn is so old it's nearly falling apart."

"I came to ask him if he could do some carpentry work for us at Honor Mansion. A carpenter is having surgery for a hernia or a kidney or something like that."

Carrie tilted her head. "A hernia or a kidney?"

"Well, something's wrong with him." Veronica waved the thought away. "So he's out for a while and we need to get the interior woodwork finished. I thought of Abel. Don't all Amish men know carpentry?"

Carrie turned to Yonnie, who was watching Veronica McCall with a curious look on her face. "Yonnie, does Abel do carpentry?"

"Oh sure," Yonnie said. "And he knows all about electric. And motors too."

"He's an electrician?" Veronica asked. "Even better! Our electrician hasn't shown up in three days. They all keep quitting. Perfect! I'll go talk to him." She blew out the door, not bothering to shut it. Hot, heavy air swooped in.

If Veronica McCall hired Abel on, Carrie

thought, maybe he would stick around and help them get through the harvest. Just one harvest, she prayed, whispering cautiously to God above, if she could just make it through this first harvest without Daniel. She closed the door and turned to Yonnie. "What else can Abel do?"

"He's good at fixing things. Abel can fix anything." She looked up to the ceiling, pensive, as if trying to pull down a memory like a book from a shelf. "I'm pretty sure he could build a nuclear submarine if he put his mind to it."

Carrie stared at Yonnie, trying to make sense of her. "Yonnie, what do you know about nuclear submarines?"

Yonnie smiled, and the wrinkles on her face fell into their natural grooves. "I know about all sorts of things."

Carrie went over to sit next to her. "Well then, what do you think Abel plans to do with himself, now that he's out of jail?"

She picked her quilting up off her lap. "Stay here, of course, and help us. We're his family. He belongs here."

"I'm not so sure that others are going to understand an English-looking fellow just set free from jail is family."

Yonnie kept her eyes on her quilt pieces. "Abel is still in his Rumspringa."

Carrie doubted that. Abel seemed a little old for running-around years. "So you think he just hasn't decided yet about joining the church?"

"Oh sure," she said, but not with conviction. She started to concentrate on a row of tiny stitches.

"Yonnie, was Abel so . . . ," she hunted for the right word, ". . . devout before he went to jail?"

She gave a short laugh. "Oh my, no."

"He's changed, then?"

Concern pulled down her wrinkled features. "Haven't we all." She started humming, which was her signal that she was done talking.

Abel didn't return for supper that night. He wasn't even home in time for evening prayers. Carrie was nearly asleep when she heard a car zoom up the driveway, skidding to a halt in front of the barn. She got out of bed and looked out a corner of the window to see who it was. In the full moonlight, she saw Veronica McCall reach out to plant a kiss right on Abel's lips. She quickly stepped away from the window and jumped back in bed, ashamed of herself for spying on them like, well, like Emma. But one thing she did notice: Abel didn't seem to be objecting to the kissing.

⚜

A few days later, about dinnertime, the bishop's grandson, John Graber, showed up at the farmhouse, carrying a big smoked ham. "My mother thought you might be needing this," he said in his awkward way.

"Oh my, yes. This will feed us for . . . weeks," Carrie said, taking it from him. Months, even.

Abel came in from the barn, bursting through the kitchen door. "Well, hello there!" he said. "Just noticed your buggy out front." He reached a hand out to John Graber. "I'm Abel, Yonnie's grandson."

John Graber looked at Abel's hand as if he didn't know what to do with it. Then his head turned from Abel to Carrie, completely confused. But then, the wheels in John's mind had always turned slowly.

"This is the bishop's grandson, John," Carrie said, filling in the silence.

John just stood there, looking ill at ease and bewildered. It was one of the many reasons Carrie thought he was strange.

He ran clean out of words after the first greeting.

Abel, not a bit put off by John's lack of loquacity, went on merrily ahead and invited him to stay for supper. Carrie tried not to let a relieved smile spread over her face when John declined and abruptly turned to leave. She could only imagine what John would report to his grandfather after hearing Abel pray like he was on a first-name basis with the Lord God Almighty.

"Another time, then, John!" Abel called out cheerfully from the kitchen door.

Carrie scowled at Abel after he closed the door.

"What? What did I do?" he asked her.

"John Graber is sweet on her," Yonnie whispered. "She doesn't want to encourage his attention. She thinks he is strange."

"He does seem a little strange." Abel grinned at Carrie. "Maybe a little weak on the social skills."

As Carrie watched John's buggy turn onto the road, she wondered how long it would be until Esther showed up. She hurried upstairs and pulled open a trunk where she had stashed Daniel's clothes. She had meant to pass them on to someone in need

but hadn't found time yet. She picked up
the shirts and trousers and held them close
to her, burying her face in them and inhaling deeply. There was still a lingering hint of
Daniel in them—the sour smell of wood
smoke mixed with the sweet smell of hay.
She took them downstairs and handed
them to Abel.

He lifted his dark brows at Carrie, puzzled.

"Perhaps you could look Plain while
you're here," she told him.

Abel frowned, scratched his chin, then
dropped one hand to rest on his dead
cousin's shirt.

The next morning, after breakfast, Esther arrived in her buggy with Emma and
a large suitcase. "I've decided you need
help," she told Carrie, eyeing Abel suspi-
ciously. "Emma will stay for a while."

At least Abel was wearing Plain clothes,
Carrie thought. Daniel was much taller so
the pants legs puddled around the ankles,
but Abel could pass for an Amishman.

Emma clomped upstairs to claim a spare
bedroom while Carrie made coffee for Esther and brought out a day-old cake. For as
long as Carrie could remember, Esther had

an effect on folks like a thundercloud that had just poured rain on their picnic. Abel stayed for coffee and did his best to try to engage Esther in conversation, but she nearly ignored him. It wasn't long before the conversation at the kitchen table drizzled to a cold stop.

Esther waved away Carrie's offer for a second cup of coffee, hurried to her buggy, and left. Carrie stood at the kitchen door for a moment.

Abel came up behind her, folding his arms across his chest as he watched Esther slap the reins to get the horse moving. "So, that's your mother."

"No, no," Carrie quickly said. "That's Emma's mother."

"So what happened to your mother?"

"My mother died right after Andy was born. My father moved us to Stoney Ridge to be closer to a hospital for Andy. When Dad married Esther, he took over managing her land."

"Oh," Abel said. "So Esther brought into the marriage her farm."

The farm and her godly self, Carrie thought but didn't say. Instead, she just nodded.

Abel gazed at her as if reading her thoughts. "She has a way of making clear her expectations."

Carrie's gaze shifted to Esther's buggy, turning right onto the street. "Even heavenly angels would find it hard to live up to Esther Weaver's expectations."

❧❧

That evening, Carrie tried to avoid Emma's glare as Abel read from his Bible, but inside, she was cringing. After he finished, she hurried upstairs to check on Andy. He always kicked off his covers as he slept, so she smoothed the sheet over him. She had just changed into her nightgown when Emma knocked on the door. Carrie braced herself.

Emma came in, wringing her hands as she sat on the bed. "Carrie, Abel ought not to be reading that Bible. It ought to be in our language. You know that as well as I do. And he shouldn't be praying like that at dinner, either. When Mother hears of this—"

"Emma, this is not Esther's home. This is my home," Carrie said sharply. "And it wouldn't do you any harm to listen to Abel." The words spilled out so fast she surprised herself with their boldness. Emma was only saying things Carrie had thought herself, just a week or so ago when Abel first arrived.

Emma's brow wrinkled, creased with worry. She drew her lips in a tight line as she folded her arms against her chest.

"I'd rather Esther not be told about Abel's way of Bible reading."

Emma went to the door. "It's not our way."

"I'm a Miller now."

"Amish is Amish. There's no difference." Emma closed the door behind her.

Carrie used to believe that, but now she wasn't so sure.

⁂

Sol had been named Pitcher of the Month for August. His image flashed up on the large screen in the stadium the day it was announced, and he was interviewed by three newspapers—one of which was the *Philadelphia Inquirer*. His baseball career was taking off, just like he had planned.

In his apartment, he kept a stack of copies of all of the newspapers that wrote about him, even though there was no one to show them to. Not yet, anyway. Soon, he hoped, when the season wrapped up, enough time would have passed that he would be able to call on Carrie. He was sure she'd have forgiven him by now and things could go back to being the way they were before. The way he had planned.

❧

It had been over a month since Abel had come. The long hot summer had flown by fast and the end of the growing season was almost in sight. The tree branches in Carrie's orchards were heavy with fat, ripening apples.

One afternoon in late September, threatening dark clouds raced across the sky. The wind blew so strong that Carrie took the clothes off of the line, still damp, before the rain started. As she took the last sheet down, she raised her face to the molten gray sky and felt a foreboding. This had the makings of a winter storm. The rain began as the day drew to a close. By supper, the rain had turned to stinging ice pellets.

"Good thing our neighbors got their third cutting of hay done last week," Emma said.

"But not good for apples," Carrie said quietly.

"What's so bad about the rain?" Abel asked, reaching for the butter.

"There's nothing wrong with rain, but it's cold enough to hail," Carrie said, more to herself than to him. "Between the wind and the hail, a lot of apples could get knocked to the ground."

In the middle of the night, Carrie woke to hear hail bouncing off the roof. She looked out the window and couldn't believe her eyes. The hail looked the size of Ping-Pong balls, ricocheting off the ground. "Oh God," she whispered. "Please help."

In the morning, the sun shone bright and cruel. Carrie dressed quickly and rushed out to the orchards. Andy heard her and followed close behind. Abel was already out there, turning in a circle, stunned. Bright red apples covered the ground like autumn leaves. Carrie picked one up. When she saw the bruise and cuts on it, she nearly cried. Most of the crop had been damaged.

Why, God? she asked silently. *Why do you have to keep knocking me down?*

Without a word to Abel or Andy, she turned to walk back to the house.

She was almost to the barn when she heard Abel yell out, "Cider!"

Carrie stopped and turned toward him.

Abel ran up to her, holding a bruised

apple, and held it out to her. "Andy said you made the best cider in the county." He spun around. "Didn't you say that, Andy?"

Andy nodded, not understanding what Abel meant.

Carrie looked at all of the apples on the ground. "You think we could salvage the crop by making cider?" A glimmer of hope showed in her eyes, but then faded as practicality swept in on its heels. "I only have one old cider press."

"I can put a gasoline motor on it to speed things up."

Carrie shook her head. "Can't. You can't have gasoline around food. I know that from working at Central Market."

Abel's brow furrowed as he scanned the farm. Then his eyes rested on the old waterwheel, attached to the barn. His face lit up. "There's nothing wrong with using water power, is there?"

Carrie nodded slowly. "But that old waterwheel hasn't been used in years."

"Just the other day I took a look at it. Nothing's broke, it just needs a little elbow grease. And thanks to last night's storm, there's plenty of water running in the creek.

Won't take much to get it turning. You clean out the cider press and get it ready. I'll work on the waterwheel—a couple of belts and pulleys and we're in business. Andy can ride Strawberry over to the Zooks' and see if Mattie's brothers can spare some time to get these apples picked up today." He turned to Andy. "If you don't mind, you might need to stay home from school today. I'm going to need a partner."

A wide grin spread across Andy's face.

Carrie looked around again at all of the apples. Maybe Abel was right. Maybe it could work. Why not try? She had nothing to lose. "I'll need empty jugs."

"Make a list. Write down everything you need and we'll get it today."

She looked at him, amazed and excited by the idea. "Denki, Abel."

By noon of that day, the waterwheel slowly creaked to life, then spun as a gust of wind sent it whirling. Abel had rigged a system of belts and pulleys to turn the screws on the cider press. As pressure pounded down on the apple mash, sweet clear cider spilled out. The Zook boys, all eight of them, even their father, had arrived to help pick up the apples and load them into crates.

Carrie and Emma had washed the apples and started adding them into the press, trying to get just the right blend of flavors, as Grace Patterson rode her bicycle up the driveway. Carrie wiped off her hands with the rag and waved to her. Though they were only a few years apart, Carrie's heart felt a motherly tug when she saw Grace. Today, Grace was dressed with a long flowing skirt and a man's shirt rolled up at the sleeves. On her feet were combat boots. Her hair was now blond, nearly white. Watching her, Carrie thought it seemed as if Grace wasn't quite sure who she really was, so she kept trying on a different façade until, one day, she might stumble on the one that suited her.

Grace bit her lip. "I came to ask you something."

Carrie filled up a paper cup with the cider and handed it to Grace to sample. "So, ask."

Grace took a sip of the cider, then her face lit up. "That is *money*! Tastes like I bit into a ripe apple."

Carrie smiled. "It's my father's recipe. The storm knocked the apples down so we had to make the cider, just to save the crop. I'm surprised at how good it tastes, though. I was afraid the apples would be underripe but they seem to be plenty sweet." She pointed to the cider press. "That old thing was made in the 1980s and still works."

"Dang, that is old." Grace filled up another cup of the cider. "So . . . ," she took a sip, throwing a glance in Emma's direction, "so my arraignment has been scheduled and I hoped . . . you . . . might be able to come to it. To talk to the judge." She swirled the cider in the cup and watched the bubbles form on top.

"I'll be there, Grace," Carrie said without hesitation. "I've already written a letter."

Grace's eyes flew up to hers. "Thank you so much," she said, almost a whisper. She drank down the cider and looked around at the filled jugs as Abel and Andy pulled up in a wagon. "Won't the cider go bad without refrigeration?" she asked Carrie. "Unless you're making hard cider. A kid in my biology class did that. Took about two weeks to ferment." Her forehead furrowed. "Then he came to school drunk and got suspended."

"The devil's brew?" Emma gasped. "Mother would never approve."

Carrie stopped suddenly and looked at Abel, who looked just as surprised. "Oh no!"

Abel blew the air out of his chest in a great gust. "No, we're not trying to make hard cider." He rubbed his chin. "Maybe we could keep the jugs cold in the creek."

"You could probably stick them in the freezers at Honor Mansion. The kitchen is empty." Grace swallowed the last drop. "I'll ask Veronica."

"That's a great idea," Abel said. "Better even to freeze it than to keep it refrigerated."

Grace crinkled up the cup and handed it to Carrie. In a low whisper she added, "Better still, get Abel to ask Veronica. She won't say no to anything he asks. She's got the hots for him."

Overhearing, Abel looked alarmed. Grace waved and hopped on her bicycle to head back to work.

"Come on, Abel," Andy said, hopping

back up on the wagon after drinking a cup of cider. "I'll go with you to ask that fancy red-haired lady with the short skirts." He glanced at his sister. "I meant, the fancy lady with the red car."

Carrie frowned at Andy. He was worrying her a little.

By the time they returned, given permission by Veronica to use the freezers, Carrie's cider mill was in production. Mattie had offered to sell the cider at Central Market, where her family had a market stand.

"Maybe Esther would let Emma sell it too," she told Carrie. "I've seen her there, working with Emma at the farm stand now and then."

Emma had been working for Esther at Central Market every other day as the crops finished up their summer bounty.

"Maybe so," Carrie said, but she doubted Esther would agree.

Carrie, Emma, Abel, and Andy pressed cider over the next few days. The Zooks loaned their cider press too, so they were able to double the output, and the weather stayed cold so the apples weren't going soft. Word spread among the neighbors that Carrie's cider was even better this year than last, and they stopped by the farm throughout the week to buy a jug or two.

After spending so much time side by side with Abel, Emma concluded that he was no longer to be viewed with suspicion. Andy, too, relinquished his lingering hostility toward him, helped along by Abel's request to skip school that week. Carrie noticed that he shadowed Abel the way he used to shadow her father, and later, Daniel. All week long, she almost never had to nag him to do chores as long as Abel worked alongside him. The sight should have gladdened Carrie's heart, but instead it made her feel sad. She was pretty sure Abel wouldn't be sticking around. And that meant one more loss for Andy.

By Friday, Mattie had sold every jug of cider at Central Market. Carrie fought back tears as Mattie handed the large wad of cash to her. Mattie had been bold enough to double the price Carrie wanted for the cider, and still, she sold every jug with people asking for more. The cider had brought in more money than selling the fancy grade apples to the packing house ever had.

Before the sun set for the day, Abel found

Carrie wiping down the cider presses in the barn. "Mattie told me that she had more customers than cider."

Carrie smiled. "Thanks to your quick thinking, Abel."

He brushed the compliment aside. "That's not what I meant. I meant that it could be we've found a niche here."

"Maybe next year we don't even bother with the packing house. Maybe we just make cider."

"I'm not talking about next year. Other varieties are coming on the market now. We could buy them and make the cider, then sell it at the Zooks' stand at Central Market. They're staying open until Christmas."

Considering the option, she asked, "I don't see how we could make much money after buying the apples."

"Hear me out. Mattie thinks she could have priced it even higher than she did." He took the rag from her and started rubbing the sides of a press. "I think we might have something here. Jacob's Cider is a hit."

It made her stomach feel funny, to hear him say *we* like he did. "I don't know. We'd need our own freezer. We can't be using

Veronica McCall's much longer. She's told me more than once that she should be charging me rent." She gathered the rags in her arms to take up to the house to wash.

Abel nodded. "I might be able to find a used freezer someplace and convert it with a generator." He opened the barn door for her and waited until she crossed the threshold to slide it shut. There, in front of her, was a wagon filled with crates of apples.

"Did I mention that I happened to stop by a farmer's market today?" he asked with a big grin. "They're not your heirlooms, but I did get five varieties of apples for your five-apple cider. The farmer said they had a high sugar content for cider. That's good, right?"

"But . . ." Carrie suddenly felt panicky about the cost of those apples. The wad of cash in her apron was about to disappear, and with it, hopes to pay the next installment of the property tax.

As if reading her mind, he added, "And they didn't cost a thing. They're misshaped apples." He held an odd-looking apple up to her. "The farmer said they taste just as good, but he can't sell them as eating apples."

"He didn't charge you?" she asked.

"Well, we bartered back and forth. He told me he needed some shelves built in his garage, and I told him I needed those apples. An even exchange."

Wrapping her shawl tightly around her, Carrie felt so grateful for Abel's help that she could hardly breathe. Maybe Yonnie was right. Maybe he could fix anything.

"I think I've settled on the right name for my home," she said, eyes shining. "Cider Mill Farm."

9

Carrie was just latching the chicken coop after throwing feed to the bossy leghorns when she heard Andy's screams coming from the barn. She dropped the bucket she was carrying and ran down to see what had happened.

When she peered inside the open door, she saw Andy doubled over, as if he was sick. Scattered around the barn were feathers and beaks and bloody pieces of meat and bones. The Cooper's hawks had attacked and killed Mattie's goslings. Carrie stood, frozen, taking in the morbid sight, unsure of what to do next. Andy picked up a broom and tried to hit the hawks, but they were too quick. They just flew above him and rested on a rafter, peering down at him with an insolent stare, mildly interested in his tirade. When Andy finally gave up, out of breath, he threw the broom down.

Abel came up behind Carrie, hearing the commotion. "No, let me," he whispered to her, as she made a move to go to her brother. "You go on back to the house." He walked over to Andy.

She turned to leave, then stopped, leaning against the doorjamb. Andy was turned in the opposite direction and didn't notice she was still there.

"The Cooper's hawks were just doing what they're meant to do, Andy," Abel said softly. "It's in their nature to hunt for food."

Andy kicked at a hay bale. "I gave them plenty of food! Why did they have to eat my geese? Why couldn't they be satisfied with what I gave them?"

"Someday, they'll be satisfied. There's a verse in the Bible that says the lion will lie down with the lamb. That's what heaven will be like."

Andy sank to the floor and leaned against a hay bale, hugging his knees. "Why does everything have to die?" Abel leaned against the hay bale, close to Andy—but not too close. "It was my fault."

"How so?" Abel asked.

"I left the goslings' door unlatched." Andy looked miserable, before resting his head on his knees. "Last night. I got watching an orb spider spin her web and catch a horsefly and wrap it up for dinner that I just plain forgot." Then he mumbled something that Carrie couldn't hear.

"What do you mean?" Abel asked, crouching down next to him, eyes fixed on him.

Andy lifted his head. "I had a dream about Dad and went to wake up Carrie. She wasn't there so Daniel said he would go get her." His voice started to break. "If I hadn't done that, he wouldn't be dead."

Abel took that in for a moment. "It was just an accident, Andy. Listen to me. It wasn't your fault. *It wasn't.* Daniel wouldn't want you feeling responsible. It just happened. We don't know why bad things happen."

Carrie leaned her forehead on the door-jamb. It broke her heart to think that Andy had carried such a heavy burden, all this time. A burden that belonged to her alone.

"It's just like my dad. It was my fault my dad died. Esther said it was. Esther said that if I don't find trouble, trouble finds me. Everything I do always goes wrong."

Abel didn't say anything for a moment. It seemed to Carrie as if he knew how important his response would be and was shooting off one of his one-sentence prayers to the Lord God before he uttered a word.

"There's a verse in the Bible that says God has the length of our days planned out. He knows when it's time for a person to pass. The psalmist wrote that God has the days of our lives all prepared before we'd even lived one day. It's all part of God's plan. Some die sooner than others, and that's hard, real hard to understand, but that's God's business. Our work is to trust him about those things." Abel stroked Andy's hair. "You are *not* responsible for Daniel's death or your dad's. I promise you that, Andy."

Andy started to weep, great sobs that shook his body. Abel pulled him close to his chest and let him cry. Carrie turned and ran to the farmhouse. She couldn't stay and watch Andy's tears; she was barely holding back the avalanche inside of herself.

Later, Carrie saw Abel and Andy carry the carnage out of the barn in a big black bag to bury in the manure pile. Then they caught the Cooper's hawks and took the cage to Blue Lake Pond to set them free. Andy came back looking taller, Carrie thought, like he'd grown a year in a day. When he went upstairs, Carrie threw on a shawl and went out to the barn. Abel was feeding hay to the horses. He threw the last of the hay in the stall, then came up to Carrie.

She searched for words, spirit-lifting words like those he had given as a gift to her brother. All she could think to say was, "Denki. For Andy."

He gave her a nod and then picked up the broom to sweep the fallen hay.

"Andy's not good at confiding his troubles. He seems to feel safe, talking to you. He's at that age where he needs . . . well, I'm not very good at . . . making Andy feel like a man."

"You're good at it." He said it so softly, while he kept sweeping, that she thought she might have imagined it. "When I first got here and saw those hawks . . . well, I've been holding my breath, just waiting for a problem." He stopped sweeping and straightened up. "At least we know they can hunt for food." He swept the rest of the hay into a stall and leaned the broom against the wall. "Kind of surprised me that Daniel would have let Andy keep those hawks. Daniel didn't like predators." He looked at Carrie as if expecting her to explain.

How could she try to explain a man she never knew? Even after all of those months together, she still had no idea who Daniel really was. "To tell you the truth, Abel, I didn't know Daniel all that well."

Abel raised his eyebrows. "I can't deny he had a jaw as tight as a beaver trap. It was hard for him to share his thoughts and feelings."

And his secrets, Carrie thought.

"At least by talking." Abel studied her for a long moment, a quizzical look in his eyes, before he cocked his head and pointed a finger at her. "Stay here. I'll be right back." He went into the workshop. She heard him pull open a drawer, rummage through it, shuffle some papers, then close it again. He came back into the barn and handed her a bundle of envelopes, secured by a rubber band. "These are the letters Daniel wrote to me while I was in jail. Maybe it would help you get to know him better."

She hesitated.

"Go ahead, Carrie," Abel said. "There's nothing to hide."

Carrie took a deep breath, still reluctant.

He pressed the envelopes into her hand. "In some of the letters, he writes about you."

Later that night, Carrie took the lantern up to bed with her and slipped the rubber band off the envelopes Abel had given to her. She looked at the postmarks of Daniel's letters and sorted them from beginning to end. She unfolded the first letter and read the pen-written note. Daniel's handwriting was angular, careful—the script of one who had been taught penmanship at school all those years ago, a skill he had never forgotten.

April 5th

Dear Abel,
After such a long and hard winter, as this past one was, I felt a small stirring of pleasure at seeing the first redwing blackbird return, and heard the clamor of northward

*winging geese, and the warbling song of the
bluebirds as they claimed their nesting boxes.
All signs that spring is coming.*

*I received your letter telling me about your
newfound faith. I can hear the change in your
voice, even through your letters. I'm glad
you've found such peace. I wish I could find
that, Abel. You've always been a 100% guy.
Whatever you've done, it's with your whole
heart. I've always admired that about you.
Me? I'm a fence-sitter. And now even my
faith has gone dormant.*

*Looks like we might have an offer on the
farm. Ervin Lapp, next farm over, wants to
buy land for his youngest son. He offered Dad
a decent price, considering land prices are low.
Dad wants to use the money and move to
Pennsylvania. His old friend, Jacob Weaver,
has been encouraging him to come, to make a
fresh start. But is there really such a thing?*

Yours, Daniel

Carrie's hands almost shook as she held the letter. It seemed as if she was reading Daniel's mind and his heart. She opened another letter postmarked a few weeks later.

May 10th

Dear Abel,

We've had a lot of soakers lately, back-to-back. Glad we got the fields plowed under before it all turned to mud. Had to stop plowing the north field for a few days until four speckled bobolinks had hatched.

Well, it's done, Abel. Dad sold this farm, with all of its memories, good and bad. We're heading down to Pennsylvania next week to stay with the Jacob Weavers and look for property to buy. It will be a small farm, no doubt, after paying off the court fine. Yonnie will stay with cousin Miriam while we're gone.

In your last letter, you mentioned that there is a grace that is greater than all of our sins. How can you be so sure, Abel? How can you truly know that we can ever satisfy God's demands for holy living?

Will write to you when we get to the Weavers and send you the address.

Yours, Daniel

Carrie slipped the rubber band around the rest of the letters. She knew Abel meant well by giving them to her, but they made her guilt over Daniel's death bubble to the surface. It was a long time before she fell asleep.

❧

A few days later, the light clop of hooves on gravel announced the arrival of the bishop and the deacon. As the buggy stopped in the driveway, Carrie threw Emma a look of disdain.

"It wasn't me! I didn't say a peep to them."

Hands hooked on her hips, Carrie asked, "And not a peep to your mother?"

Emma's lips puckered in an "Oh."

Carrie knew they were here to check up on the mysterious Abel Miller. There were organized ways of doing things—certain days and times set apart for such matters. If a concern had been brought to the church leaders, the deacon might pay a visit first. That would never be a cause for worry. Deacon Abraham was a caring man. Whenever she saw him in town or about the farm, two or three of his grandsons rode beside him in the wagon or shadowed him as he worked. He had been widowed recently and decided to move into the Grossdaadi Haus, to let his youngest son take over the farm. "Alles hat seine Zeit," he was fond of saying. *There's a time for everything.*

But to see the bishop climb out of the buggy—now that was a cause for concern. The bishop was known to be influenced by Esther. If there was any principle that Esther lived by, it was abiding by rules, the way things had always been done. It was the pattern of her life. If Esther had convinced the bishop that Abel might have a worldly influence over Andy, he would insist that Abel leave.

Carrie saw the deacon head out to the barn to talk to Abel while the bishop came inside and sat at the kitchen table. Carrie brought him coffee and a piece of shoofly pie, while Emma shared her observations about those who weren't properly dressed at church last Sunday.

"And did you notice that Amos Fisher had on his cream-colored shirt under his coat?" Emma asked the bishop. "He thought no one noticed that it wasn't white, but I saw it, straight off." She peered at him with a look that said she expected him to feel just as alarmed as she did over the gravity of the incident. He didn't.

Carrie kept trying to kick Emma under the table to quiet her from tattling on their friends and neighbors, but Emma prattled on, oblivious. Finally, the deacon came into the kitchen. He accepted Carrie's offer of coffee and pie, and happily settled in at the table.

As Emma cut the slice of pie at the counter, Carrie whispered, "Aw, Emma, why do you have to say such things? Amos Fisher probably just got busy that morning and forgot. He wasn't trying to be proud."

Emma looked injured. "I'm only trying to help the bishop. He's as blind as a bat." She poured the coffee. "Mother always said that she was the eyes and ears of the congregation."

"Mostly the mouth," Yonnie whispered, reaching behind the women to get another piece of pie.

"Carrie," Abraham said, "if there is anything you need, being a widow and all, if you have any financial worries, the church is here to help. That's what we take the alms for."

Carrie handed him the pie and reached a hand out to cover Yonnie's wrinkled hand. "Thanks to Yonnie, we had what we needed to pay the property tax bill."

"And our Abel helped us save the apple crop by turning it into cider," Yonnie added.

"Speaking of," the bishop said. "I under-stand Daniel's brother is here."

"Daniel's cousin," Emma said. "Abel is Yonnie's grandson."

The bishop nodded. "I have taken notice that Abel Miller isn't a church member."

"Abel is in his Rumspringa," Yonnie said.

The bishop raised his sparse eye-brows, surprised. "It has come to my at-tention that he reads from an English Bible. A modern one. Now, you know it isn't our way to be reading from a modern English Bible."

Carrie knew he was just speaking what he believed.

"What other English influences might Abel Miller have on this home?" the bishop asked. "What about his influence on our Andy?"

With that comment, Carrie knew for cer-tain she could thank Esther for filling the bishop's head with those worries. Just as she was about to object, Abel came through the kitchen door.

"Thought I should come in to say hello to the bishop." Abel offered a stiff, one-pump Amish handshake to the bishop as Carrie got a cup of coffee for him. She wished there was some way she could have warned him to stay in the barn.

The bishop fixed his eyes on Abel, measuring him. "You read from a modern English Bible." It wasn't a question. "The Bible has never changed."

Abel glanced at Carrie, who tipped her head toward Emma. "Well, you see, I never learned German. I came to Eli's home when I was thirteen."

Abraham slapped his knees in delight. "You see, Atlee? He can't read German! Of course!"

"If he can't read the *Luther Bible*, then he should be reading from King James," said the bishop.

Abel didn't respond to the bishop, but he looked as if reading those translations hadn't occurred to him and he was only sorry he hadn't thought of it himself.

"Abel has been away from Plain folk for a while," Abraham said. "He needs time to be reminded of our ways. We will pray he will choose to become baptized in due time." The deacon smiled. "And he'll be a fine helper for Yonnie and Carrie since our Daniel's passing. Sent by the Lord God." He stood. "Better get back to my dairy." He leaned close to the bishop and quietly added, "Ich have er gut ausgfrogt."

The bishop nodded, rising from his chair. "So then, Abel Miller, we will expect to see you in church on Sunday."

Abel had been going to an Amish-Mennonite church in town on Sundays. Carrie thought Yonnie would have minded that he wasn't going to their church service, but she never said anything to him, so Carrie didn't, either.

Afterward, as the deacon's buggy rolled onto the street, Abel turned to Carrie, "What did the deacon say to the bishop? In Deitsch?"

"That he had thoroughly interrogated you."

"That's what I thought he said." Abel gave a short laugh. "We talked about horses."

Carrie could hardly look at Emma for the rest of that day. Abel was unfazed. He acted just the same toward Emma, friendly and warm and teasing, like he understood she was a rule follower. But that night, he kept right on reading aloud from his modern Bible too.

❧❦

The next morning, Carrie slid open the heavy door of the barn and walked inside. The heady scent of hay and sweet grain was so familiar. Hope shuffled when she heard her and rolled her heavy head in Carrie's direction. Abel gave her a nod as he came in from his workshop. He unlatched the hook of the nearly empty rubber water bucket from the eye on the wall and carried it outside to the hose.

Carrie sidled into Schtarm's stall to add a scoop of sweet grain to his feed. She watched his graceful head bend to the fragrant, honeyed oats when Abel came to get Schtarm's water bucket. As she stroked Schtarm's large neck, she said, "I'm sorry Emma raised a concern about you."

"Are Esther's other daughters like Emma?" he asked, his mouth turned up at the corners.

"No. Emma is just . . . Emma. My favorite stepsister, Sarah, she lives in another district now, she always said that Emma's prayer cap was on too tight."

Carrie still wasn't sure what Abel's plans were, but she couldn't deny that she hoped he might stay on, even though the harvest was done. He spent his days at Honor Mansion doing carpentry work, but he still found time to do plenty of chores around Cider Mill Farm. He had found an old freezer for the cider that he was able to get for free if he would haul it away. It wasn't in working condition, but Abel said that was a minor detail. He fixed it and got it running with a generator.

Abel slid Schtarm's stall door shut and latched it. "So Yonnie said you're not too keen on being courted by this bishop's grandson, right?"

Carrie nodded, unsure of what he was getting at.

"Last night, Yonnie mentioned that she thought Emma and John might be a good pair."

Carrie's eyes went wide. "She wants to try her hand at matchmaking? With Emma?"

"Yonnie has a way of knowing about these kinds of things." He grinned. "So what do you think?"

She could feel a slow smile stretch across her face. "Emma would love to be married. And John would love to be loved." It suddenly seemed like such a funny coupling that she started to giggle. She could just picture worried Emma seated on a buggy seat next to John Graber, thin and long and angular and solemn. She laughed so hard, she buckled at the waist, and it felt so good. She hadn't laughed like that since—why, she couldn't even remember how long it had been. When she finally stopped laughing, she wiped away the tears streaming down her face.

"Here," Abel said, grinning, as he pulled out his handkerchief. He held the back of her head with one hand and began dabbing her face with the handkerchief. They stood just inches apart, closer than they had ever stood before. All of a sudden Abel stopped wiping, everything stood still. His gaze traveled Carrie's face, from her starched prayer cap to her lips. Carrie's heart started thumping foolishly.

Suddenly, Emma's voice rang out from the farmhouse. "Carrie? Yoo-hoo! Carrie? Where are you? Andy won't eat his oatmeal."

Abel slightly turned his head in the direction of the farmhouse but kept his eyes on Carrie. "Emma's oatmeal? Who could blame him? She's a fine cook, but her oatmeal tastes like library paste."

Carrie jumped back and hurried past him into the house.

All day long, she couldn't stop thinking of that gaze.

❧❧

Ever since Veronica McCall hired Abel to work at Honor Mansion, she stopped by Carrie's farm on her way to work to give him a ride. Early one Saturday, Veronica McCall burst into the kitchen, brushing past Carrie at the door, looking for Abel.

"He's down in the barn. I'm sure he heard you honking your car horn and will come up to the house in a minute," Emma said with a frown, as she put a match to her Coleman gas iron. "Two counties over heard you," she muttered. Emma didn't care much for Veronica's ways.

Oblivious to Emma's disdain, Veronica poured herself a cup of coffee and sat down at the kitchen table, close to the ironing board. "So what's that you're ironing?" she asked.

"My churchgoing dress. I'm getting it ready for the singing." Emma held up an organza prayer cap. "And these too." She ironed with a vengeance, making sure every little pleat in her cap was crisp and starched. Her white prayer caps sat in a row on the kitchen table, like roosting chickens.

"What's a singing?" Veronica McCall asked, picking an apple out of a bowl. She examined it, put it down, and picked up another.

"A singing is a wonderful thing," Yonnie said. "All of the young folk go, saying they want to sing hymns, but they're really stealing looks at each other when they think nobody's looking."

"So it's dating, Amish style?" Veronica McCall asked, amused. "Figures. Seems like churchgoing is the Amish's National Sport."

Emma opened her mouth to correct her for blaspheming when Veronica shocked her silent by saying, "Maybe I'll tag along. What time should I be here?"

Carrie's eyes went wide. "Why?"

"I want to learn more about the Amish."

"But . . . why?" Carrie asked again.

Veronica looked at Carrie as if she were very slow-witted. "I live and work near the Amish and I should know more about them."

Just then, Abel came through the kitchen door. An awkward silence fell over the room.

"What are you ladies talking about?" he asked as he went to the sink to wash up.

"Veronica McCall wants to come to the singing with us," Emma said to him, sounding concerned.

He spun around, hands dripping soapsuds on the black part of the floor where the linoleum had rubbed away. "Why?"

"I just thought I'd come! Why is that such a big deal?" Veronica McCall asked, frustration rising.

"It's not . . . common . . . for Englishers to go," Carrie tried to explain. "We sing hymns."

"I like music," Veronica said, putting down the apple.

"Some of the hymns are from the Ausbund," Emma said.

"What's an out band?" Veronica asked.

"Ausbund," Abel said. "It's the Amish hymnal; it's hundreds of years old. There's no music score. The verses are in high German, and songs can last fifteen to twenty minutes."

Veronica McCall's arched eyebrows shot up.

"But some of our hymn singing gets a

little lively," Emma added, eyes narrowing at her. "And downright raucous."

Veronica McCall lifted a shoulder in a careless shrug. "I'll try anything once."

Abel looked cornered, like a trapped animal. He turned back to the sink to finish washing his hands.

"What time should I arrive?" Veronica asked.

Abel winced. "Come tomorrow night at six."

Veronica stared at him, but he kept his eyes on his soapy hands. "Fine, then. Six."

"Better wear something that covers those limbs," Emma said, peering at Veronica McCall's long legs. "And button those up to keep from displaying a good bit of the Lord's bounty." She wagged a finger at Veronica McCall's blouse.

Abel froze at the sink. Carrie had been setting the table and stopped, forks suspended in midair. Emma's and Veronica McCall's eyes locked on each other, a standoff, two stubborn women with their hands firmly planted on their hips.

"Fine," snapped Veronica McCall, before scooping up her purse and blowing out the kitchen door.

"Fine," said Emma triumphantly.

Abel, Carrie noticed, didn't look so fine.

❧

That night, as Carrie was getting ready for bed, she pulled out Daniel's letters. Every few days, she steeled herself to read another letter. Tonight, she wanted to finish them.

July 8th

Dear Abel,

You'd better sit down for this.

I asked Carrie Weaver, Jacob's daughter, to marry me and she said yes. I'm still a little stunned, myself. It all happened rather fast. Ever since we arrived at the Weavers', Dad had been encouraging me—downright badgering—to take an interest in Carrie. More than an interest. She's a lovely girl— don't get me wrong—but I still have Katie in my heart. Then, suddenly, Jacob Weaver died and Carrie was grieving so, and next thing I knew, I asked her to marry me. We're to be married in September. Carrie wanted to marry quickly and move out of Esther Weaver's house. (When you meet Esther, you'll understand.) So, there you have it.

There are moments when I wonder what I've done . . . but I will tell you that it's a great relief to see Dad looking pleased. As for Carrie, I think she deserves better.

Yours, Daniel

October 7th

Dear Abel,

I'm writing this in the middle of a violent storm. Lightning is splintering the dark sky, and the thunder booms so loud it's as if the heavens have cracked open to spill forth the rain.

Carrie and I have been married for four weeks today. Strange, how one day in a person's life can change its course forever. Married life is an adjustment, though I think Carrie does a better job of it than I do. She is suddenly caring for a household of Millers—Yonnie, Dad, and me. Her younger brother, Andy, too. And she has been unfailingly kind. Dad calls her "my great blessing." I think he's right.

But for the life of me, I can't figure out why I should be blessed.

You asked me if Carrie knew of the Ohio incident. I wanted to tell her, straight off, but

Dad counseled me not to. "Some things are best left behind," he told me, and I couldn't really argue with that. I hesitated to tell her and the moment passed.

You also asked me if I have forgiven myself yet. How do I do that, Abel? I see the loneliness etched on Dad's face when he doesn't realize I'm watching. Mom should be by his side. I think of my Katie and the happy life that was robbed of her. I think of how old that little Benjamin Lapp would be by now, and if Elam Lapp would have taken him fishing and birding, like Dad did with you and me. I think of you serving time in jail when I should be there, and Dad having sold his farm to pay the fines. Both of you have paid a steep price for something I was responsible for.

How can I ever forgive myself? How, Abel? And if I can't forgive myself, how could I ever expect God to forgive me?

Yours, Daniel

February 4th

Dear Abel,
It's been over a week now since Dad died. I'm sorry you weren't here for the service. The

local church showed up, even though they hardly knew him. Quite a few folks came from Ohio on a bus, mostly greybeards. It would have pleased him.

During the service, Carrie did something that touched me deeply. When the first clods of dirt fell on Dad's coffin with a gentle thud, she reached over to take my hand. Such a simple act, but it was like she was sharing her strength. I have felt frozen, Abel, and Carrie is helping me to thaw. I wished I could have told her how much it meant to me. I tried to, but the words just get jumbled in my head, like when we used to go fishing at Black Bottom Pond and couldn't untangle the lines. When the last shovelful of dirt covered Dad's lifeworn body, I couldn't help but hope you might be right. That six feet under isn't the end.

Yours, Daniel

Carrie read and reread the letter. The part about when she reached out and held Daniel's hand nearly broke her heart. The sound of the dirt clods hitting Eli's coffin reminded her of her own father's funeral. Her mother's too. She had reached out for Daniel's hand for *his* strength, not to *give* him strength. She felt a fresh wave of crushing guilt over failing Daniel so miserably. Memories of him pressed like a pile of stones on her chest.

Her feelings about Daniel were so tangled up, his death so unexpected, that she had managed to push thoughts of him away. In fact, she had gotten pretty good at ignoring sorrows. It was in the still of the night, when she had nothing to listen to but her own thoughts, that she couldn't hide from them. Her heart echoed with hollowness and her sorrows found her, as if they were patiently waiting for her to acknowledge their presence. It was then that she had trouble shooing them away.

Daniel's letters changed all of that. They brought her sorrows out in the daylight. They revealed a side of him that she sensed was there but could never seem to find a way to break through to it. It was the very side of him that had given her the assurance to say yes when he asked her to marry him. She felt safe with Daniel. But when he finally shared his burden with her, she panicked like a skittish horse. Why couldn't she have just stayed and listened to him?

She felt a grieving for what might have been with Daniel. It wasn't just that he had lost his life; they had lost a life together. She was all mixed up inside, like pieces to one of Yonnie's crazy quilts before any sense was made of them. She kept hoping the pieces would come together into a beautiful pattern, and everything would turn out all right.

But it was too late for that. Daniel was gone.

❀

The next day was a churchgoing Sunday. Carrie got up early to start breakfast so they'd be ready to leave by 7:30. When Abel came inside, she poured a cup of coffee and handed it to him.

As he took the steaming cup from her, he cocked his head. "You okay?"

"Of course," Carrie said.

He peered at her with worried eyes. "You look awful pale."

She put her hands up to her cheeks. "Been indoors too much, lately, I s'pect."

"He's right," Emma said as she came downstairs. "You look as wilted as last night's lettuce."

Carrie went upstairs to wake up Andy, but stopped at her bedroom. She looked at the bed and felt its pull, climbing beneath the heavy quilt, her gaze on the window that framed a gray, brooding sky. She listened to the creak of the wind battering the walls and felt bruised with weariness. Her head hurt, nearly as much as her heart.

When Emma came past her door, she peered at Carrie. "What's wrong? Are you sick?"

Slowly, Carrie sat up. "I don't know. Maybe. I think I should skip church today and try to rest."

Yonnie poked her head around Emma. "I'll make up some of my sassafras tea. Whenever you're feeling poorly, sassafras tea will soon have you fit as a fiddle."

One bright spot, Carrie realized as she pulled the covers up to her chin, trying to stay warm, she had a firm excuse to get out of tonight's singing. She didn't want to encourage John Graber's interest in her. She didn't want to encourage any man's interest in her.

Later that evening, Veronica was down in the kitchen with Emma, loudly insisting that she refused to go in the buggy to the singing, saying she would freeze to death. Just as loudly, Emma told Veronica that she would only be cold because she wasn't wearing enough clothing, that she was showing more curves than a country lane. Insulted, Veronica insisted on driving her car. Emma and John Graber left in the buggy, and Abel joined Veronica in her car.

After they left, Andy came up to Carrie's room to play checkers. Two hours later, Carrie heard Veronica's car swerve into the driveway, a car door slam, then the car zoom off. Andy heard Abel come into the kitchen, so he flew downstairs to hear a recap of the evening. He couldn't wait until he was old enough to go to the singings.

Andy had left her bedroom door open, at the top of the stairs. Carrie could heard them talking as if they were just a few feet away. Abel was explaining that Veronica McCall wanted to leave early. "She was already mad that she showed up an hour early. I forgot to tell her the Amish don't follow daylight saving time. And then she complained that it smelled like a cow barn," he said.

"Wasn't it in a barn?" Andy asked.

"Yeah, but she was talking about the people."

Andy let out a hoot of laughter, then Yonnie shooed him upstairs to get ready for bed.

"How's Carrie doing?" she heard Abel ask. "Any idea why she's not feeling well?"

"It's her spirit," Yonnie said, sounding like a doctor. "She's ailing."

"Might be the flu."

"No. No fever, no stomach sickness. It's in her heart. She's struggling over something."

Carrie felt a chill run through her. Yonnie's keen perception always made her feel peculiar.

※※

Just after Andy left for school on Monday morning, Veronica McCall walked into the kitchen at Cider Mill Farm. Usually, when she picked up Abel, she didn't bother to come into the house. Only when she wanted something.

Veronica McCall helped herself to coffee and pulled out a chair at the kitchen table, prattling on about how cold it was and that the mud was damaging her new leather boots. Carrie kept looking out the kitchen window, hoping Abel would come in from the barn and take Veronica off of her hands.

Veronica McCall was talking so fast and furious it took her a minute to see that Carrie wasn't listening. "You haven't heard a word I've said! And . . ." She stopped in mid-sentence. "Why, you look terrible! Raccoon eyes. We need to get some makeup on you to cover up those dark circles." She reached for her purse and started to hunt through it. "Why don't you people have any mirrors in your houses?" Out of her purse, she pulled a small bag with a zipper.

"Because mirrors reflect vanity," Emma said, coming into the kitchen with her arms loaded with sheets to wash.

Yonnie eased out of her rocking chair and came over to Veronica. "Carrie is grieving over our Daniel," she said softly.

Veronica McCall looked up at Carrie. She pointed to a chair. "Sit, Carrie. I'm going to fix you right up." She unzipped the bag and pulled out a metal tube and a small plastic compact.

A switch tripped inside of Carrie. With one hand she swept Veronica's makeup onto the floor.

Just then, Abel came inside on the wings of a frigid swirl of air. He hung up his coat

and turned around, aware of a sudden silence as thick as blackstrap molasses. His
eyes darted between Veronica, Carrie, and
the spilled makeup on the floor, quickly sizing up the situation.

In a few quick strides, he was at Car-
rie's side. "Veronica, wait for me outside."
As Veronica hesitated, he added firmly,
"Now."

"I was *trying* to help," Veronica snarled.
She scowled at him, packed up her
makeup, snatched her purse off the table,
and went outside.

He turned to Carrie and put his hands on
her shoulders. "Carrie, you need to go upstairs and rest for a while. Yonnie and
Emma will take care of Andy. I'll take care
of the chores." He glanced through the
kitchen window at Veronica, leaning against
her car, fingers punching at her black telephone, angry. "Really, you need to rest."

Carrie jerked her shoulders out of his
grip. "Stop telling me what I need! Nobody
knows what I need."

Emma stared at Carrie with her mouth
gaping wide open, like a hooked fish.

"What do you need, Carrie?" Abel
looked at Carrie with such sweet sorrow it

took the fight clean out of her. Gently, he added, "How can we help you if you don't tell us?"

Suddenly exhausted, Carrie's fists unclenched and she turned to go upstairs.

Abel's words echoed in her head as she tried to sleep. She felt terrible for treating Veronica so rudely. It was so unlike her—unlike any Amish woman, except for Esther and Emma—to snap at someone like that, especially an Englisher. And then she was rude to Abel too, who was only trying to help. *What do I need? I don't have an answer. I don't know. I just feel weary and lonely and scared.* She shuddered as if a cold wind had blown through the room.

What do I need? Something for my soul that I can't seem to find.

❦

The next day, Veronica McCall drove up as Carrie was hanging laundry to dry. For the first time, she didn't start talking a blue streak the minute she laid eyes on Carrie. She just quietly picked up some clothespins and started hanging things.

"I'm sorry I spoke sharply to you yesterday," Carrie said. "You were just being kind."

"I was, and you did," Veronica answered crisply.

"You see, we don't wear makeup."

"Maybe you people should be a little more open-minded."

Carrie decided to not pursue that particular territory with her. "Just make sure you hang similar things together on the line."

"Why?"

"It's much more orderly to hang all the dishcloths together in a row, and Yonnie's aprons, and Abel's trousers."

"Dry is dry, if you ask me."

"It's just our way."

"It's faster if you just hang them."

Carrie stopped, exasperation growing. "I'm not in a hurry. A task takes as long as it takes."

"It's supposed to rain this afternoon. If you don't speed it up, you'll end up with laundry as wet as when you started."

Clothespins in her mouth, Carrie suddenly remembered a day with her mother, hanging the laundry out on a windy winter day, just a few weeks before her mother had died bringing Andy into the world. The clothes came in so stiff, frozen solid, that they could stand up by themselves when they brought them inside. Her mother took a pair of frozen pants, topped it with a frozen shirt, then topped that with her father's straw hat, and suddenly they had a scarecrow in the kitchen. Within minutes, that frosty scarecrow melted in a heap, like a snowman on a sunny day. Carrie and her mother had laughed and laughed.

Veronica McCall shook Carrie out of her muse when she reached for a clothespin. "You people make such a big deal about the silliest things." Veronica secured a towel to the third clothesline without any more arguing. When she finished, she picked up a dropped clothespin and handed it to Carrie. "I want you to teach me all about being Amish."

Carrie's eyes went wide. "Why?"

"I *told* you. I live near the Amish. I need to know more about them."

Veronica looked very sincere as she said it, but somehow Carrie thought this sudden interest had nothing to do with being Amish and everything to do with Abel. She had an image in her mind of a picture she'd seen in a book once: a lion tracking a gazelle.

Poor Abel. He doesn't stand a chance.

10

John Graber turned his attention to courting Emma, who was thrilled to have a
suitor. Carrie was even more pleased not
to be the object of John Graber's affec-
tion. He had taken Emma for a buggy ride
one afternoon and home from a hymn
singing on another.

In the night sky was a Hunter's moon,
round and creamy that, Emma said, beck-
oned her to take a walk. Carrie thought that
perhaps John Graber was outside doing
the beckoning. Esther would be pleased to
think the bishop's grandson might become
part of the family, after all.

Yonnie, Abel, and Carrie were in the living room; Andy had gone to bed. Abel was oiling his carpentry tools, Carrie was mending Andy's britches, and Yonnie had fallen asleep in her rocking chair, like she always did, mismatched quilt pieces spread on her lap.

When the clock struck nine, Abel and Carrie put their things away. Abel pulled out that Bible he carried with him. Carrie had stopped worrying about Abel's Bible reading and out-loud prayers. In fact, she looked forward to them. Abel's deep voice had a soothing effect. He read just like he prayed, like God was right in the room with everyone.

"This passage is from the book of Lamentations," Abel said. "Jeremiah was a prophet, a very emotional guy, who was called to speak for God during the siege and fall of Jerusalem. When he focused on the terrors around him, Jeremiah felt personally assaulted, even abandoned by God: 'He shot me in the stomach with arrows from his quiver.'"

Those words echoed in Carrie's mind. *He shot me in the stomach with arrows from his quiver.*

Suddenly, her heart started hammering. "That's it!" Her hands flew to her cheeks. "That's what I need! I need to have God stop piercing my stomach with his arrows."

Yonnie startled awake, but then drifted back to sleep.

Embarrassed by her outburst, Carrie jumped out of her chair. Why did her mouth always run ahead of her brain?

Abel jackknifed to his feet. "Carrie, wait." He whispered loudly, throwing a glance at Yonnie. "Please wait." He made her sit back down in the chair and crouched in front of her. She was trembling and didn't really know why. "Listen to me, Carrie. When Jeremiah focused on those circumstances surrounding him, he felt assaulted, even abandoned by God. But when he focused on God's past mercies, he found strength and encouragement." He opened up his Bible and hunted for the passage. "'I remember it all—oh, how well I remember— the feeling of hitting the bottom. But there's one other thing I remember, and remembering, I keep a grip on hope: God's loyal love couldn't have run out, his merciful love couldn't have dried up. They're created new

every morning. How great your faithful-
ness! I'm sticking with God (I say it over
and over). He's all I've got left.'"

Abel took Carrie's hands in his, and as
he did, she felt the peace of the moment
settle into her soul, like a leaf slowly making its way to the bottom of a pond. "Carrie,
Jeremiah had it all wrong. God wasn't sling-
ing arrows at Jeremiah. It was God who
was helping him through his troubles."

Carrie lifted her head and searched
Abel's dark eyes. She wanted desperately
to believe him.

※

During the off-season, the Barnstormer
players were required to participate in community events—speaking at schools and
Scout meetings, cutting the ribbons at new
store openings. "It's all part of building
community spirit," the manager said. "And
Sol, we want you at every event. We think
you're the reason for a surge in attendance
last summer. Everybody loves this Amish
spin."

Sol was happy to do anything he could
to solidify his worth to the coaches. He
didn't end up snagging that All-Star spot,

after all. In fact, it worried him a little that he didn't close the last two games of the season. He didn't even play a single inning. He knew that things changed fast on the roster. He'd already seen a number of players come and go.

The comment the manager made about fans' interest in Sol's Amish upbringing was spot-on. During the question-and-answer period at every event, Sol was hammered with questions about what it was like growing up Amish. It always amazed him that the English had been living among the Amish all of their life—sharing the roads with the buggies—but knew so little about them. And what they did know was usually wrong. One kid at a Cub Scout meeting even asked him if the Amish were a cult.

"No," Sol told him, surprised by the question. "The whole thing about being Amish— going all the way back to the 1600s—is to be an adult when you get baptized. Church leaders want each person to make their own decision before God. Being Amish has nothing to do with cults. Being Amish means you're trying to live a simple life that pleases God. Being Amish is about being part of a family, a big church family. It's having people care about you and look out for you, all of your life."

"So then," the kid asked, chewing a big wad of gum, "why'd you leave?"

Sol stumbled, not knowing how to answer, not wanting to say a word against his people. It surprised him to see how tightly his upbringing held him, even now. The Scout leader used the pause to wrap up the meeting because the janitor wanted to sweep up the gym and go home.

❧❧

One afternoon, Carrie climbed up the ramp to the hayloft in the barn to throw down a bale. With one eye looking out for mice, she dragged a heavy bale from the far corner as she heard Andy run into the barn. She heard him say to himself, "Box, twine, gloves. Gotta remember gloves." Then there was some scuffling and the sound of something being dragged outside.

Looking out through the small barn window, she saw Andy load the ramp to the loft onto the back of his pony cart and head down the driveway to the street. She shouted to him, but he didn't hear her. She finished pushing the bale over the loft's edge, then sat on the edge, debating her options, wondering how long a wait she would have until Andy returned home, when Abel came into the barn.

"Um, Abel?"

Abel turned in a circle, trying to locate her voice, before looking up. "What are you doing up there?" He looked around. "What did you do with the ramp? How'd you get up there?"

"Andy took the ramp."

Abel nodded. "I did hear something about a rescue."

Carrie narrowed her eyes. "What kind of a rescue? Is he bringing home another stray?"

Abel scratched his head. "How are you planning to get down?"

"I don't have a plan. I need help."

"I see, I see." He walked around the barn, arms folded against his chest, deep in thought. He kicked the hay bale she had thrown down over on its side. "Tell you what. I'll stand on the hay and try to catch you."

"It's too far. I'll break something! *You'll* break something!"

Abel ignored her protests and jumped up on the hay bale. "I'll catch you."

"Abel, that's crazy! I'll hurt you!"

"No you won't. Just jump."

"Abel, be serious."

He shrugged. "Guess you don't mind waiting for Andy to return."

Carrie bit her lip. She knew that could mean waiting for hours, if he even remembered to bring the ramp back. "Okay, fine. But you have to promise to break my fall."

"Trust me, Carrie."

She looked down at Abel, about eight feet below her, held her breath and jumped. She tumbled onto him and he fell off the hay, breaking her fall as promised, but banging his head on a barn post.

"Abel, are you hurt?" She scrambled off of him and onto her knees. His eyes were closed and he didn't respond. He started moaning, as if in great pain. She leaned closer to see if his head was bleeding. "Say something."

He groaned again and whispered in a weak voice, "I'm so . . . so . . . glad it was you falling on me like a ton of bricks and not Emma." Then he broke into a grin.

She sat back on her knees and threw some hay at him for teasing her. He sat up, laughing, then stopped abruptly as a strange look came over his face. She could almost feel his gaze moving over her hair, like the touch of a gentle breeze. Her hair! In the fall, her bandanna had slipped off, pulling hairpins out along with it. Her hair had fallen thick and loose over her shoulders and down her back. She looked around for her bandanna and scrambled to get it. Abel pulled himself up to stand. As she tried to gather her hair to tie in a knot, she dropped her bandanna. Abel reached down and picked it up, then crouched down to gently tie it around her head. He tied a knot and let his knuckles slide down her jawline, brushing his fingertips lightly over her mouth, his eyes locked on hers the whole time. Then Abel went utterly still, but the air around them seemed to vibrate.

Carrie stood and backed away from him, first one careful step and then another. The barn door rumbled open as Andy led Strawberry by the halter into the barn. In the back of the pony cart was a large box filled with three hungry, angry owlets. Next to the nest was the mother owl, angry, feet tied together with twine. Her right wing was broken, bent at an odd angle. The hayloft ramp was nowhere in sight.

❧❧

"In less than twenty-four hours, those baby owls have climbed out of their box twice to peck at my toes while I was feeding Hope and Lulu," Emma scolded Andy at breakfast. "Then their mother comes running at me, full speed, dragging that broken wing behind her, trying to protect her babies. As if I wanted them pecking at me! And the way they screech!" She shuddered. "The whole lot of them have to go!"

"They're part of our family! They need us!" Andy looked to Abel for support. Abel had set the mother owl's wing with a makeshift splint and tried to keep her tied to a post in the barn so it could heal, but she kept pecking apart the twine that held her feet.

"Soon as she's healed, Andy, they need to be set free," Abel said. "Humans can't really raise owls as well as their own parents. Fall is the time of year for great horned owls to raise a brood and teach them how to learn to hunt and fly. It wouldn't be right to keep them locked up in a barn."

"They can catch mice in the hayloft," Andy said. "There's plenty of 'em!"

"We can build an owl house and hope they'll stick around, but they're not pets." Abel took a sip of coffee and cast a sideways glance at Andy. "Any idea where my gloves went?"

Andy widened his eyes in a useless effort to look innocent.

"Speaking of missing things, Andy," Carrie asked, "when is the ramp coming back?"

Andy's face scrunched up. "See, that's a problem. I had to climb the ramp to get the nest out of the tree, but on the way down, it slipped."

"What caused that mother owl to have a broken wing, anyway?" asked Carrie.

"Beats me," Andy said, reaching over her for the raspberry jam. "Probably those English devil boys."

Carrie gave her brother a look.

"Andy Weaver!" Emma scolded. "You should be pitying those boys for their lost ways. Not blaspheming."

"Let's take Strawberry and the cart and go bring back the ramp," Abel said.

"See, that's another problem," Andy said, stuffing his mouth with bread.

"How so?" Carrie asked.

"Ramp fell into the water and sunk."

Carrie covered her hands with her face.

Abel shook his head. "Let's go down to Blue Lake Pond and you can show me where it sank." He waited until Emma left the table, then whispered to Andy, "Might have to catch a fish or two while we're there. Our last chance before the weather turns too cold. Feels like the wind is already practicing for winter." Loudly, he added, "Then we'll clean out the goslings' pen for those owlets so they'll stop thinking Emma is their mama."

It was that gloaming time of day, nearly dusk, when Andy and Abel returned home, wearing cat-in-the-cream smiles. Her brother's face, with its windchapped cheeks, shone with happiness. Andy preened like a starling, Carrie saw, feeling her heart swell.

"Took all day but we got the ramp," Andy told Carrie, sounding like a man of the world. "Happened upon Abel's gloves too." He handed Emma a string of trout and

tracked mud onto her freshly cleaned linoleum floor.

Carrie went out in the barn to help Abel
with Strawberry. "Andy said getting the
ramp took all day." She picked up a bucket
of oats to toss in Strawberry's manger.

"The ramp took five minutes," Abel said,
slipping the bridle out of the pony's mouth.
"The fishing took all day." He led the pony
into the stall and grabbed her water bucket
to fill it.

Carrie wanted to tell him how grateful
she was that he spent time with Andy and
helped him with his bird rescues. She knew
Andy could be vexing. More than a few
times, he had driven Esther to the brink of
exasperation with his careless ways. She
wanted to express all of her appreciation
for what Abel did for them, but all that came
out was, "Denki, Abel."

He grinned. "A day like this is so *good*, it
makes you want to praise God for his goodness, and thank him for giving you the life
to enjoy it," he said, watching Strawberry's
throat ripple as she drank. He turned around
and leaned against the bars, crossing his
arms against his chest. "Nicht wahr?" *Don't
you agree?*

She looked at him, unclear about what he meant. "About what?"

"About God's goodness." He pulled the stall shut, latched it, and swiveled to face her. "Carrie, do you believe God is good?"

"Of course," she replied without hesitating, hoping to stave off a preaching. She pulled her shawl around her shoulders. "I'll see to warming your dinner."

Abel put a hand out to stop her.

Oh no, Carrie thought. *Too late. Here comes the sermon.*

"For all of my growing up years, I only knew that hard side of God. His wrath and punishing ways, but I never really knew about the other side of God. The good side."

"If he is so good, then why does he make us suffer so?" As soon as the words spilled out of Carrie's mouth, she wanted them back, but of course it was too late. That was the risky thing about words—once said they couldn't be unsaid. She closed her eyes, ashamed. How dare she question the mysterious ways of the Lord?

"Carrie, God doesn't cause the suffering. He helps us bear it." Abel spoke with such gentleness that it almost hurt to hear it.

"There was a chaplain in the jail who taught me about the parts of God I had missed. He showed me how to study the Scriptures and learn about God for myself."

Abel dropped his hand and crossed his arms again. He turned and looked straight at her, leaning one hip against the railing. They stood together in silence for a long moment. "That's why I'm here. I want Yonnie and you and Andy to know about this side of God. I don't want you to miss out."

"Miss out?"

He put his hands on her shoulders and softly said, "On the part about life being hard but God being good, and not confusing the two."

Her stomach did a flip-flop, with Abel standing so close and giving her such an intense look. Nervous, she said the first thing that popped into her head: "And Veronica McCall?" she asked in an accusing tone. "Do you want her to know about this too?"

He dropped his hands and tilted his head, genuine puzzlement on his face.

Instantly, Carrie regretted her words. What was the matter with her today, with her mouth flying ahead of her brain? What

Abel did with Veronica McCall was none of her business. "She was here today, looking for you," Carrie said in a kinder tone. "She was awful mad you weren't at work today."

He didn't answer right away. Finally, he said, "God cares about Veronica, if that's what you mean."

But Carrie saw that look flash across his eyes again, the look that said he was hiding something.

❧❧

Spring training had started well for Sol, but once the season began, things had spiraled south. Other teams had wised up to his fastball pitch, and he was losing his effectiveness as a closer. He hadn't struck anyone out in three straight games. The pitching coach had told him he was relying too heavily on one pitch. The problem was, he didn't have another pitch. He hadn't grown up spending years on Little League and school teams, like the other players did. He studied the pitchers to try to pick up their junk ball or curveball tricks, but when he would ask about their grip or delivery, they avoided answering him. He couldn't really blame them. They were competing for the same playing time.

Rody, the catcher, had been his only true friend, often staying late to help him practice. Tonight, Rody finally threw down his mitt and took off his catcher's mask. "I'm done for the day. I'm gonna go hit the showers. Let's go meet up with the guys and grab a beer."

Sol shook his head. "Thanks, but no." When he first joined the team, he had gone out with the guys after practice, but the clumsy way he had played at practice the next day brought a quick end to late nights and beer. Plus, the players were like magnets for girls—fancy girls. Forward girls, who sat too close in their tight little dresses. One girl, Alicia, latched on to him and called or text messaged him on his cell phone a couple of times a day. When he got the bill that month, he couldn't *believe* it! He had to pay a dime for every time she text messaged him, whether he wanted to read it or not. Amish girls would never act in such a brazen way.

He had quickly discovered that the party life of the English wasn't all that different from Amish Rumspringa parties, and he soon tired of it. Anything that interfered with baseball just wasn't worth it to him.

He knew he had this one opportunity. The other guys had jobs to fall back on if they didn't make the cut. Sol had an eighth grade education and one fastball pitch. If he lost this chance, it was back to the farm, mucking out stables.

Sol spent the evening in his sparsely furnished apartment, eating cold pizza, icing his shoulder, and reading a book about training tips for pitchers. He fell asleep in a chair, with the book splayed across his chest.

❧❧

In the dark of an early dawn, Carrie went downstairs and set the coffeepot to brew. Abel liked to come in for a quick cup before breakfast to warm his hands. She found she looked forward to those moments she had with him, before Andy and Emma and Yonnie came downstairs and the day had started. Abel would discuss with her what needed to be done on the farm and ask her opinion before making a decision. She'd never had a relationship like that with a man before, not with her father, or Sol, or Daniel. She would catch herself, though, whenever she found herself relying on Abel, and pull herself back from the edge.

She put some eggs in a bowl and peeked out the kitchen window. The snow was falling thick and heavy. She saw Abel climb up the kitchen steps, stamping snow from his feet, his cheeks and ears raw from the cold. She met him at the door with a mug of steaming black coffee.

"Thank you," he said, pulling off his gloves. He wrapped his hands around the mug and took a sip. "Best taste in the world."

Carrie held three eggs in her hand. "How do you want your eggs cooked?"

Just then Andy galloped past Emma heading down the stairs and went straight to last night's dessert, cutting off a hunk of cake. Seamlessly, Emma grabbed the knife out of his hand and used it to slice pieces of bread to toast in the oven. As Emma went to the table to get butter for the toast, she reached over to pinch some curls back into Carrie's cap. "Those curls that keep escaping aren't becoming, Carrie."

"Actually, they're quite becoming." Abel promptly turned a shade of plum as he realized what had blurted out of him.

Carrie felt a little flutter of pleasure from what he'd said, though she knew such thoughts were vain. A deep flush spread up her neck and over her cheeks so she spun around to face the stove, clumsily knocking the hand that held the eggs. One by one the eggs landed, cracking on the linoleum, yolks and whites and broken pieces all running together. There was a moment of stunned silence, until Andy let out a hoot of laughter.

Abel stared down at the cracked eggs, then looked at Carrie. "Scrambled would be fine."

❦

A few days later, Carrie woke to the strong, sour stench of smoke in the air. As she prepared breakfast, she saw no sign of Abel in the barn like she usually did—no glow of a lantern light, no wisp of smoke from his woodstove chimney, no opening or shutting of the barn door, no wave when he saw her through the kitchen window.

For one brief moment, she thought he had left them without saying goodbye. The notion sent her into such a panic that she could barely stop her hands from trembling as she filled the coffeepot with water. But then she spotted Abel riding into the yard on Schtarm and let out a sigh of relief that surprised her with its depth.

Abel tied the horse's reins to the post and came directly into the kitchen. "Stoltzfuses' barn burned down early this morning," he said, looking concerned. "I smelled the smoke so I rode over to see if I could help, but the barn was nearly gone."

"Oh no! They're in Indiana, aren't they?" Emma asked. "Ada was over here the other day, talking about it, so excited to see her new grandbaby. They go every year about now, as soon as they close up their roadside stand for the year."

"The deacon is trying to reach them," Abel said. "I'm going to go back over there and help clear out the debris."

"I'm coming too!" Andy said, jumping up from the table to head to the door.

Carrie reached out and grabbed his arm. "Slow down. You're going to school." She smiled. "Perhaps Abel wouldn't mind seeing that you get there."

Crestfallen, Andy sat back down at the table to finish his oatmeal, sighing deeply.

"Any idea how the fire started?" Carrie asked.

He shrugged. "The police were there, looking for signs of arson."

"What?" Emma asked, alarmed. "Why would they think such a thing?"

Before Abel could answer, a car pulled into the driveway. Emma peered outside. "There's two English women, an old one and a young one."

"They're here for me," Carrie told Emma. "I'm going into town today to help the girl who . . . caused the accident." She took her black bonnet off of the wall peg. "She's having an . . ." She couldn't remember the word.

"An arraignment?" Abel said.

Carrie nodded, wrapping her cape around her. Going into a crowded courtroom scared her to death; she was already anticipating the bold stares of curious English. She felt like a fish out of water, but she had made a promise to Grace to come. "I hope to be back long before Andy returns from school," she told Emma.

"Grace told me what you did for her, Carrie," Abel said, as he reached to open the kitchen door for her. "About forgiving her. She said you changed her life."

Carrie tied the strings of her bonnet and kept her head down.

"You did a fine thing." He spoke quietly, so Emma wouldn't overhear.

Carrie kept her eyes downcast. "It was the right thing."

"Forgiveness is always the right thing," Abel said softly.

By ten in the morning, Carrie and Mrs. Gingerich, Grace's foster mother, were seated closely behind the defense table at the Stoney Ridge District Court. Arraignments were a rubber-stamp process, the lawyer explained to the women. The prosecutor riffled through a big box of files as defendant after defendant was brought in. Carrie's eyes went wide as one woman was arraigned for stealing a blender from Wal-Mart. A boy was brought in for possession of drugs. Carrie shivered. He wasn't much older than Andy. Seeing the wickedness of the world made her long to return to the safety and security of her apple orchards. It made her grateful for her people and their gentle ways.

Carrie had been relieved when she saw Grace's appearance earlier in the car. Someone—probably Mrs. Gingerich—had made her look more like a normal teenager. Her hair color had changed from platinum blond to a color that actually existed in nature. She wore a white blouse and a dark skirt. Gone were the combat boots too. In their place were dark, plain shoes and nylon stockings. Grace felt self-conscious in her clothing, Carrie noticed. She kept scratching her legs as if they itched. She could only see the profile of Grace's face, but she felt a tenderness toward her. She could see so much pain in Grace's eyes. In a way, she reminded her of Daniel. Carrying a burden.

Just as the bailiff was calling out Grace's docket number, Abel slipped into the seat next to Carrie, startling her.

"Strength in numbers," he whispered.

The courtroom doors opened again, disrupting the proceeding. Carrie turned and saw Veronica McCall, followed by Emma. Behind Emma trailed Mattie, one arm around Yonnie for support.

When the judge glanced up, his jaw dropped at the sight: a row of Amish women settling into a bench, black bonnets lined up like a row of crows on a telephone wire. Bookended on the bench were an Amish man and an English woman with carrot red hair.

After the judge shook off his surprise, he acknowledged the show of support for Grace. "But the defendant admits she was speeding on a foggy night. A careless thing to do which resulted in the needless death of a young man. Because of your request for leniency, Mrs. Miller, I'll disregard the prison time." He gave a nod toward Carrie. "It was a gracious thing for you to do, considering this accident caused your husband's death. However, the defendant must serve 300 hours of community service. And, her driver's license is revoked for three years." He banged the gavel. "Next."

Grace jumped up from the table and leaned over the railing to hug Carrie. "Thank you, Carrie. It could've been a lot worse if it weren't for you."

"So you're not disappointed?" Carrie asked, over Grace's shoulder.

Grace pulled back and crossed her arms. "No. I mean, my license getting revoked bites, but the service hours were lighter than I expected." Shyly, she added, "Thanks to you." She looked at the row of Amish people. "And to all of you."

"Don't mention it," Veronica McCall said, claiming credit. She tapped her watch.

"But now, you need to get to work. You're on the clock. You too, Abel." She took both of them by the elbow and steered them to the door.

Carrie saw Abel try to turn back to her, but Veronica slipped her hand into Abel's and pulled him along, much like someone would lead a cow to a stall.

11

The church leaders planned to build the new barn for the Stoltzfuses while the land was resting and farmers had more time, a commodity usually in short supply. When the day came, sunny and mild for a winter day, Andy was the last one in the buggy after breakfast and chores, stepping carefully around Abel's tools, paper bags full of nails, and baskets of food. They waved to Yonnie, who preferred to stay home and quilt in the warm kitchen.

The four walls of the barn lay flat on the ground, getting assembled, by the time Old-Timer trotted into the Stoltzfuses' driveway. Andy hopped out of the buggy before it came to a stop and ran to join his friends, practicing their hammering on blocks of wood. Abel reached for his tools, gave Carrie a nod, jumped down, and hurried to the site where the barn gables were being assembled. Emma and Carrie watched as he looked for an empty spot among the men. Then Emma grabbed a basket and hurried to join the ladies in the kitchen. Carrie picked up the reins to lead Old-Timer where rows and rows of buggies and wagons were parked in the pastures.

"Carrie!"

She turned in the direction of Abraham's voice. Abraham gave her a warm grin and reached up to shake her hand. He whistled for a boy to come and take the buggy. "Put the horse in the paddock with the others," he told the boy. He helped Carrie down and picked up the two remaining baskets of food. "Our Andy gets bigger each time I see him."

"And you probably see him squirming in church."

The deacon laughed. "And why not? The good Lord never expected a growing boy to be able to sit still for hours."

The good Lord might not, but Esther certainly did. At last Sunday's gathering, she sent Carrie dark looks from across the bench whenever Andy got restless, which was often.

"Just look at those colts over there." Abraham tipped his head toward the field. A mother horse was grazing, heavy head hung low, while a foal danced around her, jumping and kicking his heels in sheer joy. "God understands the young." He put the baskets on the table. "Even the young at heart."

Abraham headed back to the building site, pulling out his hammer and nails from his canvas waist pouch. For a moment, before going inside to join the women, Carrie gazed at the bare bones of a barn, flat on the ground, waiting for life to be breathed into it.

A barn raising was the most beautiful sight in the world to her. The sounds, a symphony of pounding by dozens of hammers, took her breath away. It always had, even when she was a child.

"Hello, Carrie," said a voice behind her.

Carrie stiffened, instantly recognizing

Solomon Riehl's voice. She kept her gaze fixed on the barn. "Why are you here?"

Sol took a step to stand next to her. "I heard about the Stoltzfuses' barn burning down and wanted to do my part." He kicked a stone on the ground. "They've always been good to me."

"Everyone has been good to you," Carrie said, her glance sliding at him. Maybe too good, she thought. She turned to go to the kitchen, but he blocked her path.

"I'm sorry, Carrie. About Daniel."

"What's done is done," she said, but it came out scratchy and uncertain. She felt her eyes prickle with tears. She didn't want to cry.

Softly, he said, "Please. Let's talk."

"Not here, not now," she whispered, more to herself than to Sol. She straightened and took a step back, putting even more distance between them.

His eyes searched hers. "Then when? When can we talk?"

Carrie's heart softened, just a little, as she saw the earnest ache in his eyes. Suddenly, a loud, persistent ringing noise came out of his pocket. A dozen white caps turned instantly toward Sol's direction. Panicking, he pulled out his cell phone. Carrie used the interruption to step away from him. She picked up the baskets on the table and hurried to the kitchen, feeling the onset of tears burn the back of her throat. *Just stay busy,* she told herself, *so you won't dwell on the way things turned out.*

She started emptying out the baskets, putting the desserts she had made last night on the counter with the others, as if nothing had happened. In her heart, though, she felt sore and lonely.

❧

Mattie's heart started pounding when she caught a glimpse of Solomon Riehl out of the corner of her eye. She was setting the table for lunch, determined not to look at him. She would not, would not, would not look at him.

She looked at him.

She scolded herself, feeling like she was back in sixth grade, Sol in eighth, when she would steal glances at him all day long.

She noticed that others were avoiding Sol. He was in that strange place in their community of straddling two worlds, Amish and English. He wasn't being shunned since he hadn't been baptized, but he wasn't one of them anymore, either. She wondered how Sol felt to be among his people but standing on the fringe. How terrible, she thought, to be living on the wary edge. To never feel like you belonged anywhere, to anybody.

When Carrie's buggy arrived, Mattie noticed how Sol put down his hammer, poising himself for a moment to find her alone. She tried to keep her eyes off of them when Sol approached Carrie, but she could tell Carrie seemed uncomfortable. Then his cell phone went off and Carrie turned abruptly to leave. Mattie's eyes stayed on Sol. A look of stark pain crossed his face. He turned his head and caught her watching him. Their eyes met and held. Her heart started hammering so loudly she was sure he heard it, twenty feet away, but he dropped his head and went to the building site.

As Sol swung himself up on a beam, at ease in a precarious spot, Mattie couldn't help but admire his grace. Barn raising was an activity he'd been a part of since he was a toddler. She whispered a prayer for him, asking the Lord to show him all that he was missing and to bring him back where he belonged.

❧❧

As Carrie set clean dishes on the long picnic tables, she saw one man cup his hands around his mouth and yell, "Fix un faerdich!" *All ready!* Almost in unison, the hammering ceased. The women hurried out of the kitchen, wiping their hands on their aprons. Someone hollered out a count, as a few men picked up one frame of the barn wall and hoisted it upright. A few others swarmed to the base of the wall, hammering it securely into the cement foundation of the barn. The opposite wall went up, then the two ends, puzzle pieces locking into place. The youngest men, Sol and Abel included, climbed the wooden rigging as easily as if it were a ladder, hoisting the roof gables up with ropes. Within minutes, the skeleton of the barn, raw and yellow, stood silhouetted against the blue winter sky.

Lunch was served before noon. The men laid down their hammers and nails, untied their waist pouches, and dropped their bundles of tools, right where they'd be working. Emma and Carrie had filled up an old washtub, set outside the kitchen, with warm water, soap, and towels. Even with a brisk wind, the men were red-faced and sweating as they hurried to wash up and find an empty spot at the table. With the jerk of his head, Bishop Graber gave the signal for silent prayer. Automatically, the men dropped chins to chest, quietly communing with the Lord God. Then the bishop coughed, the signal to end the prayer, and the men grabbed their forks and shoveled the food in their mouths.

Abel arrived late to the table, lagging behind after examining something at the work site. Scratching his head, he went straight up to Abraham, seated at the end of the table, eating quickly so the next group, standing on the side, could sit and eat.

"In Ohio, we're bolting the walls to the foundation."

Abraham looked up at him curiously.

"It makes the barn sturdier to bolt instead of nail. Against storms and such," Abel said.

Seated a few seats from the deacon, Sol said loudly, "And how many barns have you built in the last few years?"

Abel jerked his head in Sol's direction, a confused look on his face.

Abraham intervened. "I have heard about this new bolting from my cousin in Ohio. It helps to protect against tornadoes, especially."

"But not fires," Sol said, looking straight at Abel. "What's to stop a fire?"

Abel locked eyes with Sol.

Abraham slid down on the bench to make room for Abel. "Abel, please sit and eat. I want to hear about your bolts."

Watching the exchange, Carrie hurried to set a place for Abel. As Carrie swiveled around to return to the kitchen to fill up a platter of pork chops, she saw Emma leaning over John Graber to pour lemonade into his glass. John was eagerly working his way through a pork chop and didn't seem to notice her. She wondered if Abel had seen Emma fussing over John, but he was deep in conversation with Abraham about bolts. She could feel Sol's eyes watching her, aware he noticed how she had tried to catch Abel's eye, but she kept her gaze from meeting his.

As soon as the men and boys were finished, they returned to pick up their hammers. The volley of pounding began again as the women sat down to eat. Esther sat across from Emma and Carrie.

"So, where is Yonnie today?" Esther asked.

"She's home, working on a quilt," Emma replied.

Esther looked at Emma. "She should be coming to the quilting frolics."

"She says she likes to quilt alone. Says it's like praying to her," Emma said, taking a bite of a pork chop. She wiped her mouth with her napkin and leaned forward on the bench, eyes shining. "She's been teaching me all that she knows, all about combinations of colors. Her stitches are as tiny as baby teeth. And she doesn't even use patterns, she just makes them up out of her head—"

"Lancaster Amish do not quilt like Ohio Amish," Esther said. "And you would do well to remember the difference, Emma."

Esther's rebuke had the effect of dousing a candle. Emma's smile faded; her neck drooped low as a cygnet's. The brightness left her and her mouth tightened. Carrie had to look away.

What Esther was saying was right, Carrie

had to admit. Lancaster was the first Amish settlement, and most of the church leaders clung tightly to traditions. As settlements spread throughout the Midwest, a willingness to change and adapt spread with them. Esther's quilts were just like the Lancaster Amish, Carrie realized. Each one looked like the one before. Yonnie's quilts, well, no two were alike. She brought combinations of colors and patterns together in ways no one could imagine.

Still, Carrie's heart was touched with pity for Emma. Each night when she and Andy and Abel gathered after dinner—to read *The Budget*, or play Scrabble or Checkers—Yonnie and Emma would bend over the frame of a quilt. It was as if Yonnie was passing on all of her knowledge to Emma. Emma was a quick study too. The quilt they were making for Abel reminded Carrie of a kaleidoscope Andy had found once and brought home.

Andy ran up to Carrie and pulled on her elbow, whispering loudly enough to warrant a raised eyebrow from Esther. "Here comes that fancy red-haired lady." He pointed to the driveway. A few of the teen-aged boys who hadn't been baptized dropped their hammers and hurried over to examine the car.

Carrie left her lunch and walked to meet Veronica. "Come to see the barn raising?"

"Abel invited me."

Carrie raised her eyebrows. That didn't sound quite right to her.

"Oh fine." Veronica rolled her eyes. "I'm sure he would have if I had asked. Where is he?"

Carrie pointed to Abel's figure, straddling a gable on the barn roof.

"Are you sure that's him? They all look alike."

"That's him."

They walked a little closer to the barn, smelling the sweet smell of fragrant pine.

"Isn't it a sight to behold?" Carrie asked her. "To build a whole barn in a single day." She pointed to the sides of the roof. "The framing is completed before the noon meal. And in the afternoon, the roofing is installed. That's what Abel is working on now."

Veronica squinted in the bright sunlight. "Nothing you people do is fast. Why in the world would you be building a barn in a day?"

"The point isn't its haste, Veronica

McCall. Wonderful things can happen when people work together. A barn raising is an amazing project of brotherly love."

"Maybe I should hire them all to finish up Honor Mansion." Veronica walked closer to the barn. "Abel! Abel! Yoo-hoo!" She waved up at Abel.

The staccato of hammers drowned out her shout, so she went back to her car.

As if in a dream where her feet were caught in quicksand, Carrie slowly realized what was about to unfold. She tried to stop Veronica, but it happened too quickly. Veronica leaned over the door of her car and honked the horn, then yelled out Abel's name again and honked again. Startled, Abel turned, lost his balance, and slipped off the roof.

※

Abel's fall was first broken by a beam, then by boards laid for the loft. Before others knew what had happened, Carrie ran into the barn and scrambled up a ladder, stepping carefully on the unnailed flooring. Abel lay crumbled on his side, moaning, one arm bent at a grotesque angle.

"We need to get him to the hospital," Abraham said, peering at Abel from the top rung of the ladder. He turned to the crowd below and spotted Veronica. "Can you call for an ambulance?"

"I'll drive him!" Veronica McCall yelled, standing among the Amish men and women. "It'll be faster than an ambulance!"

Abel put his good hand on Carrie's forearm. "Komm mit, bitte?" *Please, come?*

Carrie nodded.

The men made a gurney to hoist Abel down to the ground and carried him to Veronica's car. Carrie found Emma to tell her she was leaving, to make sure Andy got home. As she hurried to Veronica's car, Sol stopped her. "I'll come too, Carrie. I could help."

The words spilled out before she could stop them. "Like you helped Daniel?" She shook his hand off of her arm and climbed into the passenger seat, avoiding the hurt in Sol's eyes.

Abel's body went stiff as he stifled a moan of pain, intensified by Veronica's wild driving. It was as if she took aim to hit each pothole and bump in the road.

❦

Sol watched Carrie leave with that Abel Miller, moaning like he was dying, the big baby. He wondered who the good-looking English woman with the sports car was. It bothered him to see that Carrie had a life filled with people he didn't know. Discouraged, he went back to work on the roof with the other men and hammered shingles until the sun started sinking in the sky. When the men were satisfied the barn was watertight, they packed up their tools. Sol handed his tools and carpenter belt to his father. He wanted to leave quickly, before his mother cornered him, asking him to come home again. It wrenched his gut, the way she asked. Almost begging.

He walked down the street to catch a bus at the crossroads. He wished he had just driven his car. He worried it would stir up trouble, but no one would have even noticed, he decided. Crossing his arms against the wind, his mind drifted to Carrie. He had been looking forward to seeing her all week, as soon as his mother had written to him about the barn raising. But it didn't go at all like he had hoped. He thought Carrie might be eager to see him, but she wasn't. Her lips held in a thin tight line as she spoke to him, all three or four words. And then the cell phone went off! He frowned, rolling his eyes. He could still feel the measuring glances of the women as he spoke on the phone. And it was that Alicia girl!

Sol sighed, discouraged. He thought he and Carrie might be able to get back to where they were before. When he saw her today, he felt a sharp pain as he realized again how beautiful she was, how big those blue eyes were. He felt such a longing for her. But his relationship with Carrie had veered off course like a runaway horse and he didn't know how to get it back on track.

Sol thought back to a conversation he had, a year or so ago, with Carrie's father. He was shining a flashlight on Carrie's bedroom window one night when Jacob Weaver surprised him.

Jacob was standing on the porch, watching him. "What's on your mind, Solomon?"

Hardly anyone called him that, only Jacob Weaver. Sol always thought it was Jacob's way of reminding him what his name represented. Sol decided to be frank with him. He turned off the flashlight and approached Jacob. "You know about Carrie and me."

Jacob's chin dropped, his bushy whiskers rested against his chest, as if he was thinking. He wasn't a big man, but he had a way of making Sol feel small. He lifted his head, as if he had decided something. "I'm sorry, son. You ought not to be expecting my blessing."

Sol looked at Jacob, shocked. "And why not? You've known me since I was a boy. What makes you think I'm not good enough for your Carrie?"

Jacob leaned on his hands against the porch railings, slowly gathering his thoughts. Finally, he said, "I've known you plenty long. That's why I'm saying no."

"What?!"

"As long as I've known you, at church and barn raisings and other gatherings, I've noticed that you always eat first, with the older men."

Sol shrugged. "I worked hard. I was hungry."

"Yes, yes, I'm sure you were. So were the other boys. But they waited, to show respect to the elders. Seems like a small thing, I know, but it's more than that. It's the reason behind it. You always think first about yourself." Jacob shook his head. "I won't let my daughter marry a man who takes care of himself first."

Squarely meeting Jacob's gaze, Sol said, "I would take good care of her."

Jacob let his gaze slide away. "I'm sorry, Solomon." After a moment he lifted his head. "But I don't believe you would." He turned to leave.

"Then who?" Sol asked him. "Who, Jacob? Who could be good enough for your Carrie?"

Jacob stopped, stood still for a moment, then walked into the house. This time, Sol let him go. By the way he squared his shoulders, Sol could tell that Jacob had someone else in mind for Carrie. He could also see that Jacob's mind was made up.

That was the first time Sol started to think about leaving, with Carrie.

All of a sudden, he realized that at the barn raising today, he had eaten with the first shift of older men. He hadn't even thought about it, he just grabbed an empty spot. He clapped his hand against his forehead, as if he had just proven Jacob's point. But on its heels came a renewed vigor to win Carrie back.

To prove Jacob wrong.

A buggy clattered past him, then pulled over to the side of the road to stop. A capped head popped out of the buggy window. "Need some help, Sol?" Mattie shouted.

Oh, you don't know the half of it! he thought, as he broke into a jog to catch a ride with her.

❧

At the hospital, Carrie helped Abel walk into the emergency room while Veronica parked her little red convertible. A nurse took one look at how he clutched his arm, face contorted in pain, and pointed toward a bed behind a curtain. Abel stretched out carefully on the bed, took hold of Carrie's hand, and wouldn't let go. He held it so tightly that her hand turned a mottled white.

"Abel, they need to examine you," Carrie told him. "You need to let go of me. I'll be in the waiting room the entire time." But he wouldn't let go.

"Just stay," the nurse said, yanking the curtain around the bed. "Men like their women right by their side."

Carrie shook her head. "I'm not—"

The nurse interrupted Carrie with questions about the accident. Then she cut off Abel's shirt. Carrie felt her cheeks grow warm at the sight of his naked chest, but what made her even more anxious to leave was Abel's arm, bent askew. Still, he wouldn't release her hand.

Veronica's voice, raised in argument with a nurse, floated in from the hallway. "What do you mean, only family can be with him? I'm his girlfriend!"

Carrie leaned over to whisper to Abel, "I think Veronica McCall would like to be with you." She hoped this would convince him to let go of her hand.

"Nee," he whispered back, wincing as pain shot through him. *No.*

"Since when have you been speaking the dialect?" Carrie asked, smoothing his hair back out of his eyes with her free hand to comfort him, the way she did with Andy when he was sick or upset.

He tried to smile but gave up.

"Okay, pal," the nurse said, wrapping a blood pressure cuff around Abel's good arm. "Let go of her hand. I need to get your blood pressure."

Relieved, Carrie pried her fingers out of his, freeing her hand from his grasp.

After recording Abel's blood pressure, the nurse took his pulse. Frowning, she asked, "Why is your pulse going so fast?"

She peered at him, then at Carrie, who was stroking his hair. "Hey, buddy, stop looking at her and look at me for a second."

Abel turned his head toward the nurse, puzzled, as she kept two fingers on his pulse.

"That's what I thought. Now it's going down." She rolled her eyes. "We're going to wheel you to X-ray, then the doctor will tell you what a mess you've made of your arm." She snorted. "As if we all didn't know that." She yanked back the curtain and jerked his gurney, pushing him down the hall to X-ray.

Abel looked back at Carrie with pleading eyes. "Bleib do!" *Stay here!*

"Druwwelt nix, Abel," she said reassuringly. *Don't worry.* "Someone will be here."

Carrie heard the nurse mutter to Abel, "Sheesh, pal. You got it bad."

❧❧

Carrie walked into the waiting room rubbing her hands, trying to get feeling back into the one Abel had squeezed for the last hour.

"Sis Schaade! Sei Dod waar ganz unverhofft!" someone called out, thinking Carrie was wringing her hands in grief. *What a pity! His death was so unexpected!*

Startled, Carrie glanced up to see a half-dozen Amish men and women from the barn raising, patiently waiting for news about Abel, Abraham and the bishop among them.

"Oh no! He's not dead," she reassured them, still wiggling her fingers. "He's got a broken arm, but he's not dead."

"Atlee, perhaps you should take Carrie home. You should all go home," Abraham said, looking around the room. "I will stay."

"Would you? He wants someone to stay, but I . . ." *I want to go home*, Carrie thought. It had been a long day.

"I'll stay with him," Veronica McCall said, rounding a corner, a cup of coffee from the vending machine in her hand. She gave Carrie a measured look.

"Thank you," Carrie said gratefully, meaning it.

Abraham called a Mennonite taxi driver who owned a van to take them all home. It was dark now, and Carrie briefly wondered about the new barn at the Stoltzfuses', but then her thoughts bounced to Sol. When the van pulled up to Cider Mill Farm, she thanked everyone for their help.

Even the bishop, not known for his sensitivity, could tell Carrie was troubled. "That boy will be fine, Carrie. He's a young fellow. They heal right quick."

Carrie nodded.

"That English gal. She's the one who ought to be feeling upset. She brought this on," Abraham said.

Carrie shrugged. At this moment, she didn't care about Veronica McCall. She didn't even much care about Abel's broken arm.

❧❧

A light snow was falling when Veronica McCall returned to Cider Mill Farm. Abel was next to her in the passenger seat, his arm wrapped in a stiff, freshly plastered cast, hanging in a blue sling. Emma and Carrie went outside to help him, but he looked like he wasn't feeling any pain at all. His eyes were dilated and unfocused.

Carrie put one arm around Abel's waist and Emma took the other side. "Emma, he shouldn't be out in the cold workshop. I think he should sleep in your room for now. You can stay in my room."

Abel started singing at the top of his lungs, something silly about leaving his heart at a Greyhound bus station.

"He's totally doped up," Veronica Mc-

Call said. "Here are the meds that the doctor prescribed." She handed Carrie a white paper bag. "He was only supposed to have one of those pink pills, but I gave him two so he could sleep." She looked at her wristwatch. "Gotta run. I have a video conference call in the morning. Tell Abel toodles!"

"Toodles?" Emma asked, astounded. "You want us to tell him 'toodles'? How about 'I'm sorry for honking the horn and causing you to fall off the roof of the barn'?"

Veronica's eyes narrowed like a cat. "It was an accident. Accidents happen."

Emma helped Carrie get Abel into bed for the night. He kept singing, one song after another, until Emma scolded him. "I'm just about ready to stick a sock in your mouth, Abel Miller, if you don't hush up! You'll wake up Yonnie and Andy!"

At that fierce reprimand, tears started trickling down Abel's cheeks. Emma threw up her hands and left the room.

Carrie slipped off his shoes and pulled the blanket over him, being careful not to put weight on his cast. "Good thing you don't touch the devil's brew, Abel Miller. You're a mess."

"Why did you leave me, Carrie?" he asked in a gruff whisper.

"Aw, Abel, you nearly broke off my hand. I stayed as long as I could. You had a whole crowd of people there. Filled up the waiting room." She straightened. "Besides, you had her. You didn't need me."

"But I wanted *you*," he said, before closing his eyes.

Carrie touched him then, on the cheek with the tips of her fingers. "Hush this crazy talk now and go to sleep." She watched as his breathing settled into an even rhythm of sleep. She took the pill container out of her apron pocket and set it on his nightstand. Two pain pills, Veronica McCall said she had given him, when there was a warning right on the label not to exceed one pill every six hours. What had she been thinking?! The logic of that woman defied her.

She leaned over to turn off the gas lamp by his bedside, pitching the room into total darkness.

When Carrie went into her bedroom, Emma was combing out her long hair and braiding it. "Is he asleep?" Emma asked.

"I think so," Carrie answered. She hung

her apron on the peg and reached for her nightgown.

Emma put down her brush and leaned her chin on her elbows. "Mother said that John Graber is now Alva's John."

"Alva Brenner?"

Emma nodded sadly.

Carrie went over to sit on the bed near her, her nightgown in her lap. "Oh, Emma. What does your mother know about such things?"

Head bowed low, Emma added, "He doesn't come around anymore."

Now that Carrie thought about it, Emma was right. John Graber hadn't been at Cider Mill Farm for the last few weeks. How could she have missed noticing that? Just the other day, Abel asked her if something was bothering Emma. When she asked why he thought so, he said, "She seems more worried than usual."

Was she getting so absorbed in her own problems that she was blind to Emma's? she wondered, pulling pins out from her hair bun, dropping them in her lap. "Are you awful disappointed?"

Emma gave a quick nod. "Yonnie promised me . . ." She clamped her lips shut.

"Promised you what?"

"Yonnie made up a special tea and gave it to John so that he would love me forever." She looked at Carrie out of the corner of her eyes. "Don't look at me like that, Carrie." Emma's eyes swam. "I only want . . ."

Carrie handed Emma a handkerchief to wipe her tears. "Want what?"

Emma blew her nose loudly. "I want someone to look at me the way, well, the way Abel looks at you."

"What?" Carrie asked, stunned. "Stop talking nonsense."

Emma finished braiding her hair. "It's not nonsense, Carrie. He's sweet on you."

"Emma, Abel has an interest in Veronica McCall."

She shook her head. "I asked him, flat out. I said to him, 'What do you think you're doing, courting that fancy English gal?' I told him it was wrong, wrong, wrong—being unequally yoked and all—and that gal has trouble written all over her. He said to me, 'Emma, I'm not courting her!' He said he was only working for her because she needed help and he needed work and that he was trying to teach her the Bible." She pointed her finger at Carrie in warning. "But she wants him like a mudhen on a tin roof wants rain."

"Well, she may be doing the wanting, but he's not doing any running, as far as I can tell." Emma didn't know about all the times Carrie caught Veronica and Abel in the convertible car, windows steamed up. Late one night when Carrie couldn't sleep, she even saw Veronica leave from Abel's workshop. Carrie stood and started to unpin her dress, then stopped. "You don't need Yonnie's silly remedies to make a man love you, Emma."

"Then what do I do?" Emma asked, a forlorn look on her face. "I don't want to be a Maedel. I'm getting old. My wrinkles are multiplying like cow flies. I want a husband and a family of my own."

Carrie went over to her and finished braiding the long rope of her hair. "Then tell the Lord God about it, not Yonnie."

Emma gave her a weak smile. "Now you're starting to sound like our Abel when he's in a preaching mood."

Actually, Carrie thought that comment sounded more like Mattie. Abel quoted Scripture and spouted theology, Mattie talked about trusting God for everything. Both of them, though, loved God with their whole hearts. She yawned, trying to get comfortable, scrunching far against the edge because Emma had taken up the entire bed.

It took a long while to fall asleep. She wished she could have started the day all over again. It had not been a good day, this day, and she felt miserable. When was she ever going to be able to be around Sol and not leave feeling all churned up inside?

As Emma's breathing settled into loud snores, Carrie covered her ears with a pillow.

⁂

Whatever pills Veronica McCall gave to Abel knocked him out. Finally, by lunchtime, Carrie worried that he might have passed in the night. She tiptoed to his bedside and laid her hand on his forehead. He stirred at her touch, then opened his eyes and blinked a few times.

"Hi," she said. "How are you feeling?"

"Don't know." He closed his eyes again. "Just woke up."

"Think you could eat something?"

He inhaled deeply. "That coffee smells awfully good."

"I'll get you some."

"Carrie, wait . . ."

She put a hand on the doorjamb and turned back to him. "I'd better get you that coffee. No doubt your throat is sore from singing last night like a lovesick coyote." When she saw the look of alarm cross his face, she added, "Silly English songs. Out of key too. They were terrible."

Downstairs, Yonnie and Emma were washing dishes.

"How's our Abel doing?" Yonnie asked.

"He's going to survive, I think," Carrie said. "He'd like some coffee if there's any left."

"That's a good sign," Emma said. "Think he's hungry? There's leftover hotcake batter."

For reasons Carrie couldn't explain, she suddenly felt shy around Abel. She handed the mug of steaming coffee to Emma. "Why don't you take this to him and ask him yourself?"

As soon as her chores were done, Carrie threw on her shawl and headed out to the orchards, walking up and down the rows of trees through the slushy snow and mud. Still unsettled from seeing Sol, she knew she needed to fix her mind on something else.

She examined the spindly arms of the apple trees and decided the time for pruning had come. Winter was halfway over. Ready or not, spring was right around the corner.

She went into the barn and started collecting the saw blades she would need to start pruning the trees. She tried to remember which saws Daniel and Eli had used. She was grateful they had pruned the trees so well a year ago so she would only need to follow the footprint they'd left behind.

She had never sharpened a blade before, but she had watched her father do plenty of them. She lit a gas lamp and sat at the grindstone, starting to tread the pedals to make the wheel spin.

Suddenly, the barn door slid open. "Just what do you think you're doing?" Abel asked Carrie as he approached the grindstone.

She stopped pedaling. "You should be in bed."

"I'm not sick. I just hurt my arm."

"I'll say." She turned her attention back to the blade.

"Carrie, what do you think you're doing?"

"I'm sharpening the blades so that I can prune the apple trees."

His jaw dropped. "By yourself?"

"If I don't, it won't get done."

"I'll do it for you. Just give me a little time to get back on my feet."

"Not with that broken arm, Abel. Can't wait that long."

Abel's frown deepened to genuine displeasure. "Carrie, a few more days won't make any difference."

She stopped again and looked straight at him. "Abel, these orchards are my responsibility. I need to do this. I need to take care of my farm."

He got that funny look on his face again, like there was something he was hiding. "I can cut the lower branches."

She thought he was crazy to even offer, with an arm in a big cast. "Suit yourself. But I'm starting tomorrow morning."

"Well, you're sharpening those blades on the wrong side, so you're going to have an awful hard time with it if you don't let me help you, now."

She jumped off the seat and swept her hand in a be-my-guest gesture.

At breakfast the next morning, Carrie explained to Emma that she and Abel were going to be starting the pruning. Emma's lips pursed tightly together, then she listed off all of the reasons why this was a foolish idea. Abel sat in his chair, eating his scrambled eggs, a smug look on his face.

Emma pointed a finger at Abel. "And what makes you think he'll be any good to you? He's a one-winged bird."

Abel's dark eyebrows lifted, but he didn't say a word.

Carrie sighed. "Emma, I need your help with chores while I prune those trees." She stood up and took her dishes to the sink.

"If Mother knew—"

Carrie whirled around. "She doesn't know and she doesn't need to know. This is my home, Emma, not Esther's."

Emma clamped her lips shut.

Carrie threw on a cape. After hitching the wagon to Old-Timer, she hurried into the barn and lugged the hayloft ramp out to the wagon. Abel lifted the back end of the ramp, helping her scoot it onto the wagon bed. He remembered the tool box and shoved it next to the ramp. She climbed up as he hoisted himself into the seat. She stopped the horse at the farthest grove of trees and didn't even bother to tie his reins to a tree. Old-Timer was too old to think about running off.

From the wagon bench, Abel was studying the endless rows of trees. "These trees are shaped well. Room for lots of light to get in. We just have to trim back the new growth."

She climbed off of the wagon and yanked the ramp down, then started dragging it to the nearest tree.

Abel climbed down carefully, moving as slow and cautious as an old man. "Listen, Carrie . . ."

She knew by his tone of voice that he was about to tell her how she didn't know what she was getting herself into. She crossed her arms and flung her head back to stare at him. "What, Abel?"

He looked at Carrie for a long moment, then gave a little nudge to the brim of his hat. "I found some clippers too. You use the clippers and I'll use the saws."

Carrie had always loved working outdoors, much more than she did the cleaning and cooking and keeping up of the house. Emma preferred doing woman's work. The menial work, Carrie thought, and then, out of habit, whispered an apology to the Lord for her prideful heart. All work was sacred in God's eyes.

But after an hour Carrie had barely pruned the upper branches of one tree. A blister had formed on the palm of her hand and her toes were numb with cold. It was harder work than she could have ever imagined. Already, the muscles in her shoulders and arms ached as she leaned on the ramp to clip the branch. She paused and looked down the long, even row of trees. Last night she had done the math: about one hundred trees per acre, and there were twenty acres. She sighed. This job was unending.

It was slow going for Abel too. He had been trying to saw the lower branches, but with his arm in a sling he was weak and off balance. Though the morning was cold, she saw beads of sweat on his brow. He even looked pale. She was sure his broken arm was aching, but he was too stubborn to admit it.

"Let's take a rest," she said, after he had stopped to wipe his face with a handkerchief.

She climbed down from the ramp and sat on a blanket against the tree trunk, drawing her knees up to stay warm. She rested her forehead on her knees. "I can't do it," she said aloud. "I can't do it alone."

Abel leaned against the wagon. "Well, thank you very much."

She lifted her head at him. "I didn't mean it like that." She sighed and bent her head down again.

"It's hard work to manage orchards, Carrie," he said.

She snapped her head up. "So you want me to just give up?"

"No, that's not what I . . ."

When she finally risked a glance at Abel, he was staring at her with that guilty look on his face. She saw his eyes lift quickly to the trees down the row, as if he didn't want to be caught looking at her.

She stood up and stretched. "Could I ask you something?"

"Ask away," he said, grabbing a rag from the back of the wagon.

"What happened to your folks? How is it you ended up with Eli?"

He looked at her, startled, as if that was the last thing he expected her to ask. Then he took the rag and started to wipe down the tree saw. "Eli was my mother's older brother. My mother left the church to run off with my father, who was English. He never did marry her, so that's why I have my mother's last name." He put the saw down and picked up Carrie's clippers. "She died in a car accident when I was five."

"What about your father?"

He shrugged. "Well, the police didn't see the potential in selling drugs that my father did. So they hauled him off to prison and I was deposited in foster care."

It was hard for Carrie to believe there were parents like that, people who could drop their responsibilities to their children like they were changing clothes. To the Amish, family is the very center of life. To have a child is a great blessing, given by God.

Abel picked up the water jug and offered it to Carrie. She shook her head so he took a drink.

"Then what happened to you?" she asked.

He wiped his mouth with the back of his sleeve. "I got into a few scrapes while I was in the system, ended up in juvey a couple of times."

"What's that?" she asked.

"Juvey? Juvenile Hall. It's like, well, sort of like jail for kids."

His eyes were laughing at her, at the shocked look on her face. Her cheeks flamed, aware of how naïve she seemed.

"So, when I got out of juvenile hall the last time, I was told that a relative was willing to take me in. An Amish uncle." He smiled. "At that point, all I knew about the Amish were buggies and beards."

"How old were you?"

"Thirteen." He rubbed the part of his neck that his sling rubbed against. "Daniel was two years older. He and I hit it off, right from the beginning." He grinned. "Not such a good thing. I talked Daniel into a lot of mischief making. A lot."

She gazed down the long row of apple trees before looking up at him. "So even back then, you weren't thinking you'd be baptized into the church?"

He gave her a sharp look. "Back then, I did everything I could to try and prove I didn't need anything or anybody." He picked up a dried, withered apple left on the ground from last year and threw it as far as he could. "Like I said, I was a bad apple."

It must be terrible to never belong to anyone, Carrie thought. Being Amish meant a certainty of always belonging, always being a part of a whole. She wondered if Abel could sustain being alone forever. She wasn't like that. She needed others, she needed that place at the table. It occurred to her that if she had left with Sol, she might never have felt again like she belonged somewhere. She was quiet for a long moment, mulling that over. Slowly she lifted her eyes to meet Abel's. "If you were such a bad apple, why did you go to jail for Daniel?"

"Carrie, you knew Daniel. You knew how sensitive he was. Do you really think he could have survived prison?"

Startled, Carrie realized Abel was right. Daniel wasn't . . . sturdy.

Abel lifted his eyebrows. "Now don't go thinking I was a saint. Daniel was the closest thing to a brother I would ever have." He kicked the ground with his foot. "I would have done anything for him."

Carrie looked at his profile, silhouetted against the canopy of a deep and endless blue sky overhead. "Abel Miller, sometimes I think you're more Amish than the rest of us."

❖❖

Early the next morning, Carrie dressed to head out to the orchards, wondering how many days and weeks it would take to get those trees pruned. Her entire body ached, muscles she never knew she had felt stiff. Since it was Saturday, at least Andy would be joining them.

Just as she was pouring coffee into a thermos to take out to the orchards, she heard buggy wheels roll into the driveway. It was still too dark to see anything but a lantern, but then she saw another lantern, then another. Then another. She threw on her cape and went outside. Abel heard them too, and came out of the barn holding a bucket, brimming with Hope's steamy milk, fragrant and fresh, in his one good hand.

Abraham greeted them as he hopped off the first buggy. "Wie geht's!" *Good day!*

Abel and Carrie walked up to meet him, puzzled.

"With Abel's arm broke, did you think we'd forget you needed help with those apple trees?" Abraham laughed. "How is that broke arm, Abel?"

As Abel answered the deacon, Emma came up behind them. Carrie gave her a suspicious look. "Did you go telling Esther I was trying to cut those trees myself?"

"No! I promise." She looked as surprised as Carrie did.

Somehow, Carrie realized, they just knew she needed help. "Well, Emma, we'd better get more coffee brewing, then," she said, barely able to contain her relief.

In one day, working together, the neighbors finished pruning every apple tree and stacked the limbs and kindling to dry in the shed, ready to use next winter. As Carrie waved goodbye to the last buggy, her heart brimmed with gratitude. It was the Plain way for neighbor to help neighbor, she *knew* that. But for the first time, she *felt* it. This is what it means to be Plain, she thought. This security, this sense of belonging. She never should have worried. She had neighbors.

She walked down to the first row of trees in the orchard. She tilted her head back to look at the deep blue of the evening sky. As darkness descended, the stars began to pop out, clear as a map of the skies. The long, even rows of trees would soon finish their winter's nap, waiting for the call of spring. She couldn't wait for those first pink blossoms. Spring had always been her favorite time of year, when the earth warmed and erupted into dazzling colors. She was as excited as she could remember being about anything. Cider Mill Farm was the first home she'd ever really had to call her own. She had grown to love it, every rock and tree. She felt as if she was just starting her life again.

Later that week, Carrie took a letter for Abel that arrived in the day's mail and a stack of his freshly ironed clothes down to the workshop. She pulled open one drawer to put away his shirts and closed it again, but something jammed. The drawer wouldn't shut. She pulled it open and reached her hand in the back to see what was jammed. It was a large yellow envelope addressed to Abel Miller, with a return address of Veronica McCall's company. She smoothed out the envelope and placed it flat in the drawer, then closed it tight.

What was in that envelope? The thought kept nagging her, like a sliver in a finger.

Before Abel returned from Honor Mansion, she went to the barn and opened up his drawer. She picked up the envelope, knowing full well it was wrong, that it was wicked. But still, she opened it up and read the papers. She read and reread until her knees went weak and her heart started pounding in her ears. It was a contract from Bonnatt Construction Company with an offer for Cider Mill Farm.

My home. My orchards.

She stopped reading as a chill shivered through her. With shaking hands, she slid the papers back in the envelope. "I don't believe it," she murmured. "I just can't believe Abel would betray me like that." But even as she said the words, doubt flickered in the back of her mind like fireflies darting in the night.

That evening, she had trouble falling asleep, until a wheel clicked over in her mind. The thought made her finally relax. Even to smile. The joke was on Abel, really. She was surprised she hadn't thought of it sooner. There was no way he could sell Cider Mill Farm.

You can't sell what you don't own.

12

On an off Sunday in late February, when church wasn't being held, a loud roar rumbled into the driveway, so loud it sounded as if a train had arrived. Abel and Andy were in the living room and hopped up to see what the racket was. Emma stood next to Carrie by the kitchen door, wiping her hands on a dish towel.

Abel came up behind Carrie and looked over her shoulder. "No way!" He shoved open the kitchen door and flew down the steps. A giant of a man with a big silver helmet on his head, wearing a black leather jacket, climbed off of a motorcycle.

"Abe!" the man shouted, spotting Abel as he approached, enveloping him in a bear hug. "Dude—you got a broken arm!"

Coughing from the man's tight embrace, Abel looked back to the house and waved. "It's Steelhead!"

Emma, Carrie, and Andy, wide-eyed, walked out on the kitchen steps.

The man pulled off his helmet, revealing a large, shiny bald head. He walked around in a circle, taking in the house and the orchards. "I feel like I just walked into a Christmas card." Then he whirled around to face Carrie and Emma, slowly appraising the two women. He whistled. "Wow. What a babe."

"A babe?" Abel asked, glancing back to the house. "Oh, that's Carrie. I wrote you about her."

"The big gal?"

"Emma?!" Abel's eyes went wide. "A babe?"

"I like a woman with a little meat on her bones," Steelhead said. "Man, she is one hot mama."

Overhearing, Emma spun around in disgust and slammed the kitchen door.

At dinner that noontime, Andy's eyes

stayed fixed on the eagle tattoo on Steel-head's right arm. When Steelhead noticed Andy's fixation, he flexed the muscles in his arm, making it look as if the eagle was about to fly. He tore off a crusty chunk of bread, dunked it in his soup, and stuffed it in his mouth. He grinned and winked at Andy.

Carrie wondered if the tattoo would look like an expired balloon, faded and sagging, when Steelhead grew old. Emma wasn't at all impressed by Steelhead's tattoo, or any-thing else about him. Steelhead didn't seem to notice. He would tell Abel a story or make a joke, then glance at Emma to see if she was paying attention. Emma ignored him and concentrated on her meal.

Andy was fascinated by him. "How did you get so bald?" he blurted out.

Carrie gasped, but Steelhead only grinned. "I like to think I've been liberated from the burden of hair," he said, elbowing Andy.

Andy pondered that answer for a mo-ment, then started laughing so hard he bent in the middle. Carrie started laughing too, just watching him. It felt so good to see Andy laugh again.

"So, Mr. Steelhead, what brings you to Stoney Ridge?" Yonnie asked. She seemed a little dazed by Steelhead, but so did Carrie.

"Well, I'll tell you ma'am, Abe and I had always talked about starting our own business someday, and he didn't seem to be coming back up to Ohio." Steelhead slapped Abel on the back so hard he winced. "When my parole officer gave me the okay to leave the grand state of Ohio, I got to thinkin', why not go find my little buddy and see what's taking him so long?"

Abel bit the corner of his lip and kept his eyes on his plate.

"Is everyone finished?" Emma asked, ice in her voice.

Abel gave the signal for a silent prayer to finish the meal, then Emma hopped up and started to clear the table, banging dishes as she set them down on the counter. She was making such a racket, slamming pots and kettles, that Steelhead looked worried, as if she might start throwing things at him.

"Are you vexed with me, ma'am?" he asked her.

Emma didn't even glance his way.

"She's always like that," Andy whispered to him. He twirled his finger beside his head like the spring of a clock. "A little crazy."

"Am I talking too much for you, Miss Emma?" Steelhead asked her.

Starting to fill the sink with hot water, Emma said stiffly, "Plain folks believe that needless words are a displeasure to God."

"Oh, honestly, Emma," Carrie said. "Steelhead is our guest."

"No, she's absolutely right," Steelhead said. "I'm known for making a short story long." He laughed and stood to stretch. "And now, I'll be on my way. I'm staying in town." He went over to Emma and took her hand gently in his. "Thank you for the meal, Miss Emma."

Emma's cheeks colored, but she gave a short jerk of her head before pulling her hand out of his.

After Abel went outside with Steelhead, Carrie turned to Emma. "Why were you so rude to him?"

Emma scowled and pointed her finger at Carrie. "You should be too! He's going to take our Abel away."

"Don't be ridiculous, Emma." But she looked out the window and saw the two men standing by the motorcycle, talking and laughing. Even though Abel was looking more Plain as his hair grew long, he still seemed English.

"You mark my words," Emma said from behind her, "that kind of man can talk anybody into anything."

Carrie rolled her eyes at Emma's worldly wise airs.

Suddenly, Andy screamed from the other room. "Carrie! Come quick! It's Yonnie! She's dead!"

Carrie found Yonnie on the floor by her quilting frame, unconscious. She was breathing, but her pulse was racing. Emma shouted out the kitchen door to Abel to come quick.

"Call 911," Steelhead said.

"Can't," Abel said, hovering over Yonnie. "No phone."

"What?!" Steelhead looked around the kitchen in disbelief. "I'll go for help. I'll take the little dude with me."

Before Steelhead could finish that sentence, Andy was out the door and on the back of the motorcycle. They returned a few minutes later with Veronica McCall following close behind. She walked into the kitchen like a football coach talking to his players before the big game.

"Everyone? Remain calm. I called for an ambulance," she said, pointing to the black clothespin on her ear.

Emma and Andy stayed at the house while Abel rode in the ambulance with Yonnie. Veronica and Carrie followed behind in the car. Carrie was so distracted she didn't even say goodbye to Steelhead. She hoped Emma wouldn't run him off too quickly. He was an odd fellow, but there was a sweetness to him.

At the hospital, Abel, Carrie, and Veronica sat in the waiting room outside of emergency for a long while as the doctor ran tests on Yonnie, trying to determine why she was unconscious. With a captive audience, Veronica McCall thought it would be a fine time to discuss selling the property.

"Not now, Veronica," Abel said in a warning voice, trying to cut her off.

"Why not now? We have time—"

"Not now," he said, giving her an angry look.

A dark cloud passed over Veronica's face. It was obvious that she didn't like having someone tell her what to do.

Just then, the nurse came in and told them they could see Yonnie. "The doctor will be in shortly. He's reviewing her initial test results."

Yonnie slipped in and out of consciousness. She lay in the bed, so tiny and frail. Carrie leaned over to smooth some wispy gray strands into her prayer cap. Abel stood on the other side of her bed, holding her wrinkled hand, his face full of worry. She was the last leaf on his family tree.

Dr. Zimmerman came in through the door, reading Yonnie's chart. When he looked up, he said, "Well, well! My favorite Amish family! My, you people seem to be in the emergency room a lot." He pointed to Abel's cast and asked him how it was mending.

"Too slow for my liking," Abel said.

"That was a nasty break, Abel. Bones need time to heal." Dr. Zimmerman turned his attention to Yonnie. He asked Abel a few questions to get Yonnie's medical history. "She's stable, but I'd like to admit her and run more tests."

Veronica, Abel, and Carrie got into the elevator, trailing behind the orderlies as they pushed Yonnie's bed to the floor where she would stay for the night. Dr. Zimmerman tagged along to answer their questions.

Just as the elevator doors were about to close, a hand reached in. The doors jerked open as Solomon Riehl stepped inside. His eyes scanned those in the elevator, then stopped when they landed on Carrie, as if he knew she was in the elevator. Shocked by the sight of him, Carrie felt her palms start to sweat and her heart pound, but no one else in the elevator had any idea of her discomfort.

Awkwardly, Sol sidled next to Carrie. "Carrie, how are you?" he asked her in a kind voice.

"Very well," she answered, lifting her chin a notch.

"Good. That's good."

Suddenly, Veronica McCall let out a gasp. "Solomon Riehl! The pitcher for the Barnstormers!"

Veronica's face was lit up like a firefly on a summer night. Carrie didn't really blame her. It wasn't so long ago that Sol had the same effect on her. Veronica rooted through her purse for a paper and pen, thrusting them at him for an autograph. Dr. Zimmerman got caught up in Veronica's excitement and reached in his pocket for a prescription pad for Sol's autograph.

"How do you know Carrie?" Veronica asked Sol, as he scribbled his name on her paper.

Sol turned to look straight at Carrie. "We go way back. Way, way back."

Veronica looked from Sol, back to Carrie, then back to Sol. "Well, small world."

Carrie inched farther away, against the wall. She kept her eyes lowered on Yonnie, but she knew that Abel was looking straight at her. That was one thing—the only thing— about Abel that reminded her of Daniel, she realized. He didn't miss a thing.

As soon as the elevator opened, Carrie squeezed past Sol and followed the orderlies. She and Veronica waited in the hallway while Abel went into Yonnie's room with the doctor. A nurse spotted Veronica using her cell phone and ordered her outside on the deck. "It's freezing outside!" Veronica wailed, but the nurse insisted. She finally complied, leaving Carrie alone.

Carrie knew Sol was waiting by the elevator for such an opportune moment. As he approached her, she stiffened and crossed her arms. "You have a habit of popping up in unexpected places."

"I'm here with the team for an autographing event in the pediatric ward," Sol said. "A couple of the players are on the ward signing baseballs and photos and things. To cheer up the sick kids."

"How nice," Carrie said in a flat voice.

Sol took a step closer to her. "Carrie, we need to talk."

She turned her head away.

"I didn't realize Daniel had died on the same day I came to your barn with that . . . information. I'm sorry, Carrie. Until Mattie mentioned the date . . . I didn't know . . ."

Carrie kept her eyes lowered. "You didn't cause his death, if that's what you mean." *I did that,* she thought. Still, the chain of events that started by a single act astounded her.

Sol leaned in toward her. "Does that fellow mean something to you? The one dressed Plain but acts English?"

Her eyes flew up to meet his. "I suppose Mattie told you about Abel too?"

Sol nodded.

For a split second, Carrie wondered when Mattie had talked to Sol. Then she caught herself and dismissed the thought; she had no claim on Sol. "It's not any of your concern."

"But you *know* what he's done, back in Ohio. Why would you be letting yourself get taken in by these kinds of guys? I'm worried about you."

"You don't know anything about the Millers, except for that old newspaper clipping."

"I know enough. I know that Jacob Weaver would never have let you near them had he known what they'd done."

"My father knew," she said coldly.

Sol was shocked silent. He put his hands on her upper arms and his voice dropped to a whisper. "Carrie, don't you see? We've been given a second chance. To get it right."

Carrie's brows lifted. "That's not the way it works."

He sighed. "One choice? One wrong choice? That's all it comes down to?"

Carrie turned her head to the side.

He dropped his arms. "When did you

get so hot hartzfich?" *So hardhearted?* His voice broke as he asked, "Did my leaving do that to you?"

Suddenly Abel stood at the open threshold of Yonnie's door, just as Veronica joined them from the patio. They gathered around Carrie and Sol, watching them curiously. As Carrie realized she had an audience, her cheeks flamed. Sol didn't seem to notice; he kept his gaze fixed on her.

"Is Yonnie dying?" Veronica asked Abel.

"Who's Yonnie?" Sol whispered to Carrie.

Abel looked at Sol, annoyed. "Who *are* you? And why are you here?"

"Yonnie is Abel's grandmother," Veronica answered Sol. "She must be ninety if she's a day." She turned back to Abel. "A body can't live forever, you know."

Abel scowled at her. "She's only eighty-one. And who is this guy?"

"This is Solomon Riehl, the famous baseball player." Satisfied that she had made the proper introductions, Veronica turned to Dr. Zimmerman as he approached them. "So, is she dying?"

Abel threw his arms up in the air in a gesture of *oh, you can't be serious!*

Even Dr. Zimmerman looked surprised by Veronica's bluntness. "I hope not. Not on my watch, anyway." He turned to Abel. "We'll call you if there's any change in her condition."

"Better call me," Veronica McCall said with a smug smile. "These people"—she nodded her head in Carrie's direction—"don't have telephones." She followed Dr. Zimmerman down to the nurse's station to give him her phone number, talking the entire way.

As the elevator door opened, a large man in a Barnstormers' jacket stepped out and spotted Sol. In a rusty and deep voice, he shouted, "Riehl! Where'd you go? Coach is looking for you!"

Sol gave Carrie an awkward glance. "I'd better go." Lowering his voice, he added, "I'll see you soon. Think about what I've said. Just think about it, okay?" He squeezed her arm and hurried to reach the elevator before the doors closed.

Abel stared at her a moment, in that intent way of his. "What was *that* about?"

Carrie kept her eyes on the ground. "What was what about?"

"What's the story with that Sol guy?"

"It's like Veronica said. He's a baseball player."

Abel crossed his arms against his chest. "So she said. What else?"

"Nothing else," she said, lifting her head to meet his gaze. But she couldn't hold his stare.

"Well, let's see. For one thing, he's clearly Amish."

"What makes you say that?" Sol didn't look at all Amish, she thought, not anymore. It was more than the shingled hair and blue jeans. He had never moved like an Amish man, slow and cautious. He had always moved quickly, with the confidence of an athlete.

"What makes me think he's Amish? One: his accent. Two: his name. Three: the way he was looking at you."

She spotted Veronica walking toward them in the hallway. "Maybe Veronica could drive us home. Emma is probably driving Andy crazy with her worry about Yonnie."

"You go. I'm going to stay here overnight."

She glanced at Yonnie's door. "Will you tell her I'll come to see her tomorrow?"

Abel nodded, distracted, and turned to go back into his grandmother's room.

Veronica McCall drove Carrie home, talking on the black clothespin the entire time. Just before they reached Cider Mill Farm, she said, "I'll call you back. I have another call. Uh-huh, uh-huh. Wait a minute." She handed Carrie the clothespin. "Here, Carrie. Abel wants to talk to you."

With one hand, she pointed to the part that Carrie should listen to.

Awkwardly, Carrie lifted it up to her ear. "Carrie?" she heard Abel ask. "Yonnie is awake now."

Carrie hesitated before answering, unsure of where on the clothespin she should speak into. Irritated, Veronica pointed to the speaker. "How does she seem?"

"Better. She's even talking a little. Dr. Zimmerman thinks she had a small stroke. They're going to put her on anticoagulants to thin her blood. He thinks she'll be fine. He said he'll probably release her tomorrow, so I'll stay the night and hire a driver to bring her home."

"Tell him I'll come and get him," Veronica interrupted, eavesdropping.

"Oh. Okay," Abel said flatly, overhearing Veronica. There was a pause. "Carrie, are you okay?"

"Everything's fine," she said briskly, not wanting to discuss Sol. She handed Veronica McCall her black clothespin telephone.

When they pulled up to the house, Carrie thanked Veronica for coming to the rescue. With one hand on the door handle, Carrie shifted her body to turn to her. "I'm grateful for your help today. But I'm still not going to sell you my property."

"*Your* property?" she asked, arching one thin eyebrow. "Abel is the rightful owner."

Carrie shook her head. "Eli left the home to Daniel. To me and Andy."

Veronica stretched in her seat like a cat. "It's a matter of public record, Carrie. Go look it up at the county. The name on the deed of the property is Abel's."

"That couldn't be right." But even as Carrie said it, a knot of doubt started to grow.

"Ask Abel who owns the property, if you don't believe me."

Carrie felt the beginning of a slow burn. "So Abel knows?"

"Of course he knows," she crooned, with a triumphant little smirk. "He's known all along. He paid the taxes on it just last week." At Carrie's bewildered expression, Veronica smiled the smile of one who knew something that another did not. "Why do you think he's staying here? Why do you think he's here at all?"

❧

Samuel Zook, Mattie's brother, was passing Cider Mill Farm in his buggy as the ambulance pulled away. He stopped for a moment as Emma filled him in on Yonnie's emergency. When he arrived home and told Mattie the news, he offered to take her to the hospital. "But you'll have to catch the bus to get home or Dad will skin me alive for missing the afternoon milking," he told her.

Mattie grabbed her bonnet and cape and hopped in his buggy before he could finish the offer.

As soon as Mattie walked through the hospital door, she looked for someone to help her find Yonnie. A hospital volunteer led her to Yonnie's floor and pointed down the hallway to the room. Mattie gently knocked on the door, not knowing what to expect, but was surprised to see Yonnie sitting up in bed, talking with Abel. His face lit up and he sprang to his feet when he saw her.

"Mattie! How did you hear? What are you doing here? Is Carrie with you?" A crestfallen look passed over his face as he realized she was alone.

For a split second, Mattie found she couldn't answer. *Why, he's falling for Carrie! Dear Lord, anyone can see that a mile away.* When Abel asked her again why she was at the hospital, she said, "To check on our Yonnie."

"The doctor thinks that Yonnie can be discharged tomorrow," Abel said, looking affectionately at his grandmother.

Mattie took hold of Yonnie's wrinkled hands. "That's wonderful news, Yonnie!" She turned to Abel. "My dad has a hired driver scheduled for tomorrow afternoon. He has a doctor's appointment across the street. I'm sure he wouldn't mind bringing you both home, if that would help."

Abel sighed with relief. "That would mean Veronica won't have to pick us up."

He winced. "She's been calling the nurse's station every fifteen minutes. They're about ready to pull the phone cord out."

❦

Sol stood outside the hospital, stunned from the news his pitching coach had given him after the event in the pediatric ward. His contract for the upcoming season wasn't going to be renewed.

"I'm sorry, Sol," the coach told him. "We found another pitcher who can match the speed on your fastball, but he's got a few more parlor tricks up his sleeve." The coach patted him on the back, as if that made it all right. "I like you a lot. You've got a great work ethic. This is nothing personal. Baseball is a business, a tough business. It was a good run while it lasted." He then said that he would look around and see if there might be a AA team that needed a pitcher, but he knew there was no interest in the Atlantic League. "And the thing is, Sol, you're going to keep running into the same problem. I even thought about having you help coach the Junior Barnstormers team, cuz I think you'd be good with kids, but what could you offer? You haven't been taught the mechanics of pitching, or hitting, or catching. You're just now catching on to keeping stats. You've had a lucky streak with one fast pitch."

Sol sat on a bench, head in his hands. A lucky streak. A good run while it lasted. Now what? He had such plans. He was going to skim the surface of the world, and here he was, stuck in Stoney Ridge.

He had no idea what he was going to do next. His baseball dream had just died. Carrie was still mad at him; she was staying mad. His folks had told him not to come around anymore. He knew it wasn't his mother's idea; she looked as if it was killing her to hear his father say those words, but they decided it was high time Sol came back to the fold. He figured a church elder, or maybe Esther Weaver, might have paid them a visit.

The thing was, he wasn't really Amish anymore. But he wasn't really English, either. He felt small and very, very alone.

Absentmindedly, he watched a young woman, dressed Plain, walking to the bus stop. Sol jackknifed to his feet and jogged over to her. "Mattie?"

Startled, Mattie spun around to see who was calling her name. Then she smiled.

Sol was grateful to see a friendly face, any friendly face would do. "What are you doing here? Would you have time for a visit? A cup of coffee, maybe?"

"I heard the news about Yonnie so I came to see if I could help. And to answer your other questions, yes and yes."

In the cafeteria, Mattie sat across from Sol as he poured out the story of getting cut from the team. He didn't mean to tell her so much, but Mattie had a way of listening and talking at just the right places. When he told her the coach wanted him to come back for "Salute to Whoopie Pie Day" because it would boost attendance among the Pennsylvania Dutch fans, she laughed so hard it made him start to laugh too. Put that way, it did sound ridiculous.

After he finished, he asked, "Any idea what I should do now?" He peered at her as if she could provide him with answers to all that plagued him.

Mattie stood, walked to the window that overlooked the parking lot, and then turned back to him. She spoke the truth that was in her heart, because that was the only way she knew how to be. "When you get to your wit's end, Sol, you'll find God lives there."

❧

"Why didn't you tell me Eli left you these orchards, Abel?" Carrie asked, then waited, hands on her hips, letting her silence demand an explanation from him.

They had just settled Yonnie up in her bed after returning from the hospital. Emma hovered over Yonnie like a bee over blooming lavender and Andy was at school, so Carrie followed Abel out to his workshop in the barn. Since Veronica McCall's revelation about the property deed, she had been waiting for this moment to come.

Abel spun around, confused. He looked exhausted from spending the night upright in a hospital chair. "Who told you that?"

She told him everything Veronica had told her.

His eyes went wide, but Carrie knew she had the truth. "That's not how things went . . . I didn't . . . I would never . . ."

She glared at him, standing her ground.

"Can you stop looking at me like that? You're sort of scaring me."

She kept glaring at him.

He raked a hand through his hair, searching for the way to say what he had to say. "The house and orchards were left to me after Daniel died, Carrie. I received a letter from Eli's attorney before I was released from jail. He's the one who told me about Daniel's death." He rubbed his face with his hands. "Eli didn't put you in his will."

She felt anger boil up like a kettle on a hot stove. "Or Andy?"

"Or Andy."

"And you knew about this, the *entire* time."

He nodded slowly, looking miserable.

She was so upset she was shaking. "I have been working to pay the next tax bill on this property all winter. We are paying our feed and gas bills one at a time. Why, even Yonnie has been parting with her quilts! It's been that way ever since Daniel passed." She took a few steps to the open door of the workshop and swept an arm out toward the apple trees. "Do you have any idea what this land means to me? These orchards are meant for Andy to have one day. You arrive out of the blue and think you're going to walk away with it? To sell it and walk off?"

Abel was stunned. "But I never knew . . . why didn't you tell me you needed money? I could have been helping. I want to help. That shouldn't be your responsibility."

"It *should* be my responsibility! All along, I've thought they belonged to me! To me and my brother!" She spun around to leave.

With his good hand, he grabbed her arm to make her face him. "I admit, I came here thinking I would sell the place. I figured you would want to live with your folks, and Yonnie would come back to Ohio with me. Steelhead and I had plans to start a business. But then, I met you, and I saw how you love this place. I see how your face lights up and how hard you work at it. I never *signed* those papers, Carrie. I could never do that to you."

"Why should I believe you?"

"Why shouldn't you?"

"For a man who keeps spouting off that the truth will set us free, I don't see you doing much truth telling. You had plenty of chances, Abel Miller."

Stung, he dropped his hand to his side. In a quiet voice, he said, "I know. I kept looking for the right time to tell you, but it never seemed to come. And then it got harder to tell you. When the property tax bill came in the mail last week, with my name on it, and you put it in my workshop, I just went ahead and paid it. I thought I was helping, but the truth is, well, I just didn't know how to tell you the truth. Not after all this time." He rubbed his jaw. "Eli left this property to me because he was trying to set things right. For me. He wasn't trying to hurt you. Neither was I."

Just then, Andy came running to the workshop to show Abel a hummingbird's nest he had found on the way home from school. Abel bent down to examine it.

"Wow, Andy, what a find!" he said with such fondness in his voice that it made Carrie's heart hurt.

Carrie watched the two heads bent over the nest for a long moment, then as her eyelashes spiked with tears, she turned quickly to go to the house.

13

Sol drove to Central Market right about the time he thought Mattie would be done working for the day. Just this week, her family had opened up their stand to sell the first fruits of the year: asparagus and spring onions. He smiled at the pleased look on her face when she spotted him. He flashed her his most dashing grin, the one he used only when girls were around. "Hello there, Mathilda Zook."

Mattie gave him a measured look in that way she had. "Sol, please wipe that dipped-in-honey grin off your face. I know you well enough to know when you're trying to charm someone. Why don't you stop playing games and just tell me what you need."

Sol's grin faded. "I could sure use a friend, Mattie."

Mattie closed up the stand and locked it, put the money in her pocket, and turned to Sol. "Let's go for a ride."

Sol drove down to Blue Lake Pond. In the late afternoon sun, it was so cold they decided to stay in the car. With their eyes facing the silver shimmer of the pond, Sol found himself spilling out everything about the turmoil he felt over the last year. Mattie was easy for him to talk to, easier than Carrie, he realized. There was a little part of him that wasn't entirely surprised Carrie wouldn't forgive him. As if he always felt he might disappoint her, after she really got to know him. Maybe that was why he went ahead and disappointed her. He couldn't deny a part of him felt relieved about trying to play baseball without worrying about a wife. But in the back of his mind he figured he and Carrie would eventually work things out, that they were meant to be together. He underestimated her stubborn streak.

He looked over at Mattie in the car. Her

face was turned to the sky, like a flower, and she smiled softly as the sun washed over her. Things felt so comfortable with Mattie. In a way he didn't understand, she knew him better than he knew himself.

"The thing is, I could always have any girl I ever wanted." He snapped his fingers. "Just like that. Amish or English. Carrie knows that."

Mattie nodded, shifting in the seat to look straight at him. "Until now."

Sol frowned. He knew what she was probably thinking, just like his mother and sisters, that he was being punished for leaving the flock. "I don't know how you can handle all of the rules, Mattie. I got so tired of bumping into rules every time I turned around."

"I guess I don't see the rules as taking something from me. I see them as giving to me."

He glanced at her, surprised. How could he describe freedom to someone who was raised in a cage? "Do you mean to tell me that you honestly think God would label you a hopeless sinner if . . . ," he tugged on a string of her prayer cap, "if you had one less pleat in your cap? Or one more? Will the wrong number of pleats in your cap send you to the devil?" He felt a twinge of guilt to say such things aloud, to cause doubt in Mattie the way it used to when he said such things to Carrie.

But Mattie didn't look to be filled with doubts. In fact, she looked as if she was trying to suppress a smile. "Sol, you're missing the point. My clothes and prayer cap, the way I look, they aren't making me *suitable to* God. They're reminding me, every day, that I *belong* to God."

Sol looked at her, amazed, as if seeing her for the first time. Before him was a girl with steady gray eyes, wide cheekbones that narrowed to a dainty chin, giving her face a sweetheart shape. Her skin was like freshly skimmed cream, her hair the pale yellow of a winter sun. Mattie had a shy innocence common to Amish girls, yet he found that nothing he said shocked her. All those years he'd known her, yet he had hardly ever noticed her. He had to admit, the reason he was spending time with Mattie now was because she was Carrie's best friend, and this was the closest he could come to Carrie.

He shook his head. "It's amazing you and Carrie are such good friends. She's always been tempted by worldly things. She wants more choices." He stopped himself. *Or was that me?* He thought Carrie wanted more, but suddenly he realized he might have blurred her wants with his. He gave a quick shake of his head. "Wanted. She wanted more choices. I guess I don't really know what she wants anymore." He cast Mattie a sliding glance, hoping she might expand on Carrie.

Mattie's eyes were fixed on the pond. "I do have one rule, Sol. I'm not going to talk to you about Carrie."

There was no mincing words with *that* girl, he pondered after he dropped Mattie off at the end of her lane, far enough away from her house that her folks wouldn't see his car. Mattie surprised him with her forthrightness. His sisters had catered to him the same way his mother catered to his father. Wasn't that the way things worked in the Amish world? He wasn't sure he liked the change.

❦

A few weeks later, as Carrie was setting the table for supper, Esther's buggy rolled into the driveway of Cider Mill Farm. She had been visiting Ada Stoltzfus, she said, who kept her longer than she should have. On her way home, she felt a wheel on the buggy come loose. Abel took out his tools to fix the wheel, while Emma invited her mother inside and encouraged her to stay for supper. Esther seemed to be in a rare pleasant mood and agreed to stay. She even asked to see Yonnie's quilts. Still, a feeling of dread rose in Carrie, the same feeling she got before a storm was due in. Well, this was going to be interesting, she thought, setting an extra place at the table for Esther. Because like it or not, chances were that Esther was going to meet Steelhead.

On the afternoon that Yonnie had her stroke, Carrie had returned to the house thinking Emma would have run Steelhead out hours earlier. Instead, she found the two of them playing Scrabble at the kitchen table and laughing over made-up words. Andy said they'd been playing for hours. Since then, Steelhead dropped by every day to see Abel, he said, but he spent his time at the kitchen table, talking to Emma while she cooked or ironed. Today, Andy had talked Steelhead into a motorcycle trip to Blue Lake Pond to see a heron.

When the two came roaring in from their adventure, it was suppertime. Carrie bit her lip. There was no opportunity to flag off Steelhead. He and Andy came bursting into the kitchen, Andy talking a mile a minute until he saw Esther sitting at the table, and his mouth clamped shut. But Steelhead, oblivious as usual, plowed through the sudden silence and walked right over to give Esther a warm welcome. As Esther shook his big hand, her pleasant mood evaporated, the way a wisp of steam vanishes above a cup of hot tea.

It was so quiet during the meal that Carrie could hear Esther's chewing and swallowing echo through the kitchen. Finally, Steelhead broke the silence.

"Would you pass me more of that shepherd's pie, Miss Emma? It's mighty fine."

Carrie noticed that it was getting so that Emma couldn't pass him a serving dish without blushing the color of a plum.

Steelhead turned to Esther. "Emma is a good cook. Really good. I've never known as fine a cook as Emma."

Esther didn't respond. She just fixed her

eyes on Steelhead, and he was looking
like a bird caught in her lair. Carrie almost
laughed out loud at the look of mild panic
in his eyes.

"She might be the best cook in the state
of Pennsylvania," he started to blather,
"certainly better than that whack job who
called himself a cook that we had in prison.
Ain't that right, little buddy?"

He nudged Abel to help, but Abel knew
enough to not step into that particular land-
mine. He tried to look off into the distant
corners of the room as Steelhead, unstop-
pable, carried on.

"Hooboy!" Steelhead continued, his
head turning shiny. "I never want to eat
another morsel of prison grub. Been there,
done that, got the T-shirt. Know what I'm
saying?"

Esther's eyes went wide with shock and
her lips puckered as if she'd just eaten a
pickle. Emma covered her face with her
hands. Carrie tried to kick Steelhead under the table but missed. Abel cleared his
throat, trying to get Steelhead to stop talking, but Steelhead was cornered. His mind
was whirring along, and his mouth dragged

along behind it, spilling out any thought that passed through his head. Finally, after he had described prison life in its entirety, he ran clean out of words.

Esther slowly stood. "I must go."

As Carrie closed the kitchen door behind her, it was all she could do to lean against it, her forehead against the doorjamb. Esther didn't even wait for the silent prayer at the end of the meal, she was *that* perturbed.

"Too bad Esther Weaver didn't stay for my snickerdoodles," Yonnie said, still seated at the table. "She could use a little sugar."

Steelhead snorted a laugh, then another. Andy's eyes went round at the sound. A slow smile spread over Abel's face. Emma's eyes darted between the two men, as laughter started to rise up and carry them away. Then, to Carrie's astonishment, Emma started to giggle.

Carrie leaned her back against the kitchen door, studying them. Emma looked positively . . . happy.

※

One afternoon, Sol had just dropped Mattie off near her home and decided to take the long way back, a route that went past Carrie's farm. To his delight, he spotted Carrie getting the mail at her mailbox. He pulled up to her and rolled down his window. "Please, Carrie?" he asked. "I've got something to tell you."

She hesitated, but got in the car. "I'm surprised this old rust heap still drives."

"My baseball contract was cancelled. It's over."

"I'm sorry," she said faintly. "I know that means the world to you."

He was trying to hold her eyes, but she looked away. "No," he said firmly. "You mean the world to me." He reached over to take her hand and slowly brought it up to his jaw. She curved her palm against his cheek; he turned into the caress. He felt encouraged as he saw the anger in her eyes dissolve. "Carrie, what is it going to take for us to find our way back to each other? Do you want me to join the church? I will, if that's what you want. I'll do anything you want."

Carrie shook her head. "I don't want you to join the church for me. If you join the church, you do it for you." But even as she said it, sounding so sure, he saw her face soften, then her stiff shoulders, then, finally, her resolve.

Softly he said, "We could pick up from where we left off last summer."

"I'm not the same person I was last summer."

"Come on, Carrie," he said, his voice gentle and kind. "I know. I know all about you and Daniel."

"What do you mean?" She slid her hand out of his.

"I know it wasn't a real marriage. I know that he slept on the floor."

She recoiled as if she'd been slapped in the face.

"I saw that fancy red-haired lady in town the other day. She told me. She said Andy told her. When I heard that, I knew. I knew for sure you still loved me." His tone was as much a statement as it was a question, but his eyes were pleading with her.

A look of utter disbelief covered Carrie's face. "You've turned my marriage to Daniel into being all about you." Her hands tightened into fists. "Daniel and I, we were finding our way to each other. The way we were, it had nothing to do with you. Nothing!"

"It had everything to do with me! I got to

thinking, why would any normal, red-blooded man agree to sleep on the floor? With a girl like you just a few feet away? Then it dawned on me . . . he knew you loved me too."

"Again, it's back to you! As if the whole world spins on your axis."

Now Sol was getting indignant. "So you think making a man sleep on the floor isn't selfish?"

An angry flush streaked Carrie's cheeks.

"Admit it, Carrie. Aren't you even a little relieved he's gone?"

She didn't say anything for a long moment. Then she turned to him, with a look in her eyes as if something just became clear to her. "No. I'm not relieved at all." She got out of the car door and ran up her long driveway.

He banged his head over and over on the steering wheel, frustrated, wondering why everything he said lately didn't seem to come out right. They were such good thoughts, they sounded so reasonable when he worked them out in his head, but when he put them into words, they sounded haughty and proud. Downright vain.

❧❧

Carrie found Andy in the barn milking Hope. "Did you tell Veronica McCall that Daniel slept on the floor?"

"What's the big deal?" Andy asked, surprised at how upset she looked. "I saw him there, sometimes, when I had a bad dream and came in to get you. I thought it was neat that he slept on the floor. Like he was an Indian or something."

❧❧

The next day, Abel took the buggy into town for an errand. When he returned, he unhooked the buggy from Old-Timer, but left the tired horse at the hitching post to tend to later. He found Carrie in the vegetable garden, filling up her apron with spring peas. He had a large manila envelope tucked under his arm. "Carrie—"

She looked at the envelope, gathered the corners of her apron, and brushed past him.

He followed behind her. "I know you're upset. You've hardly said a word to me all week. Look, about this deed—"

Something inside of Carrie snapped as anger flooded through her. "Nemme dich die Baamgaarde! Nemme dich das Haus!" she shouted, choking over her own breaths.

"Nemme dich alles!" *Take the orchards! Take the house! Take it all!* She ran from him, peas from her apron scattering on the ground. When she saw Old-Timer at the hitching post, she untied his reins and jumped on his back. She rode away as fast as she could, which, considering Old-Timer's advanced age, wasn't much more than a steady trot.

When she reached the pond, she slid off Old-Timer and led him down to the water's edge to drink. His throat rippled as he drank. Finally satisfied, Old-Timer lifted his head and whiffed the air with flaring nostrils. She sat down, her arms hanging loosely over her bent knees, and stared at the calm water. With one hand, she fingered the horse's reins. She was always amazed at the ability of those narrow leather straps to control the instincts of such a mighty beast. Did God hold such reins to this strange, sad world, she wondered?

Wrapping her arms around her legs, she rested her chin on her knees and watched a golden eagle soar over the still pond. An oriole trilled sweetly as a woodpecker drilled into a nearby tree. This was where she had come during those hard days right after her father had died and Sol had left. This was where, many years before, she had played with Mattie, skipping stones over the pond's surface. This was where she could sit and hear the music of the wild birds. This was where she could always find peace.

She didn't know how much time had passed when Abel sat down next to her on the ground, breathless. "Took me awhile to find you."

She frowned at him. "I didn't want to be found."

He ignored her comment. "Where'd you learn to ride a horse like that?"

She shrugged, her gaze straight ahead. "I used to ride bareback a lot. Made Esther mad."

He smiled and leaned back on his elbows, crossing his legs at the ankles. "Why did you ever get baptized? Sounds like you grew up breaking every rule."

She tilted her head toward him. "I know myself well enough to know that I need the rules."

They sat in more silence after that, taking in the view of the eagle, hanging above them like a kite snagged in the sky. "Whatever problem you're facing, I can help," Abel said softly.

She turned her head slightly toward him, asking in icy anger, "Before or after you sell my home out from under me?"

He sighed. "I'm not taking your home. I'm not taking your orchards. I'm not taking anything. If you'd just let a man finish what he's trying to say, you'd know these things." He handed her the large manila envelope. "This is the new deed, changed to your name. Yours and Andy's. It's official. I had a notary witness it."

Carrie took the envelope from him, speechless. She opened it up, slowly, and pulled the papers out. Right in the middle of the deed, in a boldly typed font, was her name and Andy's. Gratitude welled up inside of her, choking off the words. She needed to tell him that he could never know how much this meant to her. They had always felt like visitors in Esther's house, never family. Never truly wanted. She needed to tell him how much she appreciated this gesture, and that she knew what it cost him, but all that came out was, "Denki, Abel."

The edges of his eyes softened, as if he understood all she was trying to say. "I told Veronica the deed has been changed. She wasn't too happy." He gave a short laugh. "One time in jail we were shown a TV documentary on erupting volcanoes. Kinda reminded me of that." He grinned. "She fired me too. Said she didn't need a one-armed carpenter."

"I'm sorry," Carrie said.

He lifted one shoulder in a careless shrug. "I'll find work someplace. Surely somebody needs a one-armed carpenter." He reached into his coat pocket and pulled out a thin envelope. "There's something else. There's one more letter from Daniel. I just wasn't sure if this letter would help or . . . well, anyway . . . seems as if you should know what it said." He hesitated, then handed it to her.

Carrie's heart started to pound when she saw the postmark. It was mailed on the day Daniel died. Carefully, as if it were made of tissue, she unfolded the letter.

March 18th

Dear Abel,

Spring is late this year. We had howling wind and blowing snow yesterday. Only the downy woodpecker didn't seem to mind. He clung to the beef suet Andy and I put out on the bird feeder. He just kept pecking on the high-energy food, finding sustenance for another cold winter night.

Speaking of finding sustenance, the strangest thing happened today. After a long struggle, Andy's cow gave birth before dawn to a new calf. Carrie helped through the whole thing without complaining or fretting. Afterward, I felt so glad she was by my side. I didn't think I would ever feel anything again for a woman, not after my Katie. I married Carrie because Dad wanted me to, and I wanted him to stop suffering. To be honest, I just didn't really care. But somewhere along the way, I started feeling something for her, a fondness. I guess the plain truth is that I needed her. And then came love. I love her, Abel.

I know in the next letter you're going to be preaching me a sermon. I can hear it now, the text will be Romans 8:28, your favorite verse *in the Bible, about God working things out for our good, even things that didn't start out so good.*

Maybe you're right, Abel. Maybe there's hope for a sinner like me.

I see the mailman coming so I'll say goodbye and get this in the mail.

Yours, Daniel

Something broke inside of Carrie in a terrible gush of guilt and pain. Tears started to flood her eyes. "I let Daniel bleed. Just like Esther let my father bleed. Daniel told me about the kerosene fires that very day, just hours after he must have mailed this letter. And I turned and ran out on him. I was so upset, that he hadn't told me, that Sol—of all people on this big earth—had been the one to tell me about those fires. I felt so angry and I just . . . I just had to get away from him . . . but I never dreamed he would die that night." She took a big gulpy breath. "I failed him miserably. I'm just like Esther."

She went through her handkerchief, then soaked Abel's, and finally, he gave up patting her on the back. He wrapped his arms around her and told her to go ahead, have a good cry. He just held her until she had no more crying left inside of her. She cried for her father's death, and for Daniel's life cut short, and for her own sorry mess. In between sobs she told him about Sol leaving and about grabbing Daniel's offer to marry.

"I didn't love Daniel," she sobbed. "Not the way he deserved to be loved."

Abel rested his chin on the stiff pleats of her prayer cap and held her closer. When she was finally able to look up at him, she noticed tearstains on his cheeks as well.

"Carrie, maybe you needed Daniel as much as he needed you. I'm not sure why he died when he did. It's just one of those mysteries God sends our way. But God has a way of fixing our messes, bringing good out of them." He tipped her chin so she would look at him. "I do know that Daniel would never want you feeling like you failed him. You didn't. One moment doesn't erase all the good."

She wiped her face with her hands. "But what if that was the last moment?"

"Even then." Abel rose to his feet and walked to the water's edge. He picked up a stone and skimmed it across the pond.

Carrie was quiet for a while, watching the stone skip on the glassy surface a few times before it sank deep. "I just wish I knew, for sure and for certain, that he forgave me."

Abel turned to face her. "You knew Daniel well enough to know the answer to that."

A loud, raucous call came from the sky, and Carrie lifted her eyes to find its source.

"Hear Mrs. Mallard honking?" Abel asked quietly, eyes fixed on the V formation of the ducks. "Three quacks mean she's telling the ducks that all is well and it's safe to come down." He reached out a hand to help Carrie to her feet. "Es is alles in Addning." *All is well.*

❧❦

Sol sat on a gray plastic chair in the LaundroMat, flipping through old magazines, waiting for the clothes dryer to buzz. It always surprised him to see men doing their own laundry. Amish men took a pass on laundry. And cooking and cleaning too. Sometimes, he felt like he had arrived from another planet, he had so much to learn. He watched a man separate clothes into bundles of light and dark colors and wondered why he would bother. Then it dawned on him. *That's why my white T-shirts are always gray!*

There were many aspects to the English that bothered Sol—their obsession with television, for example. But there was one thing about the English that Sol really admired. They gave themselves plenty of opportunities for second chances. Guys on the team had started college, then dropped out to play professional baseball. When they were ready, they could go back again. People moved from house to house. Even marriages could be easily dissolved. Two guys on the teams had been divorced and were already remarried, and it wasn't a big deal. But for him, once he bent at the knee, if he changed his mind it would have harsh consequences. He hadn't even been baptized yet and he was already getting a taste of feeling shunned.

He thought the English were a lot kinder about giving people second chances, a margin of error. If the Amish were known for forgiving, why did they have to be so rigid when someone changed his mind? He was going to have to ask Mattie about that. He found his thoughts often bounced to wondering what Mattie would say about these things. Lately, it seemed that thoughts of Mattie filled his mind more than Carrie. He shook his head, as if to clear it.

✖✖

The next day, Mattie was watching for Sol's car after she was done with work. She was careful to keep her expectations in check. She never assumed he would come to pick her up—she just *hoped* he would. When she saw his car, she could hardly hold back a grin. He opened the car door for her and had barely turned the ignition when he told her his theory of second chances and the English.

Mattie listened quietly, wondering what he was really asking. It seemed as if Sol was measuring things out lately, trying to convince himself that what he was doing was the right thing. He had been asking her a lot of questions about being Amish. After praying, she decided it wasn't up to her to convince him whether to join the church or not. That would be up to God.

"So, what do you say to that?" he asked, almost accusingly, after he finished. "About how the English give people a margin of error? About how unforgiving the Amish can be sometimes?"

"The Amish aren't perfect. And there are certainly flaws in our culture, just like there are flaws in the English culture." She looked at him. "You know the flaws of the Plain way, you've thought them out. So now, Sol, what are its good points?"

※※

Sol spent his days working at the construction site where he had been hired a year ago, before he left for the Barnstormers. After he was cut from the team, he spoke to the foreman who said he'd be glad to take him on. Today he finished putting away his tools in the foreman's truck as he heard someone yell out "quittin' time." He tossed the rest of the tools in the truck and hurried to his car; Mattie would be expecting him.

For the last few weeks, Sol picked Mattie up after work whenever she was working at Central Market. It saved her bus fare and allowed them extra time together before her folks expected her home. He wasn't sure how her folks would feel about her spending time with him, but he trusted Mattie's judgment. If she wasn't worried, he wouldn't worry either. He just knew that he looked forward to their time together.

They talked about all kinds of things, important things, and he was always a little sorry when she said she had to go.

Ever since Mattie had asked him the good points about being Amish, Sol found himself flooded with memories. At the time, though, he had looked at her, unable to answer.

"But you've always known what is truly good, Sol," she had finally said. "Our families and the church."

And how could he answer—that those things weren't good? He knew they were.

But her simple words revealed a piercing wisdom. He couldn't stop thinking about his family, meals, barn raisings, hay making with the neighbors, even Sunday gatherings. It stirred something in him, deep inside; he felt something vital was missing. He was less than himself, missing an arm or a leg or a hand. But he always felt better when he was around Mattie.

The last time he dropped her off, he asked her, half teasing, half serious, "Mattie, why do you even bother with me?"

She looked at him in her solemn, frank way. "I've always thought you had so much potential."

He gave a short laugh. "Right about now, I think you're the only one who does. I doubt my dad would even think I could run the manure spreader in a straight line."

Then she said something that took his breath away. "Not that kind of potential, Sol. Not for farmwork. Not even for baseball. But this kind of potential." She rapped on her chest. "This kind. In the soul."

※※

Finishing her morning chores earlier than usual, Carrie hurried over to Mattie's to help the Zooks prepare to host Sunday church. Once a year, each family in the district took a turn hosting church and the fellowship afterward. Every female relative and neighbor would come over a few days ahead to clean and sweep and dust and scrub and cook and bake.

She found Mattie alone in the kitchen, getting things ready for when the women arrived to prepare for the noon meal on Sunday. She was trying to warm up honey in a large honey jar, placed in warm water. The honey had crystallized and she needed it to make pies.

Carrie came over to look in the pot on

the stovetop. A spoon stood straight up. "Hopelessly stuck," she said.

Mattie laughed. "I was just thinking about how it seems as if people get stuck just like this spoon in the honey."

"What?" Carrie asked, starting to fill the sink with warm water so she could wash the dishes Mattie had piled in the sink. She was only half listening.

"Think about it." Mattie tried to loosen the spoon in the honey jar. "Folks think they're traveling on the right road and something happens to stop them—something big, like a mistake they made, or a sin. Then, even though they feel so bad, they just stay stuck."

Carrie added the soap to the hot water and swished it around as bubbles started rising up.

Softly, Mattie said, "Daniel was like that, Carrie. Daniel was stuck."

Carrie stopped what she was doing, and slowly turned to Mattie, not even aware that her hands were dripping bubbles on the floor.

"Eli was trying to help him move forward, so was Abel. Without realizing it, so were you. But he just stayed stuck." Mattie was quiet for a moment, then added, "Sol's another one. He's just stopped in his tracks." The spoon loosened a little. She released it and turned away from the stovetop to face Carrie. "If you don't mind my saying so, sometimes I think you're stuck too, Carrie. Unable to move forward, just filled with regrets about the past. About things you can't change."

As tears started prickling Carrie's eyes, she turned back to the sink.

"I don't think that's what God is wanting from us. I think he wants us to get on with things." Mattie looked out the window at Abel and Andy, who had just arrived to help move furniture out of the downstairs so the benches in the church wagon could be set up. "Take Abel. Now there's a fellow who isn't stuck. He's faced some hard things, but he just keeps moving forward, doesn't he?"

Then she reached over to the honey jar and pulled out the spoon. "Well, look at that!" she said triumphantly, holding it in the air.

※

"No one will want me there," Sol told Mattie after she had encouraged him to come to church held at her home on Sunday.

"That's not true."

"No, Mattie. They'll only want me there if it means I'm coming home."

"The church is your family, Sol. They only want the best for you."

He frowned at her. "You make it sound so simple. But you know it's not."

For some reason he agreed to go. Afterward, he decided it was the worst idea he had ever let a woman talk him into. The only place to sit was on the edge in the back row, a bystander. From that vantage point, he was able to notice how often Abel Miller's gaze roamed to Carrie during the service. Carrie never even glanced Sol's way, and he knew that for a fact because he kept himself slightly turned so he could watch her. Plenty of other folks were snatching a look at Sol, eyebrows raised in disbelief. Why weren't they measuring that Abel Miller? he wondered. *He's* the new bird in the flock. *He's* the one they should be raising an eyebrow over.

Sol's mind drifted to the first time he laid eyes on Carrie, when Jacob had moved his family to Stoney Ridge to marry the starchy widow Esther Blank. Carrie was only twelve, but the sight of her snatched his breath away. She held her back as straight as a plumb line, her chin lifted slightly in the air. It was one of the reasons Esther accused Carrie of being proud, but she wasn't proud. She was just being Carrie.

When Carrie finally turned sixteen, it took Sol two full years of asking before she agreed to go home with him in his courting buggy. She told him he was a flirt and not to bother her until he was done making eyes at other girls. He couldn't help flirting with the other girls; it was just too much fun. But he never really thought about anyone but Carrie, not seriously.

Today, Carrie sat next to Mattie on the women's side, chin to her chest, as if concentrating carefully on what the minister was preaching about. Once, she reached up and tucked a ringlet of honey blond hair that had slid loose back into her prayer cap. The gesture, one he had seen her do hundreds of times, brought Sol a bittersweet ache. The only time he saw her look across at the men's side was when Andy dropped his hymnal after nodding off, causing a startling bang when the heavy book hit the floor. Carrie raised her eye-brows at her brother in exasperation, then quickly looked at Esther, who was scowl-ing at Andy. Mattie, he noticed, had to bite her lip to keep from laughing.

On the other side of Mattie was Carrie's spinster stepsister, Emma, sitting with her chest lifted high, as if she'd just sucked in a deep breath and didn't dare let go. Sol's gaze drifted to Mattie. He had never noticed Mattie in church before, though of course she'd been there. She'd always been there. He saw that her eyes were closed and her face was lifted, her lips were moving si-lently, as if praying to God. He marveled at the depth of her faith, almost envying her. Watching her, he wondered how he had ever considered her plain. She looked so filled with joy and the glory of the Lord, she could have nearly burst with it.

As soon as the service was over, every-one poured outside to help set up for lunch. Sol saw Abel Miller make a beeline toward Carrie. She was lifting a tablecloth high in the air to spread over the table and didn't notice him until he was a few paces away. When she saw Abel, Sol's belly clenched with a sick dread.

She looks at him the way she used to look at me.

Nearly everyone ignored Sol, or kept conversations with him quick and to the point, even his friends. His mother asked when he was coming home, but when he hemmed and hawed, she turned away sadly.

He felt irritated with Mattie for encouraging him to come. She didn't understand what it felt like to have those you've known and loved all your life treat you with distance. They knew he was there, he felt their curious glances. But most acted as if he were a stranger they'd met once but couldn't remember who he was or why he was here.

And he wasn't even under the ban.

Afterward, it occurred to him that might have been the very reason Mattie had wanted him to attend.

14

Carrie returned to the farmhouse late one afternoon after taking the last of their frozen cider to the Zooks to sell at their Central Market stand. She tied Strawberry and his cart to the post and hurried inside to see if Emma had started dinner. She found a note from Emma on the kitchen table, saying she had gone on an errand and not to worry if she missed dinner.

"I wonder why she went to town so late in the day," Carrie said to Yonnie, after crumpling up the note. "Usually Emma will only go into town in the morning. She's always said that any Englisher who is drunk and hungover from the night before will still be asleep in the morning and off the streets."

Yonnie gave a slight smile. "Sounds like our Emma."

Carrie started making a batch of brownies for Andy's after-school snack. "Any idea where Abel went to?"

Yonnie looked baffled. "I don't recall him saying where he was going. Or when." She pressed her fist to her mouth, as if willing herself to remember. "I think Veronica McCall swooped in. Maybe she left with him. I think I nodded off."

Carrie glanced at her, a little worried. Yonnie had been sleeping an awful lot lately. Carrie noticed how thick and swollen her ankles were. Sometimes it seemed as if she was like a clock winding down. Carrie looked around the kitchen to see what Emma had started for supper, but she couldn't find any fixings. "Yonnie, what did Emma do today?"

Yonnie looked to the ceiling, as if the answer was written up there. "She was ironing her cap."

"Oh, Emma and those pleats," Carrie said, grinning. Making dinner would be up to her today. She went over to the refrigerator and opened it, loading up her arms with lettuce and cheese and hamburger meat. As she whirled around to set things on the counter, she happened to notice a curl of black smoke coming from the back of the barn, where Abel's workshop was. Her heart started to pound. Trying to sound calm, she said, "Yonnie, I'll be back in a minute."

Carrie flew out of the house and down to the back of the barn. First she tried to get into Abel's workshop but the door handle was too hot. She ran to the barn door and slid it open, as smoke poured out. She heard terrible noises inside, noises she knew would be etched forever in her mind: Schtarm's frightened neighing, Hope and her calf's bawls of panic. She unhooked Hope from her stanchion, pushed on her to back up and then led her out the door. Her calf had enough sense to trot behind her.

"Geh!" she screamed as she opened Schtarm's stall door, stepping back as the horse lunged forward and galloped out of the barn. The other stalls were empty. She could see flames lick the stacked hay bales and knew she had to get out. She tripped over a rope and tried to get to her feet, but bent over coughing and wheezing from the thick smoke. Her raw eyes ached. She felt her way out of the barn and gasped for fresh air.

Soon neighbors started to arrive, one after another, signaled by the smell of smoke in the air. Men and boys formed two bucket lines from the water pump, where Carrie pumped until her hands were raw with blisters. The fire department turned up the driveway and took over with their long hoses. Within an hour, the fire was extinguished, but all that was left were smoking timbers, blackened beams, stone and metal. She was amazed to see the waterwheel remained untouched.

Carrie stood there, stunned by a fire's power.

The deacon came up beside her. "Go on in the house, Carrie. Let Yonnie know all is well. A few of us will stay to make sure the fire is out." He shooed her away. "Go, get some salve on those hands."

As she turned to go inside, Andy rushed up the driveway on his scooter, his eyes wide and frightened. "Where are the horses? And Hope and Lulu?" he asked, staring at the fire truck.

"Strawberry's there," Carrie said, pointing to the frightened pony, still hitched to the post with his cart attached. "The others ran off, Andy, but they're not harmed. You might be able to find Hope and Lulu in the orchards. Maybe Emma could help you look for them when she returns." *Where was Emma, anyway? And where was Abel?*

"I'll help him," Abraham said.

Carrie went inside to assure Yonnie that the fire was out. Her nose and throat kept stinging and she couldn't stop coughing. She finally went upstairs to take a long shower, to get the ash out of her hair and smoke smell off of her body. It was dark when she heard Old-Timer trot the buggy up the driveway, Steelhead's motorcycle on its heels. From the bathroom window, she saw Emma step down slowly from the buggy, stunned, staring at the blackened hole where the barn used to be. "Die Scheier is ganz verbrennt," Emma kept saying, over and over, as if she couldn't believe her eyes. *The barn is completely burned.*

Steelhead looked like Carrie felt: dazed. He just stared at the smoldering barn site.

She saw Abraham walk up to them, so she closed the window and went to her room to lay on the bed, exhausted, just wanting to close her aching eyes for a moment. She put a cold cloth over her eyes to stop them from burning. At first she thought she was dreaming when she heard the clop of Schtarm's hoofbeats pound up the driveway. Awhile later, she woke again when she heard Abel's voice, calling out frantically to the men who remained around the blackened structure, asking where Carrie and Andy and Yonnie were and if all of the animals had been accounted for. Satisfied that they were all safe, she heard him holler, "What on earth has happened to the barn?" Drifting back to sleep, it struck her as strange that he didn't ask about Emma.

The next morning, Carrie was woken by a ray of sun that filtered through her window. She eased out of bed and pulled a fresh dress off of the peg, then stopped suddenly as her tender, blistered hands reminded her of yesterday's fire. Pinning her dress as quickly as she could, she peeked out the window and saw Abel and Abraham emptying out the carriage house. Abel didn't have his sling on, she noticed. She was relieved to see Hope and Lulu tied to stakes, munching hay. Her eyes wandered to the charred remains of the barn. She shuddered at the sight.

By the time Carrie went downstairs, nearly thirty Amish men had arrived. They walked carefully around the blackened structure, tapping on the timbers to see if any could be saved, raking through the ashes. Mattie was in the kitchen, having come over early to help with her father and brothers. She and Emma had prepared hot coffee and made cinnamon rolls, knowing neighbors would be coming soon. Even Esther had arrived; she was folding mayonnaise and chopped celery into a large bowl of shredded chicken to make sandwiches for lunch.

When Emma saw Carrie, she turned her hands over, looking at them, clucking like a mother hen. "Wie entsetzlich!" *How painful!* "Let me bandage them for you." Emma looked as if she hadn't slept well, her eyes were troubled and worried.

"Let me," Yonnie said. "I have some special ointment."

"They don't really hurt that much. I was so tired last night I hardly noticed," Carrie said, holding her palms up as Yonnie covered the blisters with ointment.

"Schtarm came back last night, all on his own," Emma said. "And Andy found Hope and Lulu in the orchards."

"The deacon decided to wait until spring planting is over to have a barn raising," Mattie said, stirring a batch of cookie dough, "so he thought the men could convert the carriage house for the animals. That's why we're all here today."

It warmed Carrie's heart to hear those words. Already, her neighbors were helping her move forward. Life was meant to be lived as it came. It wasn't their way to dwell on hardships; instead, they carried on.

As Yonnie finished wrapping the gauze around her hands, Carrie asked, "Emma? Where were you yesterday afternoon? And where was Abel?"

Emma's head snapped up. She shot a glance at Esther, then looked out the window at Abel. "He said to say he was awful sorry he wasn't here."

Carrie looked out the kitchen window. She saw Abel lugging a piece of lumber off of a wagon. Andy was alongside of him, chattering the whole time. "Yes, but Emma, where were—"

Just then, Yonnie started chanting, "Gottes willes, Gottes willes." When Carrie spun around to look at her, she saw Yonnie hugging her arms around her middle. Carrie's insides seized, knowing trouble was coming but not sure from which direction.

Not a minute later, a police car pulled up to the house. Carrie hurried out the kitchen door and down the steps to meet them, Emma and Mattie trailing behind her. Two police officers got out of the car, staring at what was left of the barn.

"Anybody hurt from the fire?" a beefy officer asked Carrie, a cluster of keys jingling from his belt.

She recognized him. It was Chief Beamer, the police officer who had told her that Daniel had been in an accident. She doubted he would remember her. To the English, the Amish looked as alike as peas in a pod. "No. My neighbors came and helped to put it out."

"Any idea how it started?" he asked her.

She shrugged. "Lightning, maybe."

Chief Beamer looked doubtful. "I don't remember any lightning yesterday. Do you, Jim?"

The officer named Jim shook his head. "Mind if we look around?"

Carrie cocked her head. "Why?"

The two policemen exchanged a look. "This is the second fire in this area in the last few months," the chief said. "We think they might have been set intentionally."

"Why would you think that?"

"Arson fires have a pattern. Splash patterns of flammable liquid, and they have multiple points of origin." He put his hands on his hips. "You just have to know what you're looking for."

The two officers went down to the burnt barn and walked around, examining the area where the fire started. They used some large pitchforks, turning ashes and smoking piles over.

"Found it," Chief Beamer yelled to the other policeman. He held up a burnt-out gasoline can. When he passed by Carrie to get to his car, he said, "We found the same can at the other fire."

Carrie's bandaged hands flew to her cheeks, shocked. "Who would do this? Why would anyone do this?"

Chief Beamer glanced around at the

men. "Any chance there's a fellow here named Abel Miller?"

"What do you want with Abel?" she asked, her heart pounding.

"Is he down there?" he asked her, pointing to the group of men surrounding the barn.

Carrie remained silent.

The chief looked at her as if he knew she wasn't going to help, then walked out in the yard and shouted out, "Abel Miller? Is there an Abel Miller here?"

Thirty Amish men stopped what they were doing and looked at the policeman. They looked at each other, a silent communication passing between them, until the deacon, standing in front of the carriage house, gave a nod.

A man, carrying a piece of lumber to give to Abraham, dropped the wood and said, "I am William Abel Miller."

Another fellow put his hammer down. "I'm One-Eyed Abe. Last name's not Miller but my wife's a Miller. Folks get my name mixed up all the time."

Two more men came forward, all claiming some variety of the moniker "Abel Miller." They weren't lying. It was their given name.

But Carrie knew what they were doing. They were caring for their own.

The chief and the other policeman looked bewildered. "Now, look—"

Abel had been watching the entire thing. He slid a board back onto the wagon and walked up to the policeman. "I think I'm the Abel Miller you're looking for."

Chief Beamer breathed a sigh of relief. "Can you tell us where you were yesterday afternoon?"

Abel shot a glance at Steelhead, standing nearby. "Out birding."

The chief looked confused. "You mean, hunting?"

He shook his head. "No. I was coming home and stopped to watch a flock of black ducks heading south over Blue Lake Pond. This time of year it's a highway in the sky, with all the migrating birds heading north. Kind of a flyway."

"Black ducks?" Abraham asked, stepping forward out of the group of Amish men, clearly interested. "Why, they're getting about as scarce out here as sunflowers in January."

The chief frowned at Abraham. "Anyone see you?"

"Don't you mean, can I prove it?" Abel asked.

"Yep," said the chief.

Abel turned his head to look at Esther, standing with her arms tightly crossed against her chest. Next to her stood Emma, hands clutched together as if she was praying. Then his gaze shifted to Carrie. When Abel's eyes met Carrie's, a current passed between them. He hesitated just a moment too long. "No. I guess I can't."

It was at that moment that Carrie knew Abel was lying. She knew it.

Chief Beamer took a step closer to Abel. "Then you'll have to come down to the station."

"On what charges?" Abel asked, chin lifted high.

"No charges yet. We've got some questions we want to ask you."

"Just because I wasn't here?"

"We got a tip that you've had a history with fires," Chief Beamer said. "And a little history with the law."

From behind her, Carrie heard Emma let out a gasp. The officer called Jim put a hand on Abel's shoulder to guide him into the back of the police car.

"No!" Andy shouted. "You can't do that to our Abel!"

Abraham gently put his hands on Andy's arms, then steered him up to Carrie. Andy threw his arms around Carrie's middle, as they watched the car with Abel, head held high, pass by them.

Emma met Carrie at the kitchen steps. "He didn't do it, Carrie. He would never do anything to hurt us."

Carrie brushed past her and went into the kitchen.

Emma followed behind. "Carrie, are you listening to me?"

Carrie picked up a rag and started rubbing clean the floury countertop where Emma had made the cinnamon rolls. "I heard you."

Emma grabbed Carrie's shoulders. "You know he's innocent, don't you?"

Carrie looked right at her. "Yes. I know."

Emma dropped her arms and looked at Carrie, puzzled.

"But I also know he is lying, and if I know Abel, that probably means he is protecting someone." Carrie put the rag on the counter and crossed her arms. "So who is he protecting, Emma? And why?"

"What I want to know," Mattie asked, leaning on the kitchen doorjamb with her arms crossed, "is who gave the police that tip?"

⁂

Sol had read about Carrie's barn burning in a newspaper at work that morning, but he didn't let on to Mattie that he knew when he met her for a walk at the pond in the late afternoon. He listened carefully as she filled him in on the details of the fire.

Then she added one little piece of information that he had missed—the actual day of the fire. For some reason, he thought it must have happened a few days ago, but Mattie said it happened yesterday. He should have read that newspaper article more carefully, he realized. His stomach made a slow, sickening twist.

"Something bothering you, Sol?" Mattie asked as they walked along the pond shore. "You're awful quiet."

He looked into Mattie's soft, kind eyes, then turned back to the pond, as still as glass. Like a stone thrown into the pond, he knew his words would disturb the calm, set into motion a rippling effect he couldn't stop. Mattie had always believed the best

in him, and now he was about to change
that.

He released a puff of air. "I told the police that Abel Miller set those barn fires."

He winced, bracing himself for her fury,
but nothing stirred behind those pale gray
eyes.

Then he felt a jolt that went straight
through him, as real as lightning.

Mattie knew! She knew what he had
done.

"It wasn't a lie, Mattie," he said quickly. "I
had some information about him. Something you don't know about. In Ohio, he had
gone to jail for killing some folks in a fire. I
thought he might try and hurt Carrie."

Yesterday afternoon, Sol was sent to City
Hall by the construction site manager to
pick up some building permits. As Sol left
City Hall, permits in hand, he noticed Abel
Miller run up the stairs as if he was late for
something. When Sol read about the fire
early this morning, the more he convinced
himself that Abel was responsible. It infuri-
ated Sol to think this man could cause harm
to his people, especially his Carrie. He
asked his boss if he could take an early
break and went straight to the police sta-

tion with a copy of that newspaper clipping that he kept in his wallet.

But Mattie had just told him that the fire had been started at about the same time he had seen Abel Miller at City Hall. She added that the police had already come to take Abel away. That was when his stomach started feeling it was twisting like a pretzel. As much as Sol distrusted Abel, even he knew there was no way the man could have been in two places at once.

Mattie's gray eyes showed her disappointment in him. They almost changed color, darkening to a smoky gray. Her eyes were like that, he'd learned. A weathervane for her feelings.

"Abel didn't kill anyone. Neither did Daniel. Not intentionally. Those Ohio fires were just a terrible accident. Carrie told me all about them." She explained to Sol about the kerosene containers contaminated with gasoline.

He felt a stinging heat in his chest and eyes. What had he done? What terrible blunder had he made? "I thought I was doing the right thing, Mattie. Everything pointed to Abel Miller. I was trying to help. You're always saying that if we love someone, we want the best for that person. I only want the best for Carrie."

A trace of color rose under Mattie's fair skin. "I also said only God knows the best for a person." She looked at a duck, skimming the surface of the pond. "Sometimes, I think you aren't as interested in Carrie as you are about winning." She marched up to the road, skirts swishing, and tossed over her shoulder, "Winning her back is like a game to you."

Sol took a few quick strides to catch up with her. "That's not true, Mattie!"

She stopped. "And since when have our people ever, *ever* judged another?" She stamped her foot. "You think you can banish anyone who doesn't fit in your scheme . . . like Daniel." She shook her head, disgusted. "And now Abel."

Sol felt as if she had knocked a punch to his solar plexus. So Carrie *had* told her about his visit on the day Daniel died. He had never brought it up to Mattie, hoping she hadn't known. She had a look on her face that suddenly panicked him, a bright, painful look that glittered in her eyes. Oh God, could he lose her too? When he reached out to her, she backed up and crossed her arms over her chest.

"Sol, you sit on the fringe, not Amish, not English, and you still think you can have everything you want." She wagged a finger at him like an angry mother. "Well, you can't!"

Sol's eyes went wide. "Mattie—"

"Don't Mattie me!"

"Please, Mattie. Calm down. Don't be mad. I'm not like you, Mattie. You . . . you're like a furrow, plowed straight and deep. You always knew right where you wanted to go, how you wanted to be. I'm trying, but it's just not that way for me. I'm not . . . strong like you." The words shocked him coming out as they did, without thought or premeditation, but he knew them to be true. He suddenly knew what was making his chest hurt. It was fear. It was nothing like he'd felt before. He felt a fear of never being able to make things right with the people he loved. He felt a fear of losing Mattie. He felt a fear of God turning his back on him.

He slid a cautious glance at Mattie and watched her eyes fill with a soft pity, stinging his pride, but he could see the fight slip away from her.

"Oh Sol," she finally said. She came close to him and wiped the tears off his cheeks with her palm. She smiled again, a warm, slow smile and the warmth of it spread down deep into Sol's chest. "Don't you understand? It's never too late to be the man you were intended to be."

❧

You have to know what you're looking for.

Those words of Chief Beamer kept echoing in Carrie's mind. She spent the afternoon poking through the ashes of the barn.

Emma came down to help. "What are we looking for?"

"Anything. Anything that might tell us how this fire started."

"Carrie," Emma started, looking worried, "maybe we should let the police handle this."

Carrie looked up. "I thought you didn't believe Abel could have set this fire? The police seemed pretty sure he did."

Emma bit her lip, then gave a quick nod

of her capped head, picked up a stick, and started looking.

Covered with gray ash, hands black with soot, Carrie was just about to give up the hunt when she found something. Something that split her heart down the middle.

Steelhead arrived, but before he could dismount from his motorcycle, Emma hurried to tell him Abel needed his help. She explained quickly what had happened and where Abel had been taken.

Steelhead winked at her. "Don't you worry, little muffin. I'll see what I can do."

The neighbors returned home to do their own chores after completing the work on the carriage house, but Esther and Abraham lingered and agreed to stay for dinner. When supper was ready, Carrie found Esther at the carriage house, giving Abraham, a man known for his skilled carpentry, suggestions about how to hammer the final hinges onto the gates.

"You've got the patience of a saint," Carrie whispered to Abraham as he packed up his toolbox, out of earshot of Esther.

His eyes smiled as he said, "Always good to have a supervisor."

The way he said it reminded her so much of something her father would have said that Carrie felt a sharp pang. Her father had such an easy way about him and never took offense. Not unlike Abel, she suddenly realized.

With everyone seated at the kitchen table, Abraham gave the signal to offer silent grace for the meal, just as Steelhead returned. Hanging tightly on behind him was Abel. Andy leaped up like a puppy to greet him, opening the door and bouncing down the kitchen steps. Abel wrapped an arm around Andy's shoulders and climbed the stairs to give everyone an awkward nod.

"I just wanted you all to know that I've been released. No charges." He and Steelhead stood by the door, tentatively, as if they weren't sure they would be welcomed.

"That is a great blessing," Abraham said, smiling warmly. "I could not understand why they thought you would have started a fire in your own barn, anyway."

"Carrie's barn," Abel said, glancing at Carrie. "And Andy's."

"Our barn," Yonnie interrupted. "These orchards belong to all of us."

"Sit," Abraham said, pointing to the empty chairs. "Eat with us."

Emma and Carrie rose to set places for Abel and Steelhead. Emma filled up two heaping plates of food while Carrie set the utensils at their places. Abel went to the sink to wash up. He looked at Carrie, a question in his eyes, but she turned away.

Abel and Steelhead sat down at the table and automatically bowed their heads. "Thank you, dear Jesus," Steelhead started. Emma and Carrie froze. "Thank you for setting free my brother Abel. Thank you for this fine meal made by these two fine women."

Carrie dropped her head into the palms of her hands.

"Thank you, sweet Jesus. We love you, Lord. Amen. Amen. Hallelujah." He popped his head up, grinning widely. He patted Abel on the back. "Chow time, little buddy."

Esther sat there stoney-faced, watching Steelhead. Tonight Carrie noticed that there were deep lines around her mouth and eyes, and the hair that showed from beneath her prayer cap was turning as gray as a winter day. She was still beautiful, Carrie thought, aware that her father had always thought so too. Emma, seated next to her mother, was in sharp contrast, as plain and plump as one of Yonnie's buttermilk biscuits.

Abraham smiled broadly. "So, Abel, tell us how it came to be that you were released."

Abel looked up, exchanging a glance with Steelhead. "Turns out Steelhead had seen me, during the time of the fire. So, I had an alibi, after all."

"It's the gospel truth, I did see him," Steelhead said, before shoveling a forkful of food into his mouth.

"You couldn't have thought to tell the police officers that piece of information when they asked?" Esther asked Abel.

The same thought occurred to Carrie.

"Isn't it wonderful that Abel is done with that nonsense?" Emma asked.

"Then just as Steelhead arrived, another fellow came in and said he had seen me in town yesterday afternoon. I think you all know him." Abel cast a sideways look at Carrie. "A fellow named Solomon Riehl."

Silence fell over the table. Finally, the deacon cleared his throat. "Emma, I'd like more of your wonderful chicken pot pie." He reached over to her with his empty plate. "And in a month's time, we will build a new barn. A farm is not a farm without its barn."

"So, Abel, with the workshop gone, where do you plan to live?" Esther asked, frowning.

"Right here, with us," Yonnie said, frowning right back at Esther.

Carrie put up a hand in warning. "Actually, he might prefer to stay with Steelhead for a while."

Abel kept his eyes on his plate.

"Good," Esther said, satisfied. "We should be going. Abraham, it's time for prayer." She bowed her head.

"Not yet, Esther," the deacon said.

Meekly, Esther lifted her head.

Abraham handed Esther the casserole. "Have another piece of your daughter's chicken pot pie. It's a fine dish."

"It sure is," Steelhead said as Emma's face flamed.

Esther and Abraham left soon after supper. Carrie made Andy take a bath to wash off soot and ash after being near the barn all day. The stench of sour smoke was everywhere. As she was gathering his dirty clothes to launder, she heard Yonnie's knees creak up the stairs and her door quietly close. Carrie listened for the roar of Steelhead's motorcycle to start up before she went downstairs, sure that Abel had left with him. But there he was, at the kitchen window, staring out at the place where the barn had been. He spun around when he heard her.

Carrie stiffened. "I thought I heard Steelhead leave."

Abel's smile dimmed. "He did. He, uh, took Emma out on a motorcycle ride."

Carrie's eyes went wide. Emma was starting to worry her a little.

Abel walked over to her. "Carrie, I'm sorry I wasn't here yesterday. If I had been here, the fire wouldn't have started." He looked at her bandaged hands. "Are your hands awfully sore?"

She put her hands behind her back. "Not so much. Yonnie put some ointment on them that helped."

"You believe me, don't you?" He took a step closer to her, searching her eyes. "You know I wouldn't have started the fire."

She brushed past him to start putting away the dishes that Emma had washed.

"Carrie, look at me!"

the air. "She tried kissing me that one time and I put an end to it!" He shook his head as if he couldn't believe what he was hearing. "I've been trying and trying to teach her about what it means to have a faith!"

Carrie rolled her eyes and crossed her arms tightly across her chest. "I've seen her coming out of your workshop once or twice, late at night."

"That's where I keep my Bible and books." He scratched his head. "At least, I did until the fire." He took a step closer to her and put his hands on her upper arms. "How is it everyone seems to know but you that I—"

A knock on the front door interrupted him. He sighed, dropped his arms, and went to answer it.

For a split second, Carrie worried Veronica McCall had arrived, but the visitor at the door was Grace. She followed Abel into the kitchen.

Carrie gasped when she saw her. "Your hair!" This time, it was purple.

Grace's hand flew to her hair. "What? Is it too much?"

"No, no," Abel said soothingly, pulling a

She stopped. "I know you didn't set th
fire, Abel." She put the dishes down a
fished something out of her apron pock
She opened her palm—there was Verc
ica McCall's little black clothespin c
phone.

Abel looked puzzled. He reached c
and picked up the cell phone. "Where c
you find this?"

"I spent the afternoon raking throug
the ashes in the barn."

He turned it over in his hand. "Do yc
know what this means?"

"I do." Her chin lifted a notch. "I kno
exactly what it means. You're trying to pr
tect Veronica McCall. Same way you trie
to protect Daniel."

He couldn't have looked more stunned
Carrie had clubbed him on the back of th
skull with a two-by-four. "Protect her?" H
took a few paces around the kitchen, rub
bing his jaw, thinking something out. Stop
ping with his hands on his hips, he sai
again, "You think I'm trying to *protect* Ve
ronica?" He threw his hands up. "What, you
think I'm sweet on her?"

"I've seen you in her car, kissing!"

"One time, Carrie." He held a finger ir

chair out for Grace. "It's very nice." He flashed a warning look at Carrie to stop staring at Grace's purple hair. "Carrie, why don't you sit down? Grace said she has something she wants to tell us."

Grace tossed her bulging backpack on the kitchen table. "Dang, that's heavy. I can't stay long. But I need to show you something."

"Did you bicycle here carrying that?" Carrie asked.

"Yup," Grace said, all business. She pulled out a big steel tube from her backpack, and a stack of papers.

"What's all this?" Carrie asked.

"When I heard about the fire," Grace said, "something just kept bugging me—like stuff wasn't adding up. Yesterday afternoon, Veronica came rushing into her office. She was acting kind of odd—I mean, she acts all ADD and OCD a lot, but this was even more so, like she'd overdosed on sugar—talking loud and saying hello to everyone. Like she wanted everyone to know she was there. She asked me what time it was. Twice, she asked, like she wanted me to remember. Then she closed her door to make a phone call, but she was in such a tizzy she forgot to close the back door. Her office has two doors. I heard her talking to someone to report a fire burning. I could have sworn I heard her give Carrie's address. Then she made another call—I heard her say something about a convicted arsonist named Abel Miller, violating his parole." She pulled out a stack of papers. "So this afternoon, I went online and printed out the telephone bill that had yesterday's call log. Busted!" She waved the bill in the air. "She made a call to the fire department to report the fire and to the police department to tell them about Abel." She handed Carrie the bills.

Carrie and Abel exchanged a glance.

"There's more." Grace reached down and pulled out a metal tube. "These are the properties adjacent to Honor Mansion, the very ones Veronica is chomping at the bit to buy." Popping the cap, she tipped it over and out rolled a set of architectural blueprints. "You need to see these." She unrolled the blueprints on the table—plans drawn for Bonnatt Company's golf course.

"Carrie," Abel said, pointing to one section. "Look at how they've incorporated the Stoltzfuses' land."

"Where their barn was before it was burned down," Carrie said.

"Yup," Grace said. "The Stoltzfuses sold those couple of acres to Veronica."

Carrie and Abel exchanged a look. When the Stoltzfuses' barn was rebuilt, it was built closer to the house, but it was a smart thing to do. A good opportunity to move it, in fact. That original barn was so far from the house that a street ran between the house and barn. Abner and Ada had always complained about their barn's location.

"The Stoltzfuses never knew about the golf course," Grace explained. "Veronica gave them twice as much as it was worth and they wanted to help their son in Indiana buy a farm." Her cheeks went pink. "I, uh, happened to be eavesdropping when they were in Veronica's office." She pointed to another area on the blueprints. "Look here."

Grace pointed to surrounding properties, neighbors to Cider Mill Farm. "They're going to need a few other chunks of Amish farmland too." She put her finger on Cider Mill Farm's property. "Now look at your farm."

The golf course incorporated *all* of Cider Mill Farm. It was as plain as day.

"Grace, did you take these from Veronica's office?" Abel asked.

"Yup, and I need to get them back before she returns to the office later. She's at a business dinner with Bonnatt tonight." She rolled the papers up again. "I don't know what you want to do with this information, but I knew I had to get it to you."

"Thank you, Grace," Carrie said.

Grace bit her lip. "There's one more thing." The anxious tone in her voice made Carrie and Abel look up sharply. "I'm sunk if I lose my job. I still have court fees to pay from the accident and I'm still on probation and if I get fired, then—"

"Not to worry," Abel said. "We won't involve you."

After Grace left, Abel came back into the kitchen, shaking his head.

Carrie sat at the kitchen table, leaning on her elbows. "Could this be true? Would Veronica McCall do such a thing?"

"Could and would." He sat down in the chair across from her. "The deacon said something tonight that made it all so clear.

He said, 'A farm is not a farm without its barn.' Get rid of the barns and you have an easier time getting rid of the farmers." He leaned back in his chair. "She knew enough about the Amish to know that."

Abel was deep in thought, drumming his fingers on the tabletop. His fingers froze. "And someone had tipped the police off that I had done jail time for fires. It's like Veronica knew just enough to try to pin the fires on me. The police were talking about holding me for forty-eight hours—and calling my parole officer in Ohio because I would be violating parole even if they didn't press charges. In the nick of time, Steelhead came in, but they weren't too impressed with an alibi provided by another ex-con. But then Solomon Riehl and Mattie came in and the police decided two witnesses cleared me."

Mattie was with Sol? Carrie felt her mouth go dry. Emma had told Carrie she had seen Sol at Central Market, hanging around Mattie's stall, nearly every time she worked there lately.

Abel started drumming his fingers again. "But how could Veronica possibly have known why I had been in jail? I never told her any of that. I never even told her I'd *been* in jail."

Distracted, Carrie was only half listening, then the full sense of what Abel just said struck her. "Oh Abel, I told her!" She swallowed hard, and told him about the day in Veronica's office when she asked her to look up Abel Miller on the computer. "I'm sorry. I had a dreadful feeling about that as I left her office."

He raised an eyebrow as he listened, then gave a slight shake of his head. "It's not a secret. It would've been easy for her to find information."

Abel and Carrie disagreed about what to do next. They went back and forth, but Carrie wouldn't budge. "I won't do it, Abel. It's not our way to seek vengeance."

"I'm talking about justice, not vengeance."

"How many times have we said the prayer, 'Not my will but thine be done'?"

Abel threw up his hands. His voice had an edge of impatience to it. "Carrie, if we don't stop her, she'll just do it again. You saw those blueprints. She's after more land.

How many more people have to lose their barns?"

Carrie knew he was right; Veronica Mc-Call wouldn't quit. She stood up and went to gaze out the kitchen window, crossing her arms. "It's not our way, Abel. We don't pick and choose how and when we trust in God. We either trust him or we don't." She surprised herself, saying those words, but she knew she believed them to be true.

Abel leaned forward, kneading his strong hands together. He was quiet for a full minute, and then he rubbed his hand over his face. He stood and took a few strides toward her, his hands hooked on his hips. "Du machst mich ferhoodled." *You make me crazy.*

Her eyes met his and held just a beat too long, and before she realized what was happening, he leaned toward her and his lips, so soft and warm, found hers. She thought she might be dreaming, even as she felt the grip of his strong arms slip around her waist. He kissed her with such sweetness it was almost unbearable, a kiss that lasted forever and was over too soon.

Abel pulled away first and looked into her eyes, whispering, "I was trying to tell you something before Grace arrived: why is it everyone seems to know how I feel about you . . . except for you?"

Just as he was about to kiss her again, she heard Steelhead's motorcycle. By the time Emma had climbed off the motorcycle and came up the stairs to the kitchen door, Abel was already opening it for her. Her eyes darted from Abel's to Carrie's, sensing the tension in the air, as if they were angry.

"What's happened? What did Abel say?"

Abel's lips tightened. He adjusted the brim of his black felt hat. "Nothing. Nothing at all." He paused at the door, before giving a nod to Carrie. "It's been a long day. Sleep well, Carrie."

Carrie closed the door behind him. She could still feel Abel's lips on hers, his arms holding her tightly. Slowly, she turned around, then did a double take.

"Emma? Wu is dei Kapp?" *Where is your cap?*

15

A few days after the fire, Carrie took Andy
and Yonnie in the buggy over to the Stolztfuses'. It was a warm spring day and Andy
was eager to see their new colt, born just
a day before. After lunch, Ada Stoltzfus
shooed Carrie off.

"You go on home. I'm sure you have lots
to do. I'll have Abner bring Yonnie and Andy
back later today, after we have a good visit."
She handed Carrie a few jars of home-
made raspberry jam. Carrie smiled, accepting her kindness.

Carrie was eager to go; she had plenty of
chores waiting for her back at Cider Mill

Farm. She saw Abel working in the carriage house, so she left Old-Timer tied to the hitching post and hurried to the house to start dinner. Ever since that kiss in the kitchen, she had been taking pains to avoid being alone with Abel. As she hung up her bonnet on the peg, she heard a strange noise coming from Emma's room. Cautiously, she tiptoed upstairs and opened Emma's door. In the bed were Emma and Steelhead. Carrie backed up and knocked into the wall. Steelhead and Emma looked up, horrified.

Carrie ran downstairs and outside and burst through the open door of the carriage house, shouting Abel's name.

He dropped Old-Timer's water bucket and spun around fast. "What's happened?"

Carrie was breathing hard, in such a state that she couldn't speak, which only alarmed Abel more.

"What's wrong?"

She put the palm of her hand against her pounding heart, as if to quiet it. She couldn't move, couldn't breathe. "It's . . . it's . . . Steelhead is in . . . bed!"

Abel looked at her as if she were speaking another language.

She took a gulpy breath. "With Emma!"

The kitchen door banged open and out flew Steelhead, running toward the carriage house. He had dressed hastily and forgotten his shirt and shoes altogether. He was still putting one arm into a coat.

"Carrie!" Steelhead shouted, hopping on the gravel driveway as if it were made of hot coals. "It's not what you think!"

She whirled around to avoid looking at Steelhead's hairy chest, embroidered with another large tattoo. "Steelhead, what have you done?" she asked, her voice breaking. "How could you do such a thing?"

"I couldn't help it," Steelhead sputtered. "Emma is, well, she's like no other woman I've ever met."

Carrie spun around, then covered her eyes. "Zip your coat!" Muffled from behind her hands, she asked, "How could you take . . . advantage . . . of my sister?"

Steelhead put up his hands in warning. "I didn't! I would never hurt Emma." He took a deep breath. "I did right by her. We got married. We got our license, the other day, at the county courthouse." He gave Abel a guilty look. "We waited three days, like the law says to do, then this morning we went to the Amish-Mennonite preacher in town, to get married. Proper-like. In the eyes of God."

Carrie reached a hand against the beam, feeling as if she was nearly going to pass out. Abel's arm encircled her waist, supporting her, as he led her to sit on a hay bale.

Steelhead came closer. "I love her, Carrie. From the minute I saw her, I knew. This was the only girl in the world for me."

Carrie looked at Abel. "Did Yonnie give him her tea?"

Abel shook his head. "I don't think so. He's telling the truth. He's been crazy about her since the day he met her."

Carrie's shoulders sagged. "Steelhead, Emma is . . . she's Amish!"

Steelhead nodded. "I know. I know. We have a few things to figure out."

"A few things to figure out?" Carrie put her hands against her head; she couldn't believe what she was hearing. "She's broken her vows to the church. She'll lose everything."

Steelhead looked uncomfortable, but unconvinced. "We'll work it out." He crossed his large arms over his chest. "I've never felt like I belonged to anyone before meeting Emma. The times I've spent sitting in your kitchen, talking to her, getting to know her, I knew—we both knew—we belonged together."

Carrie stood to face Steelhead, astounded. "If you truly loved her, *why* would you . . . *how* could you . . . take everything meaningful from her?"

Steelhead looked dazed, stumped. He scratched his head, as if he hadn't thought that deeply in a long time. Slowly, he turned to head back to the house, then stopped. "We were going to tell you, Carrie. In fact, Emma was coming to tell you what we'd done, but that barn fire kind of threw us for a loop. Then Emma didn't want to tell you, on account of that little police problem with Abel, then Esther was here . . ." Steelhead snorted. "And she's a little scary. Even for me." He zipped up his coat, as if he suddenly realized he was barechested. "We came back to tell you today, but when we got here, no one was around, and then . . . well, our passion just overtook us."

Carrie clapped her hands over her ears

as Abel made a cutting motion at his throat, trying to warn Steelhead to stop talking.

Steelhead dropped his head. "Won't you at least come and talk to Emma? She's awful upset you found us like that. You mean the world to her, Carrie."

As Steelhead turned and left, Carrie plopped back on the hay bale. "Abel Miller, did you know about this?"

An awkward look covered Abel's face. She knew that guilty look on his face meant he was hiding something. Carrie fixed her gaze on him and sure enough, he just started spilling.

"I went to City Hall to try and stop them, Carrie. I knew what they had planned and I felt responsible, bringing Steelhead here. They were determined to go through with it. Emma was just as determined as Steelhead. But it wasn't my place to tell you." He paused. "That's why I couldn't tell you where I'd been."

She crossed her arms, still glaring at him. "Just how many more secrets are you keeping?"

He stiffened. "Don't go throwing stones, Carrie. You know as well as anybody how secrets get started."

She looked at him, puzzled.

"Planning to leave with Solomon Riehl was no small secret."

Her cheeks flushed, stung by his words. Yet he wasn't wrong. How many times did she lecture Andy about the seed of deceit beginning with an untruth? How often did she remind him that an untruth grows, so quickly, so quickly, into a lie?

For a long time, neither of them spoke. Then Abel sat down next to her on the hay bale, so close she could smell the faint scent of detergent on his clothes. "Aw, Carrie, she loves him. He loves her."

"Her way of life is as different from his as cheese from the moon. It isn't as simple as falling in love, Abel."

"Maybe it is," he said. "Maybe it should be."

Then a thought, a ray of hope, cut through the fog. "Maybe . . . maybe Steelhead could go Amish."

Abel looked at her as if she had lost her mind. "And give up his motorcycle?"

"A motorcycle is easier to give up than a family." Her voice dropped to a whisper. "Would it be so awful bad to go Amish?"

He shrugged. "Expecting an English guy,

especially one like Steelhead, to go Amish would be, well, it would be like asking Schtarm to be a buggy horse."

She covered her face with her hands.

He pulled her hands away from her face. "Would it be such a terrible thing to go English?"

Carrie looked him straight in the eyes. "You know the answer to that. She'll lose everything she holds dear. She'll be shunned, like she doesn't even exist anymore." She shuddered.

"So it's better that she end up alone, or with an Amish fellow she doesn't even love, than marry a man she does love? They share the same faith, Carrie, the same beliefs. They just express them in a different way."

Carrie knew he wasn't talking about Emma and Steelhead anymore, but she hadn't meant to get into that particular territory. She still hadn't sorted it all out. Each time her mind drifted to that kiss, which was often . . . oh, that sweet, sweet kiss . . . it made her feel lightheaded and her stomach all dizzy, just like she felt as a girl when she swung too high on a tree swing.

She pulled her hands out of his and stood to leave. "Maybe that's what the will of God might be for her."

He stood, facing her. "Is that really how it seems to you?"

"For the Amish, that's the way it is."

They stared at each other, a standoff. The silence between them was as thick as blackstrap molasses.

"She hasn't lost everything." Abel picked up Old-Timer's water bucket. "She has him."

The sound of wheels churning up gravel made them both turn their heads toward the road. Esther and Abraham rolled up the driveway in a wagon. Seated between them was Yonnie. Andy sat in the back on top of a bale of hay.

"Abraham brought some hay for your animals. On the way, we stopped for pecan pie at the Stolztfuses' stand and saw Yonnie and Andy, so we gave them a lift," Esther said, helping Yonnie ease out of the buggy. "Ada insisted we bring a pie for you too."

Carrie glanced at the house and saw Emma peering out the kitchen window, a stricken look on her round face. Then

Steelhead came up behind her. A cold chill shuddered through Carrie.

❧❧

The next day, Abel found Carrie hanging sheets on the clothesline. He picked up some clothespins and handed them to her. "Carrie, we still have a problem we need to take care of."

She glanced at him and took a clothespin out of her mouth to speak. "Which problem would *that* be, Abel? My sister, marrying your English friend? Or my barn burning down?"

Ignoring her, he handed her a wet sheet. "I think we need to go to the police and tell them you found Veronica McCall's telephone at the fire site."

She pinned the sheet to the clothesline. "No."

"Why not? What's wrong with just telling them?"

"Vengeance belongs only to God."

"Who's talking about vengeance? I'm talking about justice."

"I won't judge another person. It's not our way."

"Carrie, I'm just talking about telling the truth." He rubbed his face, exasperated.

Then he dropped his hands and hooked them on his hips. He was studying her as if he didn't quite know what to make of her. "Is it so wrong to want to stop her from doing this to anyone else?" He took a step closer to her and lifted her chin so that she would look at him. "Is it, Carrie?"

❧❧

Abel's words rankled her. As Carrie went about her chores that day, she prayed to God about what to do with Veronica McCall. By early afternoon, an idea came together in her mind. She felt in her heart it was the right thing to do, that God had given her this plan, but she knew she had to do it alone. She wanted to keep Abel out of this. This was between Veronica McCall and her. So she waited until she knew Abel had gone birding with Andy. She threw on her cape, put the black clothespin cell phone in her apron pocket, and hitched up the buggy to go to Honor Mansion.

When she arrived, she stood at the open door of Veronica McCall's office. "A farm is not a farm without its barn," Carrie said, in a voice so steady it could not be her own.

Veronica's eyes lit up. "So you're ready to sell?"

Carrie sat down in the chair across from her. "That's not what I meant. Do you remember I told you that Amish proverb, the very first time we met?" She placed the black clothespin cell phone on the desk in front of Veronica.

Veronica's eyes went wide in shock. Then she got up and closed the door to her office. "Where did you find this?"

"In the remains of the barn at Cider Mill Farm. I spent the day raking through the ashes. Just when I was about to give up, I found that."

She reached across the desk to grab it, but Carrie closed her fist around it. "I must have left it there when I was visiting Abel."

Carrie fixed her eyes on her.

"What?" Veronica asked. She snorted. "You couldn't possibly be insinuating that I set that fire."

Carrie held her gaze, then Veronica dropped her eyes. "You can't prove anything. A lost telephone earpiece does not implicate me."

"No, not alone, but a number of things put together do." Out of her apron pocket,

Carrie fished the page about Abel's arrest that she had printed for her, months ago. She unfolded it and set it before Veronica. "It even has the date that you printed it." She pointed to the top of the page.

"That's not much to go on."

"Your phone records show that you made calls to the fire department about fifteen minutes after the Stoltzfuses' fire had been set and then fifteen minutes after the Cider Mill Farm fire."

A stain of color spread across Veronica's sharp cheekbones. "That's outrageous! How dare you accuse me of such lies!"

"Not lies." She pulled out both sets of phone bills that Grace had given her, one from Veronica's cell phone company, the other from Honor Mansion's telephone service.

"Where did you get these?" Veronica asked, eyes narrowed in suspicion.

Carrie chose to deflect that. "There's one more thing. Yonnie saw your car at the house around three o'clock. She was in the kitchen and saw you go into the barn. Then she fell asleep and didn't see you leave." She looked at Veronica. "But she did place you at the site, at just the right time. And the police said a woman gave an anonymous tip about the fire and about Abel Miller setting it. So even though one piece of evidence alone isn't much, put it all together and it's a convincing picture. Like a puzzle, all filled in."

Veronica stared at Carrie, furious, bested. "What is it you want?"

Carrie took the paper and folded it up again. "Nothing."

Veronica raised an eyebrow in suspicion.

"It's not my place to judge you, Veronica McCall. I've made plenty of mistakes myself." She took a deep breath and looked Veronica straight in the eyes. "I forgive you. For burning my barn."

The only evidence of nervousness that Veronica showed was of a pencil, twiddling back and forth in her hand. Other than that, she remained still.

"But if anything else were to happen, I will go to the police. It wouldn't be right of me to let you continue to hurt people. Innocent people." Carrie slipped that paper back into her apron for safekeeping, then lifted her eyes to meet Veronica's. "I forgive you, but I don't trust you."

Veronica stood and walked to the window, crossing her arms tightly against her chest.

Carrie rose to leave and was almost to the door when she turned back. "I just don't understand why you would harm Abel. He's been so good to you."

"Sure you do." Veronica spun around. "You're nobody's fool, Carrie."

As Carrie's hand turned the door handle, Veronica's voice dropped to a whisper, almost a hiss. "He treats you like spun sugar."

Keeping her hand on the handle, Carrie lifted her chin a notch. "I know."

Veronica's eyes hardened. "I don't think I've given you enough credit."

And I might have given you too much, Carrie thought as she closed the door behind her.

❧❧

When Carrie returned to the farmhouse from Honor Mansion, she found Emma and Steelhead in the kitchen, seated at the table, looking solemn. Emma's suitcase was at her side.

Carrie took a deep breath. "Where's Andy and Abel?" she asked, hoping to stall what she knew was coming.

Steelhead answered. "Abel is down in the carriage house with the little dude."

Carrie looked at Emma's nervous hands, wringing her handkerchief. "Have you told Yonnie?"

Emma wiped her eyes with her hand-kerchief. "She's upstairs, resting. She said she'll miss me, but she won't be pointing a long bony finger in judgment at me. She said that she's a sinner too, of the worst kind, and she's too old to worry about shunning. She said I'd be getting plenty of that from . . . the others."

From Esther, Yonnie meant. Carrie hung her cape and bonnet on the peg. "Does Abel know you're leaving today?"

Steelhead nodded. "Just so you know, Abel tried to talk us out of it."

"So he said." Carrie pulled out a chair and sat down.

"This morning we fixed up a back room in the carriage house for Abel to stay."

"Where are you and Emma going to live?"

Emma blew her nose loudly. "Over in town. I'm going to start a quilt shop with my savings from work at Central Market." She looked at Carrie with pleading eyes.

"You could stop by. Yonnie said she would come."

Carrie's eyes dropped to her lap. She wasn't sure how to answer her. She needed time to sort it out.

Tears leaked down Emma's cheeks. "And Seymour"—she nodded her head toward Steelhead—"found a job as a sanitation engineer."

"Seymour?" Carrie asked, trying to hold back a grin in spite of the seriousness of the moment. She looked at Steelhead. "Your name is Seymour?"

Steelhead looked sheepish. "Yeah." He squeezed Emma's hand. "Carrie, I want you to know that I love Emma and just want her to be happy."

Carrie pressed her hands against her temples. "If you love her so much, then why won't you go Amish?"

Emma and Steelhead exchanged a glance.

"I offered," Steelhead said. "She said no."

Carrie looked at her, stunned. "Emma?"

"You know it's nearly impossible for the English to go Amish, Carrie. Steelhead would be miserable being Plain. Look at how our Abel is struggling. He's been living with Plain folks for years, off and on, and he can hardly string two words together of the dialect to make any sense. I can't do that to Seymour." Emma blew her nose. "Oh Carrie, this is my chance at love. A real, true, heartfire love. You know what I'm talking about."

Carrie did. She knew.

Emma squeezed her hands together. "I hope you'll forgive me. I know I've disappointed you, but I feel peace in my heart that I'm not disappointing God." Emma took a letter out of her apron pocket and handed it to Carrie. "Would you give this to Mother?"

Carrie closed her eyes. "No, Emma."

"Please, Carrie, please." Emma was nearly begging, her voice teary.

Carrie shook her head. "I can't. Esther should hear this from you. She deserves that."

"She's right, cupcake," Steelhead said. "It's just what I've been telling you. We'll go right over and tell her together."

Emma looked as if she was about to face the firing squad. As Carrie handed the envelope back to her, Emma grabbed her for a hug. Then Steelhead wrapped his large arms around the both of them, squeezing the breath out of them before releasing them.

"We'd better hit the road, lambchop," he said to Emma.

As they climbed onto the motorcycle, Abel and Andy came out of the barn to say goodbye. Just as Steelhead started the engine, Abel pulled Andy by the shoulders to get him out of the way. Emma took off her prayer cap and her apron and handed them to Carrie.

Her eyes blurry with tears, Carrie said, "I'm going to keep these for you, Emma, just in case you change your mind. You can *always* change your mind and repent and be forgiven by the church. Remember that." Then she gave Emma one last hug.

Carrie, Abel, and Andy followed the motorcycle down the driveway and watched it roar down the road until it disappeared from sight.

"You okay?" Abel asked Carrie.

Carrie looked at the cap and apron in her hands. "She's my favorite sister."

Abel smiled. "I know," he said, slipping her a handkerchief.

Then a thought jolted Carrie and stopped her tears. Even if she felt confused and heartsick about shunning her own sister, she knew Esther wouldn't think twice. "I'm guessing Esther will be rounding the corner into this driveway with a new helper by sundown."

Color drained out of Abel's face. Carrie felt the same way.

Andy, who had seemed stoic about Emma's leaving, glared at Abel accusingly. "I suppose you'll be leaving next."

Abel looked taken back. "What makes you say that?"

"Emma told me you fixed it so the house belongs to Carrie and me."

Abel and Carrie exchanged a glance.

"Yeah. That's what I figured," Andy said, running off before Abel could answer.

❧

Within a few hours after Emma left Cider Mill Farm, Esther's buggy clattered into the driveway. Seated next to her was Clara, a cousin thrice removed, tall, thin, and unhappy. "Clara will help you now," Esther said in a voice that had a vinegar tang to it.

Scarcely nodding at Carrie, Clara took

He stopped so abruptly at the door- that Andy, following close behind, ly ran into him.

hould I get an ambulance?" Abel d Carrie.

ee, nee," Yonnie whispered. "No hos- I need to make something right be- pass."

oticing how frightened Andy looked, e said quietly, "Go milk the cow." e boy's wide-eyed gaze jerked to the ow that faced the carriage house, back to her. "But I already did." o," Carrie said firmly, pointing to the "Take Clara with you." She shut the behind him, whisper-soft, as Abel knelt e Yonnie's bed, holding her hands in

nnie's voice came out in little puffs. sin . . . is like a cancer that spread choked our family."

el gently kissed her hands. "Yonnie, se—"

et me say it." She closed her eyes as thering strength. "The kerosene, con- ated with gasoline. Daniel didn't do e thought he did, but he didn't." She a deep breath. "I did it."

her bag up to Emma's empty room and started to unpack.

"She's the one who's allergic to every- thing, isn't she?" Carrie asked miserably. "Maybe I could find someone else."

"For now, she stays," Esther said, cast- ing a mutinous look at Abel.

Carrie took a deep breath. "I just found out about Emma, Esther, same as you."

Esther stiffened her spine at the mention of Emma's name. Adhering to the Ordnung, she would never again utter her name. "But he knew." She gave a brief nod in Abel's direction.

"Yes, ma'am, I knew," Abel said.

Arms akimbo, Esther glared at Abel. "This is your doing. Your English Bible, your talk about God being bigger than being Amish. Emma—" she shuddered, "—she told me about the things you've said. You turned her thinking inside out."

That wasn't true, Carrie knew that. Abel looked pained, but he didn't defend him- self nor did he back away. He just let Es- ther say her piece.

"And how long until you convince my Carrie to leave?" Esther glanced over at

Andy, standing next to Abel. "And take my Andy with her?" And then, to Carrie's shock, Esther's eyes started to well up with tears. Embarrassed, she turned to leave.

Carrie's heart swelled with an unexpected softness toward Esther. In her own brittle way, she realized, Esther loved them. She had lived her life hanging on to tight rules and didn't know what to do when those rules didn't work.

Carrie ran to her buggy to stop her before she left. "Andy and I aren't leaving, Esther. We're staying right here. I won't take him from you. You can count on that."

With one leg hoisted on the buggy step, Esther stopped and gave a quick nod. She reached a hand out to grasp Carrie's and gave it a light squeeze. Then, she lifted herself up onto the buggy seat, her face all stern and stiff again, and slapped the horse's reins.

Carrie watched her go, realizing she had just come to a final decision. She turned around to face Abel. Their eyes locked, filled with unspoken thoughts, then his gaze fell away from hers and he returned to the barn.

❦❦

A week to the day after Er nie didn't come downstairs when she usually did. Carrie of her favorite hot tea and s stairs to give it to her. Not a she heard him scream.

Carrie hurried upstairs to side and could see that she v Her breath sounds were lab spasmodic. Her skin was co blue. Carrie reached for her thin as tissue.

Yonnie grasped Carrie need . . . Abel." Her face w tired and tense.

It was the tension on her ried Carrie the most. She was dying; she recognized t she'd never seen an Amish with their face tense and t with peace.

"Get Abel," Carrie told A the carriage house." She turr "Hush, now. Don't talk. Save He'll be here soon."

Yonnie's labored breathing in the somber room until a d and Abel rushed up the sta

He raised his head, startled. "You? But how?"

Tears leaked out of the corners of Yonnie's eyes. "I needed gasoline for the washing machine."

Abel stared at her, his eyes wide open, unblinking. "Yonnie, what are you getting at?"

"I found a red can in the barn with some gasoline still in it. I was coming back to the house and heard the phone ringing in the shed." She took another deep breath, gathering strength. "Cousin Miriam was on the phone, calling about Daniel and Katie's wedding. We gabbed a long time."

Abel's expression on his face grew absolutely still.

"I must have put the can on top of the containers when I picked up the phone. When I hung up with Miriam, I noticed the can was on its side. But nothing had spilled. Oh Abel, I was sure nothing spilled out."

He was silent for a moment, then quietly said, "The spilled gas would have evaporated."

Yonnie was panting, sucking in great gasps of air like she was drowning. She pressed her hands to her cheeks. "Lieber

Gott, I didn't know what I'd done. Not till later that day, after Daniel had come back and delivered the kerosene to the neighbors. And then, the fires." She shuddered. "By the time I realized what had happened, the police were all over the farm. I was so frightened. That night, I tried to tell Eli. I tried, but I couldn't. And then it was too late."

"Yonnie . . ."

She put up a hand, heavy and swollen at the knuckles, to stop him. "Things started happening so fast. There wasn't time to think. Oh, to lose Eli's Lena, and Daniel's Katie, all at once. Four funerals, four funerals in one week. And next thing I knew, you and Daniel and Eli were standing before the judge. The longer I waited, the harder it got to tell the truth." She drew in a draught of air. "And then off you took yourself to jail. And still I didn't tell. I let my sweet Daniel think he was responsible." She gave out a gasp, as if in pain. "Oh Abel, I am the worst of sinners. The Lord God will punish me."

Abel dropped his head. His fists were clenched tight, but he remained silent. Carrie could see the pulse beating in his neck, fast and hard.

"Tell her, Abel," Carrie said softly but firmly, kneeling down beside him, resting her hand on his back. "Tell her you forgive her. You've got to let her know."

Time was running out. Yonnie's confession had sapped her energy and she was fading. Carrie saw the signs of approaching death—skin as thin as crepe paper, shallow gasps, a slowing pulse.

"Abel, we know, both of us, how secrets get started. You said it yourself . . . that we have no business throwing stones. Don't let her down the way . . . ," Carrie's voice broke on the words, ". . . don't disappoint her the way I let my Daniel down. Tell her you forgive her."

Her words fell into an empty silence. Slowly Abel lifted his head and Carrie thought he was going to speak, but then he dropped his chin to his chest.

Somebody had to do *something*. The only prayer Carrie ever said aloud was the Lord's Prayer, but she felt the need to speak what was on her heart, like Abel always did, as if the Lord God himself was standing beside her.

Carrie placed one hand over Yonnie's,

and one hand over Abel's. "Um, dear God in heaven, none of us deserve your forgiveness, but still, we're asking for it. We're hoping for it. Please have mercy on our Yonnie. She made a mistake, a dreadful mistake, and she's sorry. She's so very sorry. Please, God, have mercy. Amen."

As soon as Carrie finished, Yonnie inhaled deeply, as if filling up her lungs, then exhaled, a sigh of great relief.

One moment Yonnie was there, and the next she was not.

Abel fell on his grandmother's still chest and wept for all that had died with her, heartbreaking cries that Carrie knew would heal him in the end.

If only Daniel could have heard this truth, she thought, stroking Abel's back. If only he could have wept like Abel was weeping. If only Daniel could have known that grief was meant to heal.

16

Abel and Andy, quiet and solemn, went birding for the afternoon. As soon as the undertaker arrived for Yonnie's body, Carrie told Clara she'd be gone for a long while, and she went straight to Mattie's house. If Yonnie's passing had taught her anything, it was not to wait on important things.

One of the Zook boys opened the kitchen door when he saw Carrie marching up to it.

"If you're looking for Mattie, she's upstairs," he said, eating a sandwich.

Carrie took the stairs two at a time, just

as she had when they were girls. She found Mattie in her bedroom, whipping a sheet in the air, letting it float over the bed. Standing across the bed from her, Carrie pulled the sheet taut, tucking it into the corners.

"Yonnie died this morning."

Mattie froze. Her eyes went wide with shock. Slowly, she sat down on top of the bed.

Carrie sat next to her and told her about Yonnie's confession, choking up as she spoke about Daniel. Mattie listened carefully, wiping away tears with a handkerchief.

"I need to go, Mattie, there's so much to do to get ready for Yonnie's viewing. But first, there's something I have to ask you."

"Anything," Mattie said. "How can I help?"

"I need to find Sol. How do I get in touch with him?"

Mattie closed her eyes and moved her lips silently, as if whispering a prayer, then opened them as she slipped off the bed. "I'll get his address."

Carrie took the bus into Lancaster to Sol's apartment. She had never been to that particular part of town before; she felt apprehensive, but she knew she needed to see him. She held the piece of paper that Mattie had written on and looked for the apartment number on it. She knocked on 13B and took a step back. Sol opened the door, looking as if he had just walked in the door from work, still in blue jeans and a dirty T-shirt and work boots.

For a long moment, he blinked a few times, as if he thought he was dreaming. Then he swallowed, and opened wide the door. "Carrie, come in."

Carrie looked around the dingy apartment. She thought she saw cockroaches scurry out of an empty pizza box.

"Do you want to sit down?" Sol asked tentatively, tucking his shirt into his blue jeans, looking around to see if there was an empty place to sit.

She shook her head. "No. I need to get back soon. I just came to tell you something."

His eyes flew to meet hers.

"You asked me to forgive you," she said, her voice shaking. "You asked me several times. I'm sorry I didn't offer it to you." She folded her hands against her stomach. "It was wrong of me to hold on to that anger.

It hurt you and it hurt me and it wasn't fair to Daniel. And it just . . . it's no way to live." She looked up at him. "I forgive you. I'm not mad at you anymore. That's all. That's all I came to say."

Sol's eyes started to swim. "I don't know what to do, Carrie. Tell me. Tell me which way to turn." He looked as if his very soul ached, as if he had finally come to the end of burnt-out solitude.

In all the years she had known Sol, she had never seen him look helpless. Her every memory of him was marked by his sure smile and his confident way of handling whatever life threw at him. He looked so hurt, so frightened and broken, and she couldn't bear it. She felt something turn over in her chest.

"All that I can tell you is that I'm not afraid of God anymore. There's peace in my heart. I don't feel God's finger wagging at me. I had that part of knowing God all mixed up. But the past is the past. What's done is done. I don't want you feeling bad about it. I'm grateful for the life God has given me." She looked deeply into his eyes, hoping he understood.

Sol reached out for her hand. Carrie

smiled, a sweet conciliation, and put her hand in his.

※

Within a few days, a funeral service was held for Yonnie. Emma and Steelhead came to the cemetery, standing at a distance, on the edge. Carrie noticed that Emma still wore Plain clothes but her prayer cap was absent. Carrie exchanged a smile with her, but she didn't leave the graveside to go speak to her as Abel did. Emma was happy, Abel said. She wanted Carrie to know she was happy. Seeing her made Carrie's heart ache; she missed her sorely.

Afterward, back at the house, Carrie carried an empty plate to the kitchen to refill with cookies. She thought of Yonnie eating cookies for breakfast and felt a wave of grief, missing her quirky ways. It saddened her that Yonnie had waited so long to set things straight. Maybe, at the very end, people need the truth to be known. Abel was right, the truth did set people free. If only Yonnie had told the truth to set Daniel free. Yonnie's secret had kept Daniel in a prison, of sorts.

Abraham lingered after others left to return to their farms for chores. "Would you have a moment, Carrie?" the deacon asked her as she handed him his coat. He gave her a warm smile.

Carrie threw a shawl over her shoulders and the two went outside.

"Shall we walk to the orchards? They're in bloom, aren't they?" he asked, knowing full well they were. "Springtime is a testament to the goodness of the Lord. He maketh all things new." He clasped his hands behind his back as he walked, looking so very content. "It's been over a year now since Daniel passed."

Carrie nodded. "It was a year on March 18."

"Hard to understand why the Lord God took such a young man as he did, but it's not for us to question God's ways, is it?"

"No."

A soft, strong breeze swept up through the trees, scattering a confetti of apple blossom petals down on them. He stopped and cupped his ear. "Do you hear that mourning dove call out, Carrie?"

She listened for the familiar cooing sound.

"Did you know that some birds use the

nests of other species? Oftentimes a mourning dove will use an old robin's nest to
raise her family—a nest that is a lot sturdier and more secure than her own."

The deacon kept walking along in that
slow, thoughtful gait of his. "Great horned
owls have even taken over crows' nests.
There's a powerful instinct God put in nature to keep life going." He stopped and
looked at the curtain of flower blossoms
that covered the trees, quiet for a long time.

Suddenly, Carrie realized that he had
been praying the whole time he was talking, his head tilted to the heavens, as if
including the Lord God in this conversation.

"He put it in humans too. The ability to
love again. Not to remain so tied to the
past that we can't keep living."

He started walking back toward the
farmhouse. "I had a visitor yesterday. A
young man. Said he was ready to start instructions so he could be baptized in the
fall." The deacon fished out his handkerchief from his pants pocket and blew his
nose loudly, then put it back in his pocket.
"I can feel the Lord God's pleasure when a

young fella is ready to make that decision."
He took his hat off and rubbed the indentation on his hair that his hat had made.
"Of course, I always ask the young fellas—each one, I ask—'now, son, you wouldn't be making this decision because you're sweet on an Amish girl, would you?'" He put his hat back on. "Why do you think I ask that question of the fellas, Carrie?"

She knew how important it was to have pure motives for baptism. She had struggled with it herself. "Otherwise, one day he might regret the decision. Maybe even resent that girl."

He nodded. "That's right. So I asked him, straight off. Know what this fella said?"

She tilted her head, curious.

"He said he's been struggling a long time, a real long time, about whether he should be baptized in the Amish church."
The deacon chuckled. "He said that he loved the Lord God with all his heart, soul, and mind. Being Amish came after that. But he wanted me to know that he did love an Amish girl. He prayed about it, and God finally gave him peace. He thought God understood."

Suddenly, as understanding flooded

Carrie's mind, her heart felt too big for her chest.

The deacon nodded. "So I told this young fella, as long as he knew that God came first, above all else, then I would approve him for baptism. Because that's the most important thing of all, to know that God comes first." He took a few steps forward, then stopped to wait for Carrie, a smile lighting his eyes. "Just exactly what I told him."

Walking back toward the house, they finished the rest of their talk. An important talk.

※※

The following week, at first light, teams of men arrived at Carrie's farm, hauling in beams and boards and wooden pegs. By midmorning, wagons with women and children arrived, loaded with hampers of food. When Carrie saw Esther's buggy, she hurried to greet her and help her down. Esther gave her a thin smile, rusty from disuse.

As Carrie watched everyone working on her behalf, she felt flooded with gratitude. Watching the barn rise before her gave a catch in her heart. These were her people, her family. She almost sensed her father's pleasure, as real as the sun shining. Her mind drifted to Daniel too, wondering what he would think about this beautiful new barn. She found thinking of him didn't cause the sorrow that it used to. She gave thanks to God for bringing Daniel to her, and her to Daniel.

By late afternoon, nails had been gathered up in brown paper bags and hammers tucked beneath the bench seats of buggies. Carrie left Esther and Clara in the kitchen, cleaning out the Tupperware to return to the women who'd brought the food.

She gazed at the new barn, proud and tall against the cerulean sky, the freshly sawn boards still raw and yellow. Inside, she found Abel and Andy examining the posts and rafters. Carrie stood in the center and peered up at the thick beams that crossed over her head, inhaling the fragrance of new wood.

Andy climbed up to the loft and tossed a handful of sawdust on Abel's head. Carrie laughed—it covered his dark hair like a snowfall. He brushed it off, grinning.

"What are you thinking?" he asked her as she turned in a circle, soaking up the sight of the new barn.

"I was thinking that everyone I know has something at stake in this barn. The women brought the food, the men brought the wood and supplies, all of my neighbors gave the gift of their hard work. There's a little part of everyone here." She wrapped her arms around herself, deeply satisfied. "It's a fine barn, Abel."

Andy started climbing down the ramp, then decided to jump off, midway, but as soon as he hit the floor he doubled over, clutching his foot in pain. He had landed on a hammer that had been left behind, and the sharp edge sliced into his heel.

Carrie crouched down and pulled out a handkerchief to mop up the blood seeping out of the wound. "Why are you running around barefoot, Andy? You know better!"

Abel bent down to examine the cut. "That's pretty deep. It's going to need stitches."

Carrie took Andy's hand and placed it against the wound. Straightening up, she said, "Abel, would you mind getting the buggy ready? I'll need to take him into the emergency room." She rubbed her face with her hands. "Just the other day, I realized Andy hadn't needed an infusion of Factor IX in months and months."

"I'll go with you," Abel said.

"So will I," Esther said, standing at the open barn door.

Abraham peered around her shoulder. "I'll come too."

Carrie looked at Esther, stunned. Esther had never gone with her father or Andy to the hospital when they needed attention. Not once.

Abel smiled. "That would be nice, Esther."

Andy's eyes went wide. "But if she comes that means I can't watch television," he whispered to Carrie, who gave him a look that read, "Too bad."

Abel went down to the carriage house to get the horse. Carrie dragged the tongue of the buggy to help him hitch the horse. As Abel backed the horse into the buggy traces, Carrie looked up in surprise.

"Abel Miller, bist du narrisch?" *Are you crazy?* "You've got the wrong horse."

Abel shook his head, eyes fixed on fastening the buckles to Schtarm's bridle. "I've been working with Schtarm. He thinks he's finally ready to be a buggy horse."

Carrie raised her eyebrows. "He thinks

so? Or knows so? Because I'm not climbing in a buggy with a runaway horse."

Abel finished clasping the last buckle, then turned to her. "He knows. He's ready."

As Abel went to the barn to pick up Andy, Abraham approached Carrie, waiting by the buggy. "Abel has been bringing Schtarm to my farm for the last few weeks. We've picked up where Daniel started, getting that horse buggy broke." He helped Carrie up. "I think Schtarm has finally worked out all the things that were troubling him." He covered Carrie's hands with his big, worn ones and gave them a squeeze. "You know, about being a buggy horse."

Carrie nodded, knowing exactly what he meant.

In the emergency room of the hospital, Andy's heel was stitched up while he was given another infusion of Factor IX. Abraham kept Andy amused with stories about his boyhood. Esther seemed amused too, Carrie noticed, wondering if something sweet was brewing between Abraham and her. Abel offered to get coffee for everyone, so Carrie walked with him to the cafeteria.

Abel bought the coffees and pointed to an empty table in the crowded room. "Let's sit for a minute, since Andy has company."

"I still can't get over having Esther here," Carrie said, pulling a chair out.

Abel nodded in agreement. "God is always working to bring folks together."

He really should be a preacher, she thought. He had a way of gently redirecting people to God. "Schtarm did well, Abel. We were here in half the time that it usually takes." She stirred cream and sugar into the coffee in her cup. "Yonnie was right about you."

He lifted his eyebrows in a question as he took a sip of his coffee.

"She said you could fix anything. Engines, motors, horses." Carrie blew on the top of the Styrofoam cup to cool the coffee. "People too." *Like me*, she thought. *He helped to fix me.*

Abel shrugged off her compliment, but seemed pleased. "Grace bicycled over this afternoon while you were cleaning up after lunch. She was on a break and had to get back to work, but she wanted you to know that someone new is managing Honor Mansion. Veronica has been promoted and is moving to New York City. In fact, Grace said she had already left." He took another sip of coffee. "Grace also mentioned that you paid a visit recently to Honor Mansion."

Carrie made her eyes go all round and innocent, like Andy's did when he tried to act as if he didn't know what she was talking about.

"So, were you planning on telling me anytime soon about that particular visit?"

Carrie inhaled, as if she was about to say something, then shook her head.

Abel leaned forward on the table. "Let's make a pact. No more secrets." He held out his hand to her. "Deal?"

She smiled and took his hand, giving it the one-pump Amish handshake. "Well, then, since we're not keeping secrets, I suppose there's something I should tell you. Mattie gave me some news today when she came over to help with the raising. Sol is moving back home. Come summer, he's starting baptism instructions."

"This summer? He's taking the baptism classes this summer?" A strange, almost sickened look came over Abel's face.

She nodded. "That's what Mattie said."

Carrie looked down at her coffee. "She said they're to be married in November."

"What?" Abel inhaled sharply, leaning back in his chair. He whistled. "I never saw that coming."

"My dad used to say that folks marry for all kinds of reasons."

Abel gazed at Carrie, his eyes dark and fathomless. "So what do you say about it?"

"I'm happy for Mattie and Sol. I really am." She and Mattie had time for a long heart-to-heart talk while cleaning up today's lunch dishes. She admitted to Mattie that she had loved Sol like crazy for a while, and in some ways she always would. "But it wasn't you who came between us, Mattie," she told her sincerely. "That was God's doing." She and Sol weren't meant for each other. And one thing Carrie knew: no woman but Mattie could ever help Sol to be his best self.

When Abel didn't respond, she glanced at him and saw him quickly look away. He was holding his hat in his hands, running it around and around by the brim. When he finally looked at her, his face was solemn. "Things haven't exactly turned out the way you thought they would, have they? It isn't exactly what you asked for."

In Carrie's mind, she reviewed the day, this wonderful day, of barn building and family building, a day filled with hope. "No. It's not. It's more. My life is more than what I ever could have asked for."

Their eyes caught and held, and held and held, and this time they both knew that neither one was letting go. He reached out a hand, palm forward, and she placed her palm against his, weaving their fingers together. Her stomach did a flip-flop; she'd been waiting for this conversation since the walk with the deacon last week. She could tell Abel was measuring his words carefully. She saw him swallow hard.

"Carrie, I can't imagine living the rest of my life without you. I love you. Be my wife." He grinned that crooked grin. "Be my Amish wife."

Carrie studied him for a moment, his brown hair curling at the ends around his collar, his beautiful melted-chocolate eyes, the cleft in his chin. Sometimes, she realized, the very thing we think is a problem turns out in the end to be God's protection.

When Sol left her for baseball, she thought her heart was permanently broken. God had a different idea for her, a better one. God led her to Daniel, who led her to Abel.

She tilted her head. "Is it as simple as that? You love me, I love you."

"As simple as that."

They shared a smile, as deep and as intimate as a kiss.

Questions for Discussion

On the surface, Carrie appeared to be a person who wasn't firmly grounded. Describe the changes she underwent.

Aside from providing Carrie with a home, what did Daniel give to her? What did she give to him?

How did Carrie's perceptions of faith and prayer change? At what point did she have a sense of her own self? What caused that growth?

Jacob Weaver, Carrie's father, never wanted Solomon Riehl to marry Carrie. He said, "I won't let my daughter marry a man who takes care of himself first." Was his opinion of Sol too harsh? Why or why not?

What kind of a person was Esther Weaver? What compels her to adhere so strictly to the laws and traditions of the Amish faith?

What core beliefs did Mattie have that allowed her to be a loyal friend to Carrie despite loving Sol?

Did it surprise you when you read that Mattie and Sol had become engaged? Did you think Sol loved her? Or needed her? Or both?

How would you describe Carrie and Abel's relationship? What drew them together?

Why did Emma choose eloping with Steelhead over being Amish? What kind of future do you see for them?

Did it bother you that Carrie had evidence to pin arson charges on Veronica McCall but chose not to? The Amish prefer to suffer injustice rather than to instigate legal suits. Do you think Carrie stood her ground? Or did Veronica McCall get the upper hand?

If you had to identify yourself with just one of the characters in this novel, who would it be? Why?

Did you learn anything new about the Amish life in reading this novel?

Acknowledgments

First, last, and always, to the Lord God, for giving me the opportunity to write for his sake.

A special thank-you goes to the Lancaster Barnstormer baseball team for letting Solomon Riehl pitch his fastball for their team. And also for sharing time and knowledge, answering my questions, and reading through the manuscript to help correct errors.

Thanks also to my favorite first readers who graciously agreed to read and critique that first draft. The Ugly Draft. Lindsey Ciraulo and Wendy How. Your keen insights and guiding comments ("Now, did you happen to notice that Carrie has three arms in that scene?" and "Why are there two Mondays in that week?") are invaluable!

Thanks to my dream team: agent Joyce Hart of The Hartline Literary Agency and those at Revell: Andrea Doering, Barb Barnes, Janelle Mahlmann, Twila Brothers Bennett, Claudia Marsh, Deonne Beron, Carmen Pease, Sheila Ingram, Donna Hausler, and everyone else who has worked so hard on my behalf.

Many thanks to the Amish families I met, who graciously opened their homes and their hearts and let me share their world for a little while.

And, of course, thanks to my family for being so supportive of this writing gig: Steve, Lindsey and Josh, Gary, Meredith and Tad.

Suzanne Woods Fisher's interest in the Anabaptist cultures can be directly traced to her grandfather, W. D. Benedict, who was raised in the Old Order German Baptist Brethren Church in Franklin County, Pennsylvania. Benedict left the colony amicably and eventually became publisher of *Christianity Today* magazine.

Suzanne is the author of *Amish Peace: Simple Wisdom for a Complicated World*. Her work has appeared in many magazines, including *Today's Christian Woman*, *Worldwide Challenge*, *ParentLife*, *Christian Parenting Today*, *Marriage Partnership*, and many others. Fisher lives with her family in the San Francisco Bay Area.

Visit Suzanne's website at www.suzannewoodsfisher.com.